Books Can Be Deceiving

**Center Point
Large Print**

*Also by Jenn McKinlay and available from
Center Point Large Print:*

The Misadventures of Miss Aggie series:
Miss Aggie's Gone Missing
Miss Aggie Cries Murder

Books Can Be Deceiving

Jenn McKinlay

CENTER POINT LARGE PRINT
THORNDIKE, MAINE

This Center Point Large Print edition is published
in the year 2011 by arrangement with
The Berkley Publishing Group,
a member of Penquin Group (USA) Inc.

ISBN: 978-1-61173-226-9

Library of Congress Cataloging-in-Publication Data

McKinlay, Jenn.
Books can be deceiving / Jenn McKinlay. — Center Point large
print ed.
p. cm.
ISBN 978-1-61173-226-9 (library binding : alk. paper)
1. Librarians—Fiction. 2. Murder—Fiction. 3. Connecticut—Fiction
4. Large type books. I. Title.
PS3612.A948B66 2011
813'.6—dc22

2011030281

For my brilliant agent, Jessica Faust

ACKNOWLEDGMENTS

Perhaps no place in any community is so totally democratic as the town library. The only entrance requirement is interest.
                                    —LADY BIRD JOHNSON

I have been very fortunate to spend my formative years and my adult years working in a variety of positions in many different libraries. There is no way to acknowledge every person I've worked with, so I just want to give a nod to the places I've worked and the people within them: East Lyme Public Library, Cromwell Belden Public Library, Phoenix Public Library, Maricopa County Library, Desert Botanical Garden Library and Scottsdale Healthcare Library. The librarians and staff in these libraries are truly some of the most brilliant and dedicated people I've ever met. The world is a better place because you all make a difference in people's lives every single day!

And now to thank those people who helped to make this book shine. I want to thank my manuscript readers: Sheila Levine, Jan Buckwalter, Carole Towles, Wendy Resnik, Sue McKinlay and Susie Matazzoni. Thanks for catching the details in the library world that I missed. And to my amazing editors: Kate Seaver, Katherine Pelz and Eloise L. Kinney; wow, you really made this book tight. Well done! Also, I have to thank the cover creators, Rita Frangie for design and Julia Green for art, for making the most spectacular cover ever. I really want to work in that library. I wonder if they're hiring . . .

Finally, to my families, the McKinlays and the Orfs, thanks for always cheering me on. It means the world to me! And for my men, Chris, Wyatt and Beckett, thanks for all the hugs and unwavering belief that I could do this. I love that we are a book-loving, library-loitering family!

CHAPTER 1

"Oh, I just love that Maxim de Winter," Violet La Rue said, her knitting needles clicking together as if to emphasize her words. "He gives me the shivers."

"Him?" Nancy Peyton asked. "He's not nearly as scary as Mrs. Danvers."

Lindsey Norris glanced up from her knitting at the two ladies sitting across the circle from her. It was crafternoon Thursday, where members of the crafternoon club gathered at the Briar Creek Library to do a craft—currently, they were knitting—and discuss the assigned book of the week.

Lindsey was the director of the library, and this group had been one of her ideas to make the Briar Creek Library the place to be in the small town. Unfortunately, she had discovered that her ability to knit and talk at the same time was about as good as her ability to pat her head and rub her tummy at the same time. Which meant it took great effort, and the results were not pretty.

"Oh, that Mrs. Danvers," Violet clucked. "Someone should push her out of a window."

Violet was a tall, thin black woman with warm brown eyes and gray hair that she wore pulled back from her face in a tight bun at the back of her head. She dressed in colorful, flowing caftans that whispered around her when she walked. She was a retired actress, having starred on the Broadway stage most of her life, who now volunteered her time at the Briar Creek Community Theater.

She was an expert knitter, and it irked Lindsey to note that she wasn't even looking at her needles while she spoke.

"I read that Mrs. Danvers is one of the most infamous female characters in literature," Nancy said, also not looking at her needles. She was Lindsey's landlord and Violet's best friend.

Lindsey dumped her knitting into her lap and said, "*Rebecca* is Daphne du Maurier's greatest work and frequently draws comparisons to *Jane Eyre*."

"Oh, she's getting irritated with her knitting again," Violet whispered to Nancy.

"I am not," Lindsey protested.

"It's all right, dear," Nancy said. "You always put on that scholarly voice when you're frustrated with your knitting."

"I do not," Lindsey protested.

A widow in her midsixties, Nancy was a delightful landlady. With her short gray hair and sparkling blue eyes, she didn't miss much that went on around her. She liked to bake cookies, she was teaching Lindsey to knit, and she never nagged about the rent, but sometimes she mothered Lindsey, and at thirty-five, Lindsey wasn't really sure how to tell her to knock it off, especially when it was kind of nice to have that maternal softness in her life.

"Do not what?" a voice asked from behind her.

Lindsey glanced over her shoulder to see a giant teapot standing behind her. A few months ago, she would have found this odd but not now.

"How was story time?" she asked.

"Full house," Beth said. "The kids loved my Mrs. Potts outfit, and of course I taught them all to sing 'I'm a Little Teapot.' "

"Naturally," Lindsey said.

If Beth weren't a librarian, Lindsey was pretty sure she would have been a circus performer. She could just see her balanced on a pony, riding around the ring in a tutu with a feather on her head. Beth brought that over-the-top energy to her role as a children's librarian and in fact to her whole life.

Lindsey had met Beth Stanley more than ten years before when they both were attending Southern Connecticut State University to get their master's degree in library science. They had ended up rooming together in a small second-floor apartment on the Boulevard in New Haven.

It had never been dull living with Beth. Lindsey still remembered the day she had come home from class and found Beth painting a life-size mural of a rabbit warren on the living room wall. She had just read *Watership Down* and was

11

inspired to get a pet bunny, which she named Blackberry after her favorite character in the book, and was decorating the living room to look like a rabbit's habitat so that Blackberry would feel more at home.

Upon graduation, Beth had come right here to Briar Creek to be the children's librarian, while Lindsey had pursued a more academic career path, becoming an archivist at the Beinecke Rare Book and Manuscript Library at Yale. Her under-graduate work had been in literature, and she had originally thought that she'd go on to pursue a degree and position to become a museum curator, but she'd found the library world to be a better fit. It wasn't hard for her to guess why. She'd been a nerd to the tenth power as a kid. A bookworm, who played the flute in the band, wore thick glasses and kept her blonde hair cut short in a frizzy bob, she was a bit of a loner, preferring the company of the characters in her books to actual people, the only exception being her brother Jack.

Things had been going just as she'd planned right up until six months ago. Suddenly her personal life had imploded, and the economy tanked. Budgets had been slashed at the university and positions eliminated, one of which had been Lindsey's.

When Beth heard that she had been let go, she encouraged her to apply for the open position of library director in Briar Creek, a quaint town perched on the shore of Connecticut. Lindsey had been charmed by the library and the town, and when they'd offered her the job, she had agreed and had been the director of the small public library for the past several months.

"So, what is it that you don't do?" Beth asked.

"I do not put on my scholarly voice when I get frustrated with my knitting," Lindsey said.

"Yeah, you do," Beth said as she shimmied out of the enormous teapot. She was short and curvy. Her cropped black hair was arranged in wispy spikes, a disarray-on-purpose sort of hairdo. The spray of freckles across her upturned nose made her seem younger than she was, but it was her childlike exuberance that really rolled the years back from her true age of thirty-two. Lindsey knew whenever she heard laughter in the library, it was usually because Beth was in the building.

"Where's Mary?" Beth asked.

"She said she was shorthanded at the café and would be running a little late. I hope she brings some chowder with her," Violet said.

"That would be perfect on a cold, rainy day like today," Beth agreed as she plopped into the cushy seat beside Lindsey and pulled her knitting out of her Friends of the Library tote bag. She was working on a sapphire blue cardigan that just begged to be snuggled in.

"Honey, what exactly is that?" Violet asked Lindsey as she leaned forward to get a better look at the pile of heather-blue yarn on her lap.

Lindsey held up her knitting. "Socks. Well, a sock."

Violet and Nancy exchanged a look, and Beth glanced at her out of the corner of her eye.

"What?" she asked. "Come on, spill it."

"Nothing," Violet said. "But . . . um . . . who are you knitting it for?"

"My dad."

"Oh, so he is real," Nancy said. There was a twinkle in her blue eyes that should have warned Lindsey, but she missed it.

"Of course my father's real," she said.

"Wow, so how does it feel to be a descendent of Bigfoot?" Beth asked. She muffled her laugh with her knitting.

"What?" Lindsey asked and then looked at the sock on her two circular needles and frowned. "Oh, you. It's not that big."

All three of them stared at her.

"Did you check your gauge?" Nancy asked. To her credit, she didn't add "duh" to the question.

"I . . . um . . . no," Lindsey admitted.

All three of the other ladies shook their heads.

"You have to check your gauge," Nancy said.

"Swatching; it's a rule," Violet said.

"Like not wearing white shoes before Memorial Day," Beth added.

"Amen," Violet and Nancy said together.

Lindsey heaved a sigh. She'd been planning to

have these socks done for the holidays, and given that it was October, the holidays were rapidly approaching, but the way it was going she wouldn't get them finished until spring. She reminded herself that she was as new to knitting as she was to Briar Creek, but still.

She considered the sock from all angles and an idea struck. She continued knitting.

"You're really going to keep going with that?" Beth asked.

"Yes, because now it's a hat," she said. She chuckled, and the others joined her.

Their laughter was interrupted when the door to the crafternoon room opened. They all glanced up, expecting to see Mary. Instead, it was Ms. Cole. She sniffed in disapproval at the copies of *Rebecca* on the table, the knitting needles, and the small fire roaring in the fireplace.

Ms. Cole was in charge of circulation at the library. She was what Lindsey considered an old-school librarian who had been miffed ever since the card catalog went the way of the dinosaur.

"Can I help you, Ms. Cole?" she asked.

"If you can tear yourself away from your knitting," Ms. Cole said. Her voice was sharp with disapproval even though Lindsey made sure to participate only during her lunch hour.

"Talk about perfect casting for Mrs. Danvers," Violet whispered to Nancy, who turned her laugh into a cough.

Just then a dripping-wet Mary pushed through the door around Ms. Cole.

"Sorry I'm late," she said. "But I come with chowder."

Mary put a large paper sack down and shrugged off her raincoat, hanging it on the coat stand by the fireplace.

"I was hoping you would have extra chowder after the lunch crush," Violet said. "The Blue Anchor has the best clam chowder on the East Coast."

"That's a fact," Beth said.

"I don't suppose there were any extra clam fritters?" Nancy asked.

"Just for you, Nance," Mary said. "They're in the bag."

She shook out her shoulder-length dark brown curls and hefted the bag over to the table and started unloading it. Then she took her knitting out of her backpack, a fisherman's sweater for her husband, Ian, and sank into one of the cushy upholstered chairs. "So, Rebecca; was she awful or what?"

"But she's dead," Nancy said. "Is she awful, or is it just the memory of her that is awful?"

"I think she was," Beth said. "She was pregnant by another man."

"And she taunted poor Maxim," Violet said. "I'm glad he found a new wife, although the poor thing has to contend with the ghost of her memory."

"The new wife is the narrator," Lindsey observed. "She's an interesting character, yes?"

"Very," Nancy agreed. "She is quite a sympathetic figure."

"Remind me, what's her first name?" Lindsey asked.

The others exchanged glances. Mary opened her mouth and then closed her mouth. She and Beth dove for copies of *Rebecca* at the same time.

Lindsey smiled as they flipped through, trying to find the name of du Maurier's narrator.

"Honestly, food in the library, knitting, a fire in the fireplace," Ms. Cole said. "Our former director Mr. Tupper never would have allowed such goings-on. I really have to protest, Ms. Norris."

"You can call me Lindsey."

Ms. Cole said nothing. She merely looked at the food and the books and the happy women clustered around the roaring fire and looked pained.

"Ms. Cole, I know you find this difficult," Lindsey said. "But this room was never used before, and it's such a lovely space. It's perfect for little groups like the crafternoon club to gather. There are no books in here to be damaged by food, and the fireplace is more than a decoration. It actually gives heat."

Ms. Cole gave her a flat stare, and Lindsey sighed. "All right, what is it that needs my attention?"

"Follow me, please," Ms. Cole said and led the way out of the room. Her sensible shoes didn't make as much as a squeak on the highly glossed wooden floors. In a brown skirt, thick beige stockings and a white blouse under a tan cardigan, Ms. Cole was the picture of nondescript. Her gray hair was worn in fat sausage curls on her head, and a pair of reading glasses hung from a chain around her neck.

She looked as if she'd been frozen in time since 1955.

Lindsey followed her stout figure as she strode back to the main library. She could only imagine how Ms. Cole was going to take it when she invited the gardening club to use the room or, even worse, had Mary host a cooking class in there.

They approached the circulation desk, which was currently being staffed by their part-time clerk Ann Marie Martin. The mother of two rambunctious boys, Ann Marie only worked a few days a week. It was what she called her "grown-up time."

"You need to talk to her," Ms. Cole said. "Mr. Tupper always said, 'A fine is a fine, and we don't make any exceptions.' "

Ann Marie glanced up at them. She was a little older than Lindsey and wore her brown hair in the standard mom ponytail and dressed in corduroy jumpers with pretty blouses underneath. She always smelled like apples and was quick with a grin and quicker with a laugh. Lindsey thought her boys were pretty lucky to have her.

Right now, Ann Marie was not grinning, however; in fact, it looked as though it was taking all of her self-restraint not to roll her eyes.

"He didn't have any money," Ann Marie said. "I made a note on his record that he would pay his fine the next time he comes in, but yes, I let him check out the books he needed for his school project. I take full responsibility for the two dollars and twenty cents that he owes."

Ann Marie spun the flat computer screen on the desk so that Lindsey could see it. She looked at the circulation record and saw Matthew Carter's name and information as well as the note Ann Marie had said she'd put on his account.

"Seems okay to me," Lindsey said. "Our policy is that we don't revoke borrowing privileges until the patron owes more than ten dollars. Matthew's a good kid. I think we need to give him the opportunity to prove himself."

"If he would return his items on time, he wouldn't need that opportunity," Ms. Cole said with a sniff.

"That's why we value you so much," Lindsey said. "You help us to be better than we are, Ms. Cole, by keeping your expectations high."

Ms. Cole blinked at her as if uncertain whether she was being mocked or not.

"If you'll excuse me," Lindsey said. "I'm just

going to finish up our book talk, and I'll be right back."

"Have fun," Ann Marie said. "Oh, and Milton wanted to talk to you."

"Is he in his usual spot?" Lindsey asked.

"Yep," Ann Marie said. "Same corner as always."

"Thanks," Lindsey said.

She turned away from the desk and scanned her library. It wasn't huge, but it was a wonderful space all the same. The old stone building was two hundred years old. Before it had been the town library, it was the private residence of a ship builder. It had been renovated numerous times over the years, but it still retained a nautical charm with its wooden floors and beamed ceilings and long tall windows that overlooked the bay.

The children's section was Beth's domain, and she had designed it to look like a small enchanted island. There was a couch that looked like a big sand dune, the floor was soft blue carpet, fake palm trees were stationed around the room and a large pirate's treasure chest was filled with puppets and dress-up clothes and building blocks.

And, of course, there was Fernando, Beth's colorful toy parrot, who lived in a large birdcage in the corner. The kids especially loved that he had a sound-activated recorder programmed to repeat everything they said. He was of particular delight to Ann Marie's boys, who liked to teach Fernando naughty words.

Lindsey cut through the children's area to the adult section, which was much less fanciful. Cushy armchairs were scattered around this space, with small tables to accommodate laptop computers; study carrels with soft green banker's lamps lined one wall, and a bank of computers with word-processing and Internet capability lined another. Shelves and shelves of books, fiction in one section and nonfiction in another, filled out the remaining space in the room.

Lindsey passed by the computers and books and arrived at the small lounge area for the adults. Magazines and newspapers filled freestanding racks circled by a big sofa and several armchairs. And there in the corner, standing on his head, was Milton Duffy.

CHAPTER 2

It had taken Lindsey a few weeks to get used to Milton—okay, it had been months, and she was still getting used to him. He was a certified Yogi and was frequently found doing an asana wherever the mood struck him: the grocery store, the café, the pier, wherever.

He was also the heart of Briar Creek, serving as chairman of the library board and the tourism board, and he had been president of the historical society for the past fifteen years. He was the institutional memory of the town, and he had been invaluable in helping Lindsey get acclimated to her new position as director of the library.

"Hi, Milton," she said.

His eyes popped open with a flash of bright green, and he said, "Ms. Lindsey, always a pleasure. Are you coming down, or shall I come up?"

"I'll come down," she said.

"Excellent," he said. "Uttanasana increases the blood flow to the brain. It's an excellent way to fight off dementia."

Lindsey positioned herself beside Milton and exhaled as she lowered herself into a forward bend. Milton had been coaching her on her posture, and she could feel how much more limber her body was compared with a few months ago. If she aged as well as Milton, then that was fine with her.

At eighty-two, Milton had more energy than a man half his age. Short, with a wiry build and no hair on his head, he sported a thick silver goatee and dressed in designer workout clothes. Every single woman over the age of fifty had the hots for Milton, but he remained loyal to the memory of his late wife, who had passed away just two years before. This loyalty did not stop him from accepting every dinner invitation that came his way, but still, he never favored one lady over another, for which Lindsey admired his tact.

"You wanted to see me?" she asked. She noticed her voice sounded different when she was upside down, as if her head was stuffed with cotton, but maybe that was just all of the blood rushing to her brain in its quest to fight off senility.

"I've been thinking about our annual book sale," he said. "We usually hold it in February, but I was thinking we should do it before the holidays this year. Times are tough, and people are looking for bargains. They might be more in the mood to shop then."

Lindsey mulled it over. She had not been here long enough to witness the annual book sale, but she had heard it was quite a moneymaker for the Friends of the Library, who in turn used the money to help the library fund reading programs and such. She didn't think there was a problem with moving it, and she trusted Milton's judgment.

"Sounds fine to me," she said.

"Fabulous. I'll bring it up at the next meeting and mention that we have your approval. Some of our people are very resistant to change, you know."

Lindsey thought of Ms. Cole. "I know the type," she said. She began to unwind out of her forward bend.

"Slowly," Milton coached. "Remember to go vertebra by vertebra."

Lindsey eased out of her stretch, and she had to admit that she felt amazingly refreshed. "Always a pleasure, Milton."

"Likewise," he said and his eyes closed as he went back to his meditation.

Strands of Lindsey's long blonde hair had slipped from the clip at the nape of her neck. She reached back and undid the barrette, raked her hair back into a semblance of order with her fingers and reclipped it. She had inherited her mother's hair: pale blonde and unruly. Well, her mother called it curly, but Lindsey had always thought it had a mind of its own. She had worn it short as a young girl, but given her strong features courtesy of her father, as a grown-up she felt it made her look too mannish. So in college, she grew it long and wore it tied back. Life was a compromise.

She headed back toward the cozy little room where the crafternooners were holed up. Her stomach grumbled, and she really hoped there was some chowder left.

The ladies were all packing up their knitting, but to Lindsey's delight, there was one container of soup still on the table.

"We saved it for you," Beth said.

"Thanks," she said. "So what was the conclusion about our narrator? What is her first name?"

"She is never given one," Violet said. "I can't believe I didn't catch that. It's a technique I'm familiar with in theater, used to give the narrator no past or future but to keep her solely in the present."

"Also, the reader can identify more with a narrator who is not named," Mary added.

Lindsey smiled. There was nothing better than sharing her love of a great book with people who felt the same.

"So, what are we reading next?" Beth asked. "We have suggestions for *The Last Time I Saw Paris*, by Lynn Sheene, or *The Sea, the Sea*, by Iris Murdoch."

"Let's read *The Last Time I Saw Paris* and then *The Sea, the Sea*," Nancy said. "This rainy weather makes me long for a jaunt in Europe, and *The Last Time I Saw Paris* is a period piece set during World War II."

"Sounds good to me," Lindsey said. "Agreed?"

Everyone in the circle glanced at one another and gave a nod. "I'll go ahead and get the copies. Violet, will Charlene be joining us?"

"I'll ask her, but I'm pretty sure she will. You know how she likes to talk," Violet said. Her eyes widened as if it mystified her that her daughter could be so chatty. No one pointed out to her that the acorn had not fallen far from the oak.

Charlene was a local television news reporter in New Haven. She and her husband owned a house on one of the Thumb Islands that surrounded Briar Creek and frequently came to town with their three kids for weekends away from it all.

"Beth, are you still working on that children's picture book?" Nancy asked. "The one about the hamster that lives in the library?"

"When I get the chance," Beth said. "It's almost finished, but I need some time to polish it. Why?"

"Well, I heard from Jeanette Palmer at the Beachfront Bed and Breakfast that an editor from Caterpillar Press just booked a stay with them for this weekend."

"What is Caterpillar Press?" Mary asked.

"A children's book publisher in New York," Nancy said. "I think you should show her your work, Beth."

"Oh, I couldn't." Beth shook her head. "I don't even know how you approach a person like that. I've heard editors can be very prickly. Rick has told me about authors who pester editors and how they're banned from the industry for life."

"That's ridiculous," Violet said. "You're not going to pester her. You're just going to show her your work, and she should consider herself fortunate. You are very talented. They'd be lucky to sign you."

"You sound just like my mother," Beth said with a wry smile. As if sensing their collective doubt, she added, "I'll think about it. Really."

The other women exchanged glances. Beth was a terrible liar, and it was obvious she was putting them off. Despite her art background, she had very little confidence in her work. It drove them all crazy that they couldn't get her to be more aggressive about submitting her work to publishers.

Beth and Lindsey set to cleaning up the room, waving away the offers of help from the others. Lindsey switched off the gas fireplace and the room felt instantly colder. They rearranged the cushy chairs so that they were back in their haphazard arrangement and threw away all traces of Mary's chowder and fritters, except for the container Lindsey was keeping for herself.

"There, now the lemon has nothing to complain about," Beth said.

She had been calling Ms. Cole "the lemon" since she'd gotten her job, ten years ago. She said it was because Ms. Cole frequently looked as if she'd been sucking on a lemon. Lindsey knew that now that she was Ms. Cole's boss, she should discourage the nickname, but it was hard when it was so spot-on.

"Beth, I don't want to pressure you, but I am curious. Why don't you show the editor your work?" Lindsey asked. "Do you not want to get published?"

"No, I do," she said. "I really do, but . . ."

Lindsey waited, and when Beth said nothing, she prompted her. "But what?"

"Well, I showed my book to Rick," Beth said with a frown. "He said it is far too amateurish."

Lindsey felt her jaw clench, and she had to

force herself to unclamp her teeth. Rick Eckman, Beth's boyfriend, happened to be an award-winning children's picture-book author. He had arrived in Briar Creek five years ago, and Beth had been completely swept off her feet by his interest in her and their mutual love of children's literature. When he won the Caldecott Medal for his first book shortly after they started dating, Beth had taken it as a sign that he was her soul mate. Lindsey had never really seen it herself.

The truth was that Rick was an arrogant horse's patoot, and Lindsey had never managed to warm to him. She failed to see what Beth saw in him, but being a good friend, she had never said as much, although it about killed her not to.

"I know that Rick is an author and illustrator himself," she said. "But I don't think he has the same eye toward other artists' work as an editor would."

"Maybe," Beth said. "I really would love to hear what an editor thinks of my story."

"Then let's at least entertain the idea of querying her," Lindsey said. "What do you say?"

"All right." Beth laughed. "But only because I know you'll just keep bugging me and bugging me if I don't."

"Don't what?" a voice asked from the door.

Lindsey and Beth spun to find Ms. Cole poised in the doorway. She had her usual stern look about her, and Lindsey found she didn't want to tell her what was going on, although she couldn't say why.

"Oh, we're just talking about following through on a project," she said.

"What project?"

"Weeding," Beth answered. Lindsey looked at her out of the corner of her eye. Surely she knew the very idea of weeding sent Ms. Cole into conniptions.

"Mr. Tupper didn't feel the need to weed," Ms. Cole said with a sniff. "He felt that all materials once acquired were a part of the collection."

"I know," Beth said with a frown. "Which is why I was never allowed to pitch any of my picture books, even if they had spit-up on them."

"Ew," Lindsey said.

"Indeed," Beth agreed. She glanced at Ms. Cole with a sly look. "So, Lindsey, shall I make a list of all of the reference books we're going to pitch? I was thinking I'd start with the *Oxford English Dictionary.*"

Ms. Cole went red in the face, and she clutched her chest as if she were having palpitations. For a second, it appeared as if she might keel over, but instead she shook her gray curls and gave Lindsey her most stubborn glare.

"Mr. Tupper would never remove the *OED* from the collection," she said.

"I know," Lindsey said in a placating voice. "And neither will I. Beth was just teasing."

"Is that so?" Ms. Cole asked, looking very much like she didn't believe her.

"Oh, look at the time," Beth said and glanced at her wrist, where a watch would be if she actually wore one. "Gotta run."

"Beth . . ." Lindsey called a warning after her friend, but Beth clearly was not finished teasing Ms. Cole and did not turn around.

"She really was just kidding," Lindsey said. Ms. Cole said nothing, and Lindsey followed Beth, feeling distinctly uncomfortable.

She could feel Ms. Cole's eyes burning on her back, and she thought of Violet's observation that Ms. Cole was very much like Mrs. Danvers in *Rebecca*. She was suddenly very grateful that the library had long ago done away with most of the second story and was now made up of vaulted ceilings instead. Perhaps it was the rainy weather giving her gothic thoughts, but she was grateful there were no nearby windows to be pushed from.

At the door, she glanced over her shoulder to see Ms. Cole still staring at her with a forbidding frown. Lindsey clutched her container of chowder to her chest and gave her a faint smile. Then she put on a burst of speed, which brought her back to the lively warmth of the main room of the library.

CHAPTER 3

"The library will be closing in ten minutes," Lindsey called out. There were a few patrons still using the public-access Internet computers, and a young couple was squabbling over which DVD to check out. None of them seemed inclined to move toward the exit. It was Friday evening and as much as the patrons would have liked the library to stay open, Lindsey and her staff were ready to go.

Lindsey patrolled the small library, making sure the copier and online computer catalogs were off, books were put on cleanup trucks and all the puzzles and toys in the children's section were in their proper places.

Ms. Cole was standing at the last checkout station glaring at the young couple. Lindsey knew only too well that if they didn't get there before the stroke of five, Ms. Cole would shut off her terminal and refuse them service.

Lindsey wandered over in their direction. "Can I help you find anything?"

"I want a romantic comedy," the young woman said. She looked to be in her late teens, with long, straight black hair and pale skin. She wore heavy eye makeup and was rail thin.

31

"And I want action adventure," her companion said. He looked to be the same age as the girl. He wore very baggy jeans, had the scruffy start of a beard on his chin and sported a crooked ball cap on his head. "No chick flicks."

"Why not?" the young woman asked. "It's supposed to be our date night."

Lindsey scanned the shelves. The movies were filed alphabetically by title. Yes! There was one copy available. She snatched it and handed it to the man. "Here. It's the best of both worlds."

"*True Lies*?" he asked. One of his eyebrows lifted in doubt.

"Schwarzenegger and Curtis, explosions, romance, comedy, chase scenes, the works. Trust me," she said. "Now get moving, or you won't even get that."

She pointed to Ms. Cole, who was still glaring daggers, and the young couple hustled over to the checkout counter. As soon as they had their film, Lindsey took a deep breath and called, "The library is now closed. You don't have to go home, but you can't stay here. Have a nice night."

The last of the patrons shuffled out the door. Ann Marie quickly shut off the computers, while Beth locked the front door. Ms. Cole deposited the cash drawer into the safe, and they all gathered their things from the workroom and trooped to the back door.

Lindsey let everyone out and then set the alarm

behind them. She had fifteen seconds to get through the back door or the alarm would go off, bringing the town police screeching into their parking lot. She had discovered this the hard way her first week on the job.

She and Ms. Cole had been closing when Ms. Cole said she was sure she had left the coffeepot on. Lindsey went back to check, not knowing she only had fifteen seconds, and sure enough, the alarm sounded, scaring her half to death, and when she came out the door, there were two town police officers, Chief Daniels and Officer Wilcox, standing with guns drawn and Ms. Cole smirking behind them. It was a small miracle that Lindsey had not disgraced herself completely and peed her pants.

"Good night, everyone," she called after her staff. Ann Marie gave her a cheerful smile, but Ms. Cole said nothing. She strode to her compact car without so much as a wave.

"I don't think I'm being overly sensitive when I say that woman loathes me," Lindsey said to Beth.

"Don't take it personally. The lemon loathes everyone."

Beth and Lindsey both rode bicycles to work and left them chained to the bike rack on the side of the building.

As they turned the corner around the stone building, the breeze blowing in off the bay just yards away was like a cold slap against the cheek, leaving its briny smell lingering in the nostrils. It woke Lindsey up better than smelling salts, and suddenly, she wasn't that eager to go home and cook.

"What about grabbing a bite at the Blue Anchor?" she asked Beth. "My treat."

"Here." Beth held out her arm, and Lindsey looked at her in confusion. "Go ahead. Give it a twist."

Lindsey laughed and looped her arm through Beth's and dragged her down the sidewalk to the crosswalk. There was no traffic, and they hurried across the narrow two-lane road to the small town park. The benches facing the bay were empty, and so were the picnic tables. Obviously, the promise of more rain from the steely gray clouds overhead was keeping most people indoors. A lone seagull perched on the back of a bench and looked at them inquiringly.

They had no food to give him. Realizing it was not his lucky day, he took off with a flap of wings and a disgruntled cry.

They followed the stone path that led through the park to the large pier beyond. Tour boats were docked there as well as several fishing boats.

The Blue Anchor, Mary's café, had once been a fish market that sat on the concrete slab that abutted the pier. Thirty years ago, it had been turned into a bar, frequented mainly by fishermen.

Ten years ago, Mary and her husband had bought it from the owners and turned it into a café.

As it was the only restaurant in Briar Creek, it did very well for itself. Of course, it helped that Mary really did make the best clam chowder in the county if not the state.

The breeze pushed them through the door into the dimly lit restaurant. The windows, which were hinged to be propped open in the mild summer months, were closed against the chilly October air. The tables were vintage Formica on chrome, cream colored with flecks of gold. The seats were padded red vinyl. Laminated menus were used as place mats, and seating was catch-as-catch-can.

Beth scanned the crowded room, looking for an empty table while waving to a few people that she knew. Finally, she spied a table in the back corner that was being vacated, and she pulled Lindsey in that direction.

"What are you going to have?" Beth asked as soon as they sat down.

"Lobster roll," Lindsey said. She shrugged out of her jacket and placed her purse on the floor. "Mary's lobster roll always drips with butter, and she uses those split-top rolls that she toasts on the side. Okay, I think I'm drooling."

Beth laughed. "Don't forget the coleslaw with those diced green olives in it. It's the best."

"And a glass of wine," Lindsey said. "We've earned it."

"Indeed," Beth agreed.

Their waitress wore a pale-blue, long-sleeved polo shirt, with the Blue Anchor insignia embroidered on the left, over khaki pants. She had her long brown hair tied back in a ponytail. She looked to be about college age.

"Hi, Miss Stanley," she said.

Beth tipped her head and studied the girl. "Oh my, is that you, Eva?"

The young woman nodded.

"But you're all grown up," Beth said. "Lindsey, this is Eva Hernandez. She was one of my first teen volunteers at the library ten years ago. Eva, this is Lindsey Norris, the new library director."

"Hi, Eva." Lindsey held out her hand, and the young woman gave it a firm shake.

"It's nice to meet you," Eva said. "You're much younger than Mr. Tupper, like, by a century."

"I don't think that's been a selling point with Ms. Cole," Lindsey said.

"No kidding?" Eva asked, her tone light and teasing. "With her being so hip and all? Shocking!"

Both Lindsey and Beth laughed.

"So, are you still in school?" Beth asked.

"I'm graduating next May," Eva said. "But there's been so much going on, it's really hard to concentrate."

"Like what?" Beth asked.

Eva gave them a small, close-lipped smile and

waved her left hand in front of them and said, "Oh, this and that."

A person would have to be stone-blind not to see the rock sparkling on the ring finger of her left hand—or be a man, Lindsey thought sourly.

"Oh!" Beth let out a squeal and jumped out of her seat to examine the ring more closely. "Princess cut and in a platinum band. It's gorgeous."

"Very nice," Lindsey agreed in a much more subdued manner. She thought it spoke well of her that she didn't advise the girl to run while she had the chance.

"Have you set a date?" Beth asked.

"Next June," Eva said. "Right after graduation. We've only been together for a year, but when you know, you know."

"Eva! You have an order for pickup," a passing waitress said.

"Oh, right," she said. "What can I get you two?"

Beth placed their order, and Eva dashed off, promising to bring their wine as soon as possible.

"How old is she?" Lindsey asked.

"Twenty-two," Beth said.

"Awfully young to be getting married, isn't she?"

They both smiled when Eva returned with their wine and watched as she hurried back to the kitchen.

"Well, like she said, when you know, you know," Beth said.

"Really?" Lindsey asked. "Because sometimes you think you know and you even have the Harry Winston on your finger, but then you come home and find out someone's been sleeping in your bed. And you really wish it was Mama Bear and not Goldilocks because then she might at least have ripped the head off of the rat bastard who's been cheating on you . . . but I digress."

Beth hid her smile by taking a sip of her wine. "I am really glad your breakup with John hasn't made you bitter."

"A little tart, perhaps, but not bitter," Lindsey assured her.

"Have you talked to him at all?"

"Not since I gave him his ring back, packed up and left. It was all sort of cosmic since I'd just been let go and the position here opened up. Sometimes, I think it was the universe at work."

"Milton would certainly say so," Beth said. "I still can't believe John asked you to marry him and then turned around and cheated with his graduate assistant. What a jerk! You can do so much better than him."

"Bleah. I'm not interested," Lindsey said. "Now, enough about me and my cheating ex-fiancé; how are you and Rick doing?"

"Good . . . really good," Beth said. She ran her hand through her short black spikes, and Lindsey knew she was full of baloney. Beth always fussed with her hair when she was feeling edgy;

besides, she was a horrible liar. She always broke eye contact.

"Good?" Lindsey repeated. "Good is having a slow leak in your tire instead of a blowout, a migraine instead of a stroke or a nibble on your fishing line instead of catching the big one . . ."

"All right, enough with the metaphors," Beth cut her off. "I get it. Things are better than that. It's just . . ."

"What?" Lindsey prompted her. She took a long sip of the dry white wine and felt it warm her insides.

"I just can't help feeling a little jealous," she said. "Eva is ten years younger than me, and she's getting married. And Rick, well, when I mention marriage . . . no, I'm just being silly."

Lindsey studied her friend. This was one of those moments when she felt it was her duty as a longtime friend to be completely honest. Too bad she was too much of a spineless blob to do it.

After all, it was one thing to trash someone's boyfriend after they broke up; it was quite another to trash the person she was currently dating. The risk of alienating Beth and destroying the friendship was too great.

"Tell me again; how long have you been dating?" she asked. Maybe she could give Beth a nudge in the right direction without actually dissing Rick.

"Almost five years."

"And you really want to marry him?"

"Yes . . . I think so . . . No, I mean yes."

Lindsey reached across the table and put her hand on Beth's arm. "Stop. You're giving yourself whiplash."

"I do," Beth said with a laugh. "I do want to marry him. I'm pretty sure."

"Then tell him," Lindsey said. "Give him the old 'it's now or never' speech."

"Oh, I don't know. He doesn't like pushy women."

"Asking where your relationship is going after almost five years is not being pushy," Lindsey said. "It's making an overdue inquiry."

Just then Eva arrived with their lobster rolls, and all thought of relationships dissipated under the delightful deluge to the senses of melted butter and juicy lobster meat in a toasted bun.

They left the subject of their love lives behind and instead talked about things more conducive to good digestion, like what Beth's programming plans were for the children's area during the holidays and whether they could get the town's computer support staff to let them maintain their own website instead of having to submit everything for approval and wait an eternity for the changes to be made.

They were just finishing a decadent dessert of crème brûlée, when the door to the café was blown open and in came Beth's boyfriend, Rick

Eckman. His lime-green rain gear was soaked, and he stood dripping a puddle in the entranceway as he scanned the small restaurant.

When he saw Beth, he stomped across the café to their table. Without so much as a hello, he turned to her and snapped, "Why didn't you answer your phone? I've been calling and calling."

"Oh, sorry," Beth said. She glanced down at her purse with a frown. "I never heard it."

Rick glared at Lindsey as if this was her fault and then turned back to Beth. "I thought *we* could have dinner together."

"Oh, when we talked earlier, you said you were going to be working all night," she said.

"Well, if you'd bothered to answer your phone, you would know I finished early and wanted to join you for dinner."

"I'm sorry," Beth said. She gave him an apologetic look. "Why don't you sit and join us? We'll chat while you eat."

"I wouldn't want to interrupt any girl talk," he said. He looked like a petulant child, and it was all Lindsey could do not to excuse herself and leave.

"There's nothing to interrupt," Lindsey assured him. "We're done."

He grudgingly took a seat. Shrugging out of his raincoat, he draped it on the back of his chair. His dark hair was in need of a trim, and his glasses had rain splatters on them. He wore beat-up sneakers, grubby jeans and a ratty gray sweatshirt. Living alone on one of the Thumb Islands in the bay, he obviously did not feel the need to maintain his appearance or basic personal hygiene.

He took off his glasses and dried them on the edge of his sweatshirt. Lindsey noticed that his fingers were long and thin, almost too feminine for a man living on an island by himself. She supposed a bestselling children's picture-book author didn't have to do much hard labor, but she would have thought maintaining his boat, the one that brought him to shore to see Beth, would have given him at least a hint of a sailor's build. But no.

Eva stopped by their table and took Rick's order. He was one of those "on the side" types. He wanted his salad with dressing on the side and a baked potato with butter on the side. When his meal arrived, he tucked into his steak, after sending it back once because it was too rare, and proceeded to chew with his mouth open, while Lindsey and Beth discussed some ideas for the crafternoon club.

Mary poked her head out of the kitchen, and when she saw them, she hurried over to their table.

"How is everything?" she asked.

Before Beth and Lindsey could assure her that it was excellent, Rick spoke through a mouthful of potatoes. "You're too skimpy with the butter, and I had to send my steak back."

"I'm sorry to hear that," Mary said. Her voice was polite, but Lindsey was pretty sure she heard the sharp edge of a knife buried in it.

"You might want to comp my meal, since I was so inconvenienced," he said. "After all, I am a local celebrity."

Lindsey felt her mouth pop open. The sheer nerve of this guy bowled her over. Beth looked dismayed and embarrassed, but Mary just tipped her head and considered him with a small smile.

"No, I don't think so," she said.

"Good evening, everyone."

They turned as one to see Carole Towles standing by their table. She was dressed in an elegant olive-green silk suit, with her strawberry-blonde hair in an updo. Diamonds flashed at her ears as well as her wrists, and Lindsey would have bet a week's salary that Carole had better plans than all of them for the evening.

Still, Lindsey smiled. Carole was on the library board and always had such a positive outlook. As a former public librarian herself, Carole had become a mentor to Lindsey, and her knowledge had proven invaluable.

"I just wanted to thank you for making Mr. Bingley's favorite chicken dish," Carole said to Mary. "I'm going to the theater tonight, and I know this will cheer him up while I'm gone."

"Anything for Mr. Bingley," Mary said.

Mr. Bingley was Carole's Chihuahua. She had

rescued him as a puppy, and he was quite the favorite in town, as he had a disposition as sunny as his owner's.

"Oh, you're sweet," Carole said. "Now, Beth, I wanted to let you know that I met a woman today at Tilly's Salon who is spending the weekend at the Beachfront. We were both getting manicures." Carole paused to study the polish on her fingernails. "I think I like the color she got on hers better."

"And?" Lindsey encouraged her.

"Oh, yes." Carole glanced back up. "She's an editor with Caterpillar Press, so I told her about you and the book you've been working on. She was very eager to meet you once I mentioned that her boss is a dear friend of mine from my days at the American Library Association. Isn't that fabulous?"

Mary and Lindsey turned to look at Beth, who stared at Carole with an expression that seemed to be equal parts terror and excitement.

"Oh no, look at the time," Carole said with a quick glance at her watch. "I've got to run or I'll be late. I told her, her name is Sydney Carlisle, that you'd meet her here for lunch at noon tomorrow. I hope that's all right?"

Beth looked frozen, so Lindsey answered for her. "It's perfect. She'll be here and thank you so much."

"My pleasure," Carole said. "Let me know how it goes!"

With a flash of dimples and a wave, she hurried out the door.

Rick's head jerked back and a piece of steak fell from his mouth onto his plate with a splat. "She's having you meet Sydney from Caterpillar Press? But she's *my* editor."

"Is she?" Beth asked. "I thought the name sounded familiar."

"Why on earth would she do that?" he snapped.

"Because she's seen Beth's book, and she thinks she has talent," Lindsey said.

Rick turned his astonished face toward her and then he huffed a breath and looked furious. Lindsey felt as though she'd just jumped in front of the firing squad to save Beth.

"This is your doing, isn't it?" he snapped. "You're giving Beth ideas beyond her abilities."

Mary, who'd been silent, sucked in an audible gasp. One look at the daggers she was glaring, and Lindsey knew she was about to erupt. Mary was known for her hot Irish temper.

"I disagree," Lindsey said. "I think Beth's work is terrific; otherwise, I wouldn't encourage her to show it to an editor."

"I'm sorry," Rick said. He carefully placed his knife and fork on the edge of his plate, folded his hands in his lap and studied Lindsey through his spotty glasses. "I wasn't aware that you had become an expert on children's literature."

Mary's eyes looked about ready to pop out of

her head, but as the child of two college professors, Lindsey had spent her formative years in academia. She knew a pretentious blowhard when she saw one, and she knew exactly how to deal with him.

"I never claimed to be an expert," she said. "But I am a librarian, and I have studied children's literature, and I know quality work when I see it."

She let her words dangle in the air. Judging by the red that suffused Rick's cheeks, her meaning—that his work was inferior in her opinion—was not lost on him.

He turned back to Beth. "I was under the impression that there was one artist in our relationship and that it was me. Obviously, I was mistaken."

"Oh, no," Beth said. She put her hand on his arm, but he shrugged her off like a pouty toddler. "I'm just curious to see what an editor would think of my work. That's all."

"Because my opinion, which I've given you, is of no value to you?" he asked. His voice was a whiny tenor of hurt.

Lindsey reached for her wineglass and drained it. Mary gave her a nod of understanding and went to fetch more.

"You know I value your opinion," Beth said. "I'd just like to see if I could go anywhere with my stories."

Rick wiped his mouth with his napkin and

tossed it onto the table. "Well, I guess you've made your decision then. Have a nice life."

He rose and Beth gaped at him. "You're breaking up with me?"

"You've given me no choice," he said. He shrugged on his rain gear, looking like a giant pea pod in the soft glow of the café's candlelit tables.

Mary returned with a bottle of wine, and Lindsey filled Beth's glass and her own. Mary held out a third empty glass and Lindsey nodded, filling one for her as well. It appeared they were going to need it.

"Why you narcissistic, arrogant, self-centered son of a . . . sea dog!" Beth shouted as she hopped up from her seat and jabbed Rick in the chest with her pointer finger.

Mary took Rick's empty seat, and she and Lindsey watched the drama unfold before them as if it were on television.

"Really, Beth, there is no need to get violent," he said.

"Violent?" she shouted. "I'll give you violent."

She reached behind her and grabbed an empty chair by the back. Using it like a lion tamer in the ring, she jabbed at Rick with the legs.

"Five years," she said with a jab. "Five years of listening to you snivel and whine about your career. Five years of wanting to get married and having you put me off. Five years of never being invited onto your island but always being off island waiting for you. Five years of you telling me that I'm not good enough to write children's stories, and I believed you. Well, I am over it and you."

She jabbed at Rick, forcing him toward the door and the storm outside. He yelped and opened the door. The wind snatched it back and doused him with a blast of cold rain.

"Oh, it's really bad out there," he said.

Beth glared at him. He straightened his glasses and gave her a weak smile.

"I don't think I should risk going back to the island in my boat. I'll just stay the night with you one last time, don't you think?"

He gave her a smarmy look that was obviously supposed to woo her. Beth let out a low growl that sounded as if it resonated from the back of her throat. Mary gave Lindsey a wide-eyed stare, but Lindsey shook her head. This was Beth's battle; of course they'd give her backup, but she needed to make the final break herself.

"I am so over you," Beth said. "Enjoy your island all by your lonesome."

Rick blinked at her in confusion. "Is that a no?"

Beth's face went red and she raised the chair, looking like she might conk him on the head with it. Lindsey and Mary were half out of their seats when, luckily, a strong pair of hands plucked the chair out of Beth's grasp.

"My guess is that's a no," said a deep voice that brooked no argument.

CHAPTER 4

Captain Mike Sullivan, or Sully as he was known in Briar Creek, put the chair down and gave Rick a gentle push out the door, pulling it closed after him.

Beth spun around and nodded at him. "Thanks."

"Any time," Sully said, and he ambled back to the small bar at the back of the restaurant. He'd been talking to Mary's husband, Ian, his business partner in the Thumb Islands tour-boat company, when he'd stepped over to help Beth out.

"Way to go, big brother," Mary said, and she raised her glass in Sully's direction.

He gave her a small smile, and Lindsey saw two deep dimples bracket his mouth. With the same square jaw, mahogany curls, and bright-blue eyes as his sister, Sully was not exactly hard on the eyes, and Lindsey had to force her gaze away.

She was off men; she had to remember that. She turned her attention to Beth, who stomped back to their table.

"Can you believe that?" she asked as she plopped down in her seat and sipped her wine. "I mean, really—how thick can one man be?"

"That's a rhetorical question, right?" Mary asked.

49

Beth raised her wineglass. "Well, here's to meeting that editor. Since Carole went to all that trouble to set it up, the least I can do is show up."

"Absolutely," Mary said. "I'll use my chowder to woo her into a happy place before she looks at your work."

They clinked glasses, and each took a long sip. Lindsey studied her friend. Had it only been an hour ago that she'd said she wanted to marry Rick?

"Are you sure you're okay?" she asked. "Personally, I think I have whiplash from that turn of events."

"I'm fine. You know, when you asked me earlier if I wanted to marry him," Beth said, "I had an epiphany. I don't think I wanted to marry him as much as I wanted to get married. And you know what? I'm not sure I want that anymore either."

"When it's the right one, you will," Mary said. Lindsey glanced at her and saw she was looking at her husband with a fondness that was touching.

Ian Murphy was short and bald with glasses and freckles. He was not exactly the dashing-prince type. When she had first met him, she didn't think he was the sort of man who Mary would date, never mind marry. But then he had cracked a joke and smiled at her, and by the time they had finished their introductions, Lindsey was half in love with him herself.

Ian was funny and charming, and his smile lit up any room he happened into. Everyone loved him, and Mary considered herself lucky to have him for a husband. And as for Ian, Mary was the love of his life, and he treated her with a reverence that let everyone know he assumed she'd come to her senses any day and leave him, but she never did, and Lindsey doubted she ever would.

Lindsey and Beth exchanged a look of commiseration. If they could find someone and have half of what Mary and Ian had, they'd consider it a success.

Mary refilled their glasses, and they all took a healthy sip. "Trust me. You'll find the right man. You just have to be patient."

"I'll have to take your word for it," Beth said. "As for now, I'm going to take a page out of Lindsey's book and swear off men."

"Who has sworn off men?" a voice asked from behind them.

They spun around to find Ian and Sully standing there.

"Lindsey has sworn off men," Beth said. "And I'm going to join her."

Sully glanced at Lindsey. His blue eyes studied her face for a second before he said, "That's a shame."

Lindsey felt suddenly parched, and she looked at her empty wineglass with regret. She cleared her throat and tried to ignore the warm flush she felt creeping into her cheeks as Sully continued to watch her. She glanced away and noticed Mary studying them with interest.

"Well, as long as it's not Mary," Ian said. He turned a chair around and sat down at the table with them.

"I've sworn off all men except for you," Mary said.

"Whew." Ian wiped his forehead with the back of his hand. "I'd hate to be single and try to get my girlish figure back at this late date in life."

"Oh, I don't know," Sully teased him with a smile. "If we put a high gloss on that dome of yours, I bet we could put you out in the bay, and you'd bring the ladies in by the boatload."

Ian hopped to his feet and did a fair impression of a lighthouse, complete with foghorn sound effects. It was impossible not to laugh at his antics.

"Come on, foggy," Mary said as she rose from her seat. "Help me lock up."

Lindsey glanced around to see that the other diners had all left. A busboy had come and cleared their plates, and the rest of the staff was putting up chairs and wiping down the café.

Lindsey stopped by the register to pay their tab, but Mary refused to take it. She said it wouldn't be right to charge them on the night of a big breakup.

Lindsey waited until she turned her back, and then stuffed the money she owed, plus a healthy tip to cover the bill Rick had walked out on, into the tip jar on the counter.

"I'm telling."

She turned to find Sully standing behind her. He stood a head taller than her, so she tipped her chin up to look him in the eye.

"If you do, then I won't hold the next Harlan Coben novel for you," she said.

"That's harsh."

"Librarian's privilege."

"Are you ready?" Beth asked Lindsey as she joined them. She handed Lindsey her jacket, and they waved good-bye to Mary and Ian as they headed for the door.

Lindsey pushed the door open, and the wind ripped it out of her hands and slammed it against the wall. The rain stabbed her face with icy little pinpricks as she tried to pull the door back.

Sully reached around her and pulled it shut.

"Did you two walk here in this?" he asked.

"It wasn't like this when we left the library."

"Our bikes are still there," Beth said.

"You can't ride or walk home in this storm," Sully said. "Let me bring my truck around, and I'll give you both a lift."

He pushed the door open and headed out into the storm before they could protest.

"It's really bad out there," Beth said with a frown.

"Don't even think it," Lindsey said. "He's a big boy. There are plenty of places for him to stay in town. He doesn't need to stay at your place."

"You're right," Beth said with a nod. "I know you're right. Rick can take care of himself."

Despite these words, Lindsey noticed that Beth paused before getting into Sully's truck to check the pier and see if Rick's boat was tied up. When it wasn't in its usual spot, a look of concern flashed in her eyes.

"He probably docked it somewhere else," Lindsey shouted over the wind. "Like the marina."

Beth nodded but looked unconvinced. They hustled into the cab of Sully's truck. He shut the door behind them and hurried around to the driver's side. Heat was blasting out of the floor vents and fogging up the windows, and Lindsey was grateful, as the damp cold had begun to seep into her bones.

Sully used a rag to wipe down the inside of the windshield and put the truck in drive. They wound their way down the narrow two-lane road to the shore road beyond. When they reached the fork in the road, he turned left, which would lead them out to a stretch of small bungalows built during the postwar fifties, one of which Beth had bought a few years after she took the job as children's librarian.

Lindsey loved all of these small houses. They were painted bright colors and sported funky names like "License to Chill," "Buoys and Gulls" and "Dune Nuthin." Of course, Lindsey's favorite was Beth's. A small two-bedroom box of a house, it had a petite porch and was set back from the water with several houses between it and the well-worn path that led to the private beach. Beth had painted it sea-foam green with white trim and named it "A Shore Thing."

Some of the houses were vacation homes for wealthy New Yorkers, but most were family owned by Briar Creek residents who lived in town year-round. Lindsey wasn't sure what her future held, but she did keep an eye on the bungalows just in case one came up for sale. Over the past six months, she'd become very fond of the small town and thought it might not be so bad to spend her life in a cottage by the sea.

"Thanks for the ride, Sully," Beth said. "See you tomorrow, Lindsey."

She hopped out of the truck and bounded through the sheets of rain up onto her porch and into her house. Once the door closed behind her, Sully backed out of her small drive and headed back the way they had come.

Lindsey realized this was the first time she'd ever been alone with him, and the realization made her feel abruptly awkward. The wind that lashed the rain against her windows seemed mocking, and she felt a sudden need to fill the silence.

"This is very nice of you," she said.

He gave her a sidelong glance. "Does that mean you'll hold my favorite authors for me again?"

She grinned. "Oh, that was just a hollow threat. I could never deny a reader his favorite author."

"I suspected that, but I'm relieved to hear you say so."

The truck hit a pothole, and they bounced around a curve. Lindsey glanced out at the darkness that she knew was the churning sea.

"How do the islanders get through these storms?" she asked. "It must be scary."

"Only during the hurricanes," he said. "Mary and I grew up on Bell Island. We had a tree house in an oak tree at the water's edge. We used to love to camp out in it during summer thunderstorms."

"And your parents let you?"

"They didn't say no."

"Meaning you didn't ask."

He grinned, and Lindsey shook her head. She had a feeling Mary and Mike Sullivan had been a trial to their parents. They were both very much like the island they had grown up on. They had a streak of wildness in them that no amount of time living off island would ever tame.

"I've been reading up on the islands and their history. It's fascinating."

"Don't believe everything you read. Creekers are known to have vivid imaginations."

"Creekers?" she asked.

"Don't tell me you haven't heard that term," he said. "That's what we call anyone who lives on the islands or in town."

"Creekers," Lindsey repeated. "As in Briar *Creek.*"

"Exactly," he said. "Once a Creeker, always a Creeker, no matter where life takes you."

"Was it hard to leave your island when you grew up?" she asked.

"Yes and no," he said. She waited, but he added nothing more.

Lindsey let out an exasperated huff and said, "And you were doing so well."

"What do you mean?" He looked perplexed.

"I mean that this is the most I have ever heard you say in the six months I've been living here. Getting words out of you is harder than shucking a pearl out of an oyster. Now let's try it again; was it hard to leave your island?"

By the light of the dashboard, she saw his dimples deepen. He was clearly amused, but he took a deep breath and said, "I was ready to go when I went. I knew I wanted a career on a ship, so it was the U.S. Naval Academy and then fifteen years of active duty. When I finished serving, I was ready to come home, and the folks aren't as young as they used to be, so the timing was right."

They had reached the three-way intersection, and Sully took the road that would lead to her house, or rather Nancy's house, where she was a tenant. She didn't wonder that he knew where she lived. Briar Creek was such a small town that if Mrs. Isaac on Grover Street baked a pie, the whole town knew it in a matter of moments. Of course, given that she baked an amazing apple pie, it wasn't such a surprise.

Sully parked the truck in front of the tall white captain's house. It had reminded Lindsey of a triple-layer cake the first time she had seen it; with three stories trimmed in gingerbread, it had a festive air and bespoke a happy residence. She had wanted to move in immediately.

The wind was fierce, and it slammed against the windshield. Lindsey glanced up at her apartment on the third floor, afraid she might have left some windows open, but was distracted by something moving on the roofline. Something white, illuminated by a flash of bolt lightning, was up on the widow's walk. She gasped and Sully followed her gaze.

"What is that?" she asked.

Sully squinted and then his face turned grim.

"Oh no, not again. Stay here," he ordered. He jumped out of the truck and raced toward the house.

CHAPTER 5

Lindsey watched him dash through the rain to the house. She was out of the truck and following him before the thought had fully formed in her mind.

The front door opened into a small vestibule. A

wide staircase led up to the second floor. Sully was already on the landing above as Lindsey pounded up the stairs after him.

He paused to bang on the door to the second-floor apartment. This was Charlie Peyton's apartment. He was Nancy's nephew, and he worked for Ian and Sully's tour-boat company.

"Charlie!" Sully called. He banged again, but there was no answer.

"I think he's out," Lindsey gasped as she caught up to him.

The storm's fierce wind rattled the shutters on the dormer window at the end of the landing. Sully broke into a run, taking the stairs that led up to the third floor, and Lindsey's apartment, two at a time.

At the end of the landing, a narrow door stood open. It banged against the wall as the wind blasted past it. Lindsey could feel the bitter wind tugging at her hair and clothes as if trying to push her away. Rain pelted onto the wooden floor, making it slick.

Sully hurried up the narrow stairs, which led to the small widow's walk on the top of the roof. Lindsey followed. She had to squint to be able to see against the assault of the storm, but it took only a moment to make out the huddled shape of a person, leaning against the short wrought-iron rail and staring out at the sea.

Sully caught the woman in his arms and pulled

her back from the edge. She didn't resist. When he turned her toward the stairs, it took Lindsey a moment to recognize her landlord, Nancy.

With her gray hair plastered to her head, her bathrobe sodden with rain and her face looking pale and strained, Lindsey could hardly reconcile her with the woman who always had a fresh batch of cookies in her oven and a twinkle in her eyes.

"Let's get her inside!" Sully yelled.

It broke Lindsey out of her trance, and she hustled down the stairs ahead of them. Sully put Nancy gently on her feet, and Lindsey grabbed her and kept her upright so that he could close the hatch and latch the door behind them.

Nancy's lips had a tinge of blue, and her skin was icy to the touch. She needed a warm bath immediately.

"It's all right, Nancy," she said. "I'm here."

Nancy looked at her without recognition.

"Come on, Nance," Sully said. "He'll make it home. Don't you worry."

Nancy turned to him, and the last of her strength seemed to give way. Sully scooped her back up into his arms and carried her down the two flights of stairs to the first floor, where she lived.

"I'll start a bath for her," Lindsey said. She hurried ahead and charged into Nancy's apartment, which was thankfully unlocked, heading straight for the master bath.

As she fussed with the tap and started filling

the tub, Sully brought Nancy in and sat her on a small dressing stool at the vanity table in the corner.

"I'll go make some hot chocolate," he said. "And I'll see if I can track Charlie down."

Lindsey glanced up from the tub. "Good idea. We'll be out as soon as I've got her warmed up."

Lindsey poured in a healthy dollop of lavender bubble bath, hoping the smell would soothe and the bubbles would maintain Nancy's modesty. When the water was ready, Lindsey helped Nancy get out of her wet things and climb into the tub.

Nancy didn't say a word. She sat in the water and let Lindsey fuss over her. There were so many questions Lindsey wanted to ask, but she knew now wasn't the time. Nancy leaned her head back against the tub and closed her eyes. As Lindsey watched, a tear slipped down her right cheek and splashed into the bubbles.

Without opening her eyes, Nancy reached for Lindsey's hand, and when her sudsy, wet fingers closed over it, her voice was low and husky as she whispered, "Thank you."

When the bathwater started to cool, Lindsey helped Nancy dry off and get dressed in fresh nightclothes and then tucked her into bed. The storm still howled outside, but as soon as Nancy's head landed on her pillow, she fell into a deep slumber. Lindsey drained the tub and shut off the light. A small night-light was on in the bathroom, giving off just enough of a glow to allow Lindsey to navigate the furniture.

She pulled the bedroom door halfway shut behind her. A short hallway led past two other rooms, a spare bedroom and a home office. A large living room, filled with plants and paintings of the sea, as well as a large fireplace, was next. Lindsey was about to turn the corner, which led to the kitchen and dining room, when Sully appeared bearing a tray of hot chocolate.

"She's already asleep," Lindsey said.

"Oh, well." Sully glanced at the tray and then at the two armchairs in front of the fireplace. "It'd be a shame to let it go to waste."

"And we should stay for a bit to make sure she's okay," Lindsey said. Meanwhile, she was thinking there was no way Sully was setting one toe out the front door until he explained to her what the heck had just happened.

"Excellent. I'll start the fire." Sully handed her the tray.

Lindsey placed it on the short table between the two brown-leather wing chairs. Nancy's fireplace was gas, so Sully only had to flip it on and turn it to low, so as not to waste gas.

They sat across from each other and cradled their mugs of chocolate while the heat of the small fire washed over them.

Lindsey took a sip of her chocolate and glanced

at Sully in surprise. It was thick and rich without being too sweet.

"What?" He raised his eyebrows. "Did you think my sister was the only one who could cook?"

"This is delicious," she said.

"Thank you," he said. "I learned how to make it when I was overseas."

Lindsey studied him over the rim of her mug. He looked as windblown and soggy as she felt, and somehow that only added to his attractiveness. She pushed a sodden hank of hair out of her face and had a feeling it did not add to hers. As much as she had sworn off men, she had to admit that she found Captain Sully very intriguing.

"Why was Nancy up there?" she asked. "And why did you say 'not again' when we saw her?"

"I was wondering how long it would take you to ask me that," he said. "I'm not sure it's my story to tell, but . . ."

"But?"

"If you're going to be living here, you should probably know, and it might be too hard for Nancy to tell you herself," he said. He was quiet for a moment. He stared into the fire as if trying to come to a decision and then glanced up at her. "You know Nancy is a widow?"

Lindsey nodded.

"Her husband was a ferryboat captain. Back in 1979, he was returning across Long Island Sound and a sudden storm blew in. His ship went down

63

in the Sound. There were no survivors."

"Oh, that's terrible."

"The night he died, when they came to tell her that his ship had gone down, they found her up on the widow's walk," Sully said. "Somehow, she knew."

"Oh, poor Nancy. That must have been horrible."

"I remember her husband," Sully said. "Captain Jake—he was great. He'd take all of us island kids out on his boat. He was always laughing and telling bad jokes, like, what did one candle say to another?"

"I don't know," Lindsey said.

"Are you going out tonight? Ba dum bum."

"Oh, that's awful," Lindsey said. "No wonder you kids loved him."

"I was seven when his boat went down," Sully said. "I'll never forget it. It was an awful storm with fierce wind, pelting rain, booming thunder and lightning that ripped open the sky."

"A lot like tonight then," Lindsey said. She glanced at the large bay window where the rain hammered against the glass pane as if looking for a way in.

Sully sipped his cocoa and said, "Captain Jake should have been home before the storm hit, but it surprised them out in the Sound, and on his last run of the day, his ship got swept off course and ran aground miles from where it should have been. The hull was ripped open on the rocks, and the big waves caused by the storm took the ship down."

Lindsey blew out a breath. They both took long sips of their rapidly cooling cocoa.

"It's been thirty-two years, and every now and then, when there is a storm like that one, she takes to pacing the widow's walk again, as if she's still looking for him."

Lindsey tipped her head and considered him. "Is that why her nephew lives here?"

"Yes, Charlie is supposed to keep an eye on her," he said. "He's usually more responsible than this."

As if their conversation had beckoned him, the door from the vestibule burst open, and in came a young man, soaked to the bone and looking scared.

"Aunt Nancy!" he cried.

"She's fine," Sully said. He stood and took in the sight of the soggy young man in front of him. "What happened to you?"

"My car broke down," he said. "I had to run all the way here from the Post Road."

Charlie was whip slender with dyed black hair that usually stood on end but was now plastered to his head. He had so many piercings and tattoos that he looked like the poster child for body art gone wrong. Although he worked for Sully by day, his ambition was to be a famous rock star, and most of his free time was spent rehearsing for gigs, playing gigs or recording new songs.

"She's all right," Lindsey said.

His shoulders sagged with relief. Lindsey rose and handed him the third cup of cocoa, which had been for Nancy.

"Come sit by the fire," she said. "We'll be lucky if we don't all catch pneumonia."

"Thank you both," Charlie said. "If anything had happened to her . . ."

"No worries," Sully said. "You did your best to get here."

Charlie let loose a shudder, and Lindsey had the feeling it wasn't just from the cold.

"I'd better get going," Sully said. "See you tomorrow, Charlie?"

"Yes, sir," he said. "And thanks again."

Lindsey walked Sully to the door. Now that they were all home, she wanted to lock the front door.

"Thanks for the ride," she said. "And for helping with Nancy. I don't know what I would have done if I'd been by myself."

"You'd have managed," he said. He studied her for a moment, looking as if he wanted to say something more, but he didn't.

He crossed the porch and stepped out into the rain. Lindsey watched him go. She wondered how Nancy had felt saying good-bye to her husband every time he went to sea, and she wondered what sort of love they had shared that Nancy mourned his loss more than thirty years later.

CHAPTER 6

"Are you nervous?" Lindsey asked. "There's no need to be. Your work is great. She's going to love it."

"I wasn't nervous until you asked," Beth said. She cradled her art portfolio under one arm and ran her free hand through her hair. "Don't you think this is a little pushy?"

"Not at all. Carole said the editor wanted to look at your work," Lindsey said.

"That's because Carole knows her boss," Beth protested. "Ms. Carlisle was probably just being nice."

"Maybe, but she still could have said no," Lindsey said.

"I suppose," Beth said.

They crossed the street and headed through the park toward the Blue Anchor Café. It was a perfect late morning Saturday. The sky was a pristine blue, the water in the bay sparkled, the sun was warm and the breeze was cool and gentle. It was impossible not to feel optimistic on such a gorgeous day.

The café was quieter than usual. Lindsey assumed everyone was out making the most of the weather. They sidled up to the bar and scanned the room. There was a family of four, a few people who looked to be tourists and one dark-haired woman, sitting alone in the corner.

Mary hustled over and whispered, "That's her."

"Oh, I think I'm going to be ill," Beth said. "What if she hates my work?"

"She won't," Mary said. "Now come on. She's been waiting for you. I'll walk you over."

Mary grabbed Beth's hand and crossed the room, half dragging her behind her. Lindsey brought up the rear and took the opportunity to study Ms. Carlisle.

She was wearing a pair of Rag & Bone skinny cropped jeans with an equally expensive-looking peach-colored top and a pair of Cazabat flats. Her chestnut hair was done up in a casual twist, with long strands hanging down on either side of her face. A pair of reading glasses perched on her nose as she typed frenetically on the Netbook in front of her. She was the very picture of a New York editor on vacation.

"Excuse me, Ms. Carlisle," Mary said as she approached the table. "Your party is here."

Sydney Carlisle looked at her watch as if checking to see how on time they were. It was exactly noon. Lindsey felt Beth shrink on the spot and stepped forward to make the introductions.

"I'm Lindsey Norris," she said and held out her hand. "I'm the director of the Briar Creek Library."

"A pleasure," Ms. Carlisle said. She took

Lindsey's hand, but her grip was cold and clammy, and Lindsey had to resist the urge to wipe her palm on her pants.

"This is Beth Stanley," Lindsey said. The two women shook hands, and Lindsey added, "She's the one Carole Towles told you about, the one whose work she wanted you to see."

"Well, to be honest . . ." Sydney began but Lindsey cut her off, "Can I recommend the chowder? Mary is known for it. Isn't she, Beth?"

Beth was looking at her as if she'd recently sustained a head injury. It was very clear that Sydney Carlisle had been about to beg off, but Lindsey had grown up watching her father, a researcher, blithely ignore any wishes that went against his own. As an underfunded researcher in an academic setting, he lived by the credo that it was easier to receive forgiveness than permission. Lindsey wasn't his daughter for nothing.

"Actually, I've already ordered lunch," Sydney said. "But I'll keep the chowder in mind for next time."

Lindsey put a heavy hand on Beth's shoulder and pushed her into a seat. She took the remaining one and smiled at Ms. Carlisle.

"So, Ms. Carlisle," Lindsey began but the editor interrupted her.

"Call me Sydney."

"Terrific. Well, Sydney, what brings you to our tiny town?"

"Would you believe solitude?" Sydney asked.

"Tough to find in a town like Briar Creek," Lindsey said. "The minute you booked your room, the whole town knew an editor was on her way here from New York."

"I'll have to have a chat with Mrs. Palmer," she said. She looked very unhappy, and Beth was visibly cringing now.

"It wouldn't matter," Lindsey said. "The minute you stepped outside of the Beachfront, the town was intent upon discovering who you are."

"Don't you people have cable?" Sydney asked.

Beth laughed, tried to stifle it, and laughed harder. It was obvious her anxiety was giving her a case of the giggles.

Sydney swiveled her head in Beth's direction for the first time. "Why don't we get this over with so you can stop being terrified?"

Lindsey was pleased that Sydney's voice was not unkind. Beth had been a basket case all morning. Lindsey wasn't sure how much more her nerves could take.

"I'm giving you fair warning, however, that I am very harsh, so if you can't handle it, you'd better leave now."

Beth sat up straighter. "I can handle it."

Sydney held out her hands and Beth handed her the black case. Despite her bravado, Lindsey saw sweaty handprints on the case where Beth had been clutching it. She had no doubt that Beth was scared to death.

Sydney untied the portfolio and opened it wide. She flipped through the pages, muttering "uh-huh" but showing neither pleasure nor displeasure at the work.

"You have talent," Sydney said. "Your story is age appropriate for your intended audience, and your illustrations are engaging without being overdone. The idea of a hamster detective who lives in the library is charming. I see a future for you as a children's book author, if you want it, but not with this book."

"Why not?" Lindsey asked.

She could tell Beth was warring with herself over reveling in Sydney's compliments about her work versus having her hopes dashed at the rejection of her book. She hadn't decided which way she was going yet.

"Unfortunately, this type of story has already been done," Sydney said. Mary arrived with their food just then, and Sydney said nothing until she left. "You have the ability, Ms. Stanley. You just need to do something fresh." Maybe she felt badly for crushing Beth's dream because her voice was noticeably nicér now than it had been when they first sat down.

Beth nodded and excused herself to go to the restroom. Lindsey could tell she was disappointed, and she felt a twinge of guilt. Maybe she shouldn't have pushed her so hard.

Sydney put aside her Netbook and tucked into her lunch, a platter of fried clams with french fries and coleslaw on the side. She didn't seem to care whether Lindsey joined her or not.

Lindsey picked up her spoon and pushed it around in her chowder. "Do you think it would be worth Beth's time to query another children's book editor?"

Sydney glanced up and gave her a considering look. She swallowed her mouthful, wiped her lips with her napkin, and said, "Not with that idea. In fact, if she shops it, she'll be ruined."

"But she's worked so hard on it."

"Did she really?"

"What's that supposed to mean?"

Sydney gave her a long look. "I didn't want to get into this with her, because this is supposed to be my free weekend and I am really trying to avoid any sort of drama."

She let the rebuke wash over Lindsey, but it held no sting, as Lindsey was too annoyed on Beth's behalf to care much about Sydney's free time.

"But . . ." Lindsey prompted her.

With a sigh, Sydney leaned over the armrest of her chair and rifled through the briefcase at her feet. She came back up holding a glossy book catalog. Post-its marked several of the pages, and she flipped to one at the back.

"Look familiar?" she asked.

Lindsey scanned the page, and halfway down she saw it. In full color there he was, the same chubby, brown hamster sporting a monocle as the one Beth had created and dubbed Sherlock Hamster, detective.

"But I don't understand," Lindsey said. She flipped the catalog over to scan the cover. It was for the winter, meaning this was a preview of books to come. But how had Beth's gotten in here? She flipped back to the page that described the book. The name of the author leapt out at her—Rick Eckman.

"I think it's fairly obvious, don't you?" Sydney asked as she kept eating. "Your friend plagiarized her book idea from my author Mr. Eckman."

"Beth would never do that," Lindsey said. "That's preposterous."

Sydney suddenly looked weary. "I don't want to get into a debate about what is plagiarism. I'm just telling you that he has a book coming out with virtually the exact same story line and characters. I know you want to help your friend, but she can't steal other people's work to get ahead. It will get her blackballed from the industry."

"Beth didn't steal anything from him," Lindsey said. She knew she sounded defensive, but she just couldn't believe what was happening. This was a nightmare.

"He's a Caldecott-winning book author," Sydney said with a sigh. "Surely you're not suggesting he stole his idea from her. Why would he? No one would ever believe it."

"That may be true," Lindsey said. "But that's what happened."

She snatched up Beth's portfolio and pushed back her chair. "Thank you for your time."

"I'm sorry," Sydney said. It was the first time Lindsey thought she might actually be sincere.

"May I keep this?" Lindsey asked, holding up the catalog.

"Oh, it has all of my notes," Sydney said with a grimace. "Do you want to just tear out the pertinent page?"

"That will work. Thank you," Lindsey said. She opened the catalog to the page she wanted and carefully tore it out, making sure not to damage the page or the book.

She glanced up and saw Beth headed their way. "I hope you enjoy your stay with us, Sydney, and thank you for your time."

"No problem." Sydney took the remainder of her catalog and stuffed it back into her bag. She returned to her lunch while Lindsey crossed the café to Beth.

She noticed that the tip of Beth's nose was bright pink, and her eyes looked puffier than usual. She'd been crying. Lindsey really hated that she was about to make a bad day much worse for her friend, and it was all Rick Eckman's fault. If he were here, she'd give him a swift kick in the pants or possibly a solid punch to the nose.

"Beth, let's go take a walk," she said.

"Oh, no, I don't want to seem like a big baby," Beth said. "It's rude to walk out on Ms. Carlisle. We should finish our lunch with her."

"Oh, I think she'll be fine," Lindsey said.

"I guess I can call Rick now and tell him he was right. I was rejected and crushed by it."

"Not so fast," Lindsey said. "I've got something to show you."

Chapter 7

"What is it?" Beth asked as Lindsey hustled her out of the café and across the parking lot to the town park.

A seagull was perched in its usual spot on the back of one of the benches, and seeing that they had no food, it gave them a sideways stare of disapproval before lifting off onto the air currents that swept in from the water. Feeling duly chastised, Lindsey promised herself she would remember to bring some stale bread the next time she came to the park.

An elderly couple was parked on a bench down the way, sharing a newspaper and drinking coffee out of paper cups. A mother with two young ones was sitting under a tree on a blanket while the baby had some tummy time and the toddler collected leaves.

"Sit here," Lindsey said. She gestured to an empty bench.

"What's going on?" Beth said. "You look angry, and not just a little angry but more like a swarm of killer bees angry."

Lindsey took a steadying breath. She *was* humming like a swarm. In fact, she was so mad, everything was going fuzzy and she was beginning to see spots.

"Here," she said. She couldn't trust herself to say anything more. She handed Beth the glossy page from the Caterpillar Press catalog and sat beside her.

"I don't understand," Beth said. "What is this?"

"Sydney gave it to me," Lindsey said. "It's from the publisher's catalog of upcoming books."

"But that's my book," Beth said. She pointed to the picture. "How did they . . . and why is Rick's name . . . ?"

Her voice trailed off as the ugly truth came into focus.

"He stole my story, didn't he?" she asked.

"I'm afraid so," Lindsey said.

"But that's . . . he told me it was too amateurish," Beth protested.

"Well, I guess we know why he didn't want you to show it to anyone," Lindsey said. "He'd already sold it under his own name."

"What did Ms. Carlisle say?" Beth asked. "She must be furious that he's deceived them."

Lindsey did not want to have this conversation. She really didn't. If Beth's feelings had been hurt before, she could only imagine how upset she was going to be now. But there was no need to explain. Her silence was telling.

"Oh, no—Ms. Carlisle thinks I plagiarized him!" Beth cried.

"I'm afraid so," Lindsey winced.

Beth stared out at the Thumb Islands. The breeze coming in from the water ruffled the spikes of her black hair. Her large, gray eyes narrowed. Lindsey wondered if it was to hold back tears.

"I'm going to murder him!"

The elderly couple glanced over from their bench, obviously startled by her outburst.

"I'm going to deep-fry him in oil," Beth ranted. "No, that's too messy. I'm going to chop him up and feed him to the sharks, piece by miserable piece."

Now the mother by the tree with the young ones was looking at them with her eyebrows raised up to her hairline. Lindsey recognized her as a regular at story time. Uh-oh.

"Beth," she said. "Get a hold of yourself."

She looked at the older couple and the mother, still watching them, and forced a laugh. In a loud voice, she said, "You're such a kidder."

But Beth wasn't going to be diverted. She stood

up with her portfolio under her arm and began to stomp toward the pier. "When I get done with him, Rick Eckman is going to wish he was dead."

Lindsey followed in her wake with a feeling of dread. Her own breakup with her fiancé had not been pretty, but at least he'd only cheated on her, not stolen her work. She had no idea how she would have handled it if he had, but she couldn't blame Beth for being furious. She'd been working on that picture book for years, and for Rick to take it and submit it as his own was unconscionable.

Beth churned across the pavement, past the Blue Anchor and out to the tour-boat office. The dock was empty, meaning both Ian and Sully were out giving tours.

Ronnie Maynard, the tour coordinator, was in the little storefront office, sitting at her desk.

Beth slammed through the door. "I need a boat."

"Well, hello to you, too," Ronnie said as she lowered her nail file and glanced at the pair of them.

"Hi, Ronnie," Lindsey said. "Don't mind Beth, she's a little upset."

"A little upset?" Beth repeated. "I am more than a little upset. I am crazy mad. I need a boat, and I need it right now."

"What happened, hon?" Ronnie asked. Her voice was kind, as if there wasn't any trouble she hadn't heard before that couldn't be fixed by a sympathetic listener.

Beth took a deep breath and told her. Ronnie clucked in all the right places, calming Beth down with her genuine understanding.

Lindsey had gotten to know Ronnie over the past few months. She was a regular at the library and liked to check out the latest romance novels. She was a particular fan of Amanda Quick and Linda Howard.

If the term Sully had taught her was accurate, then Ronnie was one of the older Creekers, as she had to be about the same age as Milton, making her around eighty years old as well.

Looking at her, it was hard to tell. She wore her cranberry-red hair in an updo reminiscent of a beehive. Huge neon-green plastic rings decorated her fingers, and she wore matching bauble earrings and a necklace. Her neck and face were wrinkled from years out in the sun, but she was fit, wearing khaki capri pants with Keds and a knitted sailor's top. She favored green eye shadow and bright-pink lipstick, and she had a heavy hand with the foundation.

"So, that's why I need to borrow a boat," Beth said, finishing her monologue.

"Sully just took the water taxi out," Ronnie said. "He's picking up the Ginowskis on Split Island. Both Charlie and Ian are out on tours and not expected back until later today."

"Could I rent a boat?" Beth asked.

"All I have left is a kayak," Ronnie said.

"I'll take it," Beth said.

"No, you won't," Lindsey said. Enough was enough. It was time to rein her in before she got herself killed.

"Excuse me," Beth said. "If I want a kayak, I'm taking a kayak."

"You don't even know how to kayak," Lindsey said.

"Paddle right, paddle left; how hard can it be?"

"There are some pretty strong currents out there," Ronnie said. "Besides, it's high tide, the rocks are covered by water and you could smash up on one if you don't know where they are."

"See?" Lindsey asked. "Now you're just going to have to calm down and wait. We can take the water taxi when it returns."

"Fine," Beth said but her cranky tone made it clear that it wasn't.

The small office had a tiny waiting area made up of three deck chairs and a glass coffee table covered in boating magazines. Beth sat in one of the chairs and turned to stare out the window.

Lindsey blew out a breath. There were at least five hundred other things she'd rather be doing on her day off, but Beth was her best friend. She took a seat and picked up a magazine.

"You don't have to go with me," Beth said. "I can handle this on my own."

"Normally, I would agree with you," Lindsey said as she paused to sniff the cologne sample in the magazine. Too citrusy; why was men's cologne always heavy on the citrus? "But given that you threatened to feed him to the sharks in front of a listening audience, I'm thinking I should be there."

"Thanks," Beth said. "You're right. You may have to sit on me if he gets within punching distance."

"Well, after I let you get in a few kidney shots, maybe," Lindsey said.

Beth grinned, and Lindsey was pleased to see a glimmer of the old Beth sparkle in her eyes.

Forty minutes later, Sully arrived with the Ginowskis. They waved at Ronnie through the glass window and headed into town. Sully gave Lindsey a puzzled look as he entered the office.

She hadn't seen him since Nancy's bad spell the night before, and she wondered if he thought she was here because of that. His first words confirmed it.

"Is everything all right?" he asked. "Do you need Charlie?"

"No," Lindsey said quickly. "Nancy's fine. We're here for a different reason."

"I need a boat," Beth said.

Sully glanced at Ronnie, and she shrugged. "We're booked out."

"Do you need a lift?" he asked. "I can take you in the water taxi."

"That would be perfect," Beth said. "I'll double your rate."

"You don't have to do that," Sully said. "Where do you need to go?"

"Gull Island," she said.

Sully's eyebrows rose. He clapped a hand on the back of his neck. "You know that's a private island. I'm not supposed to dock there without permission."

"Just get me within swimming distance then," Beth said, and she led the way out the door.

Sully glanced at Lindsey, and she said, "I'll explain on the way."

Beth was already sitting in the boat clutching her portfolio to her chest. It was a midsized inboard motorboat that had a canopy. Sully helped Lindsey step down into the boat, and he untied it from the dock, pushing off as he jumped in.

He turned the motor on low, and they puttered out past the end of the pier through the no wake zone toward the islands.

Lindsey sat in the seat beside Sully, who turned to her and asked, "So, what's this all about?"

She gave him the short version.

"Suddenly, I'm not feeling so polite about not docking," he said. He leaned close to Lindsey and lowered his voice and asked, "Did she know all this last night, when they had their tiff at the café?"

"No, we just found out this morning."

They had motored out into the channel now, and Lindsey noticed he gave the engine more power, and a good-sized wake formed behind them. This was her first time out on the water, and she reveled in the fresh, cool spray against her face and the wind tugging at her hair.

They rounded a small cluster of islands. The first one had a large granite boulder jutting up that indeed looked like a big thumb, thus, the name of the islands. A bit farther was a flatter one that had a small house perched on it, and then several others that barely qualified as more than rocks. Depending upon who you asked, there were either seventy islands out here or more than a hundred. Sometimes the rocks counted and sometimes they did not.

Lindsey had read up on the history of the Thumb Islands and knew that the archipelago had formed thousands of years before during an ice age. They passed by another large island, and an older woman with short gray hair, wearing an apron and carrying pruning shears, waved at them as they passed. Sully waved and grinned back at her.

"My mom," he said. "That's where I grew up, on Bell Island."

Lindsey studied it as they passed. Sure enough, a large granite boulder on the east side of the island looked like an enormous bell. The island had three large houses on it with large lawns that were turning brown with the coming winter and tall trees whose leaves had turned and were beginning to fall. It looked like an idyllic place to spend a childhood.

"How big is it?" she asked.

"Almost ten acres," he said. "It's the second largest island out here."

They headed farther out into the Sound. The waves got choppy, and their boat slapped hard against the water until Sully slowed it down. They passed several hazardous-looking rocks, a few small uninhabited islands and then a series of islands where the houses looked like charming summer getaways.

Lindsey could see the appeal to having your own island. No door-to-door salesmen, no traffic, no home-owner's associations. If you wanted to be left alone, an island was a good way to go.

The boat took a wide turn around one island. Wider than Sully had swung around other islands. She glanced over the side to see if there were rocks they were avoiding, but she couldn't make out any in the water's rocky depths.

She glanced at Sully and saw him studying the island as they passed. It was then that she realized that this one looked to have been burned. The skeletons of charred tree trunks stood sentry around the shell of a stone cottage, which was roofless and blackened by fire.

"What happened there?" she asked.

"Lightning strike," Beth said.

Lindsey glanced at Sully for confirmation. She

noticed he shifted in his seat, and she narrowed her gaze.

"Lightning didn't do that, did it?"

He turned and studied her for a moment and then seemed to come to a decision. "No, it didn't."

CHAPTER 8

"What?" Beth gasped. "But in all of the books about the islands, it says that it was the storm of 1983. There was record lightning, and one of the bolts hit the Ruby house, burning down the house and killing the family, who were asleep and trapped inside."

"That's what the books say," Sully agreed. "But they never explain why the body of Peter Ruby wasn't among the rest."

"Who's Peter Ruby?" Lindsey asked.

"The father," Sully said. He didn't go into details, but he didn't have to, Lindsey could tell by his tone that he hadn't liked the man.

"The speculation is that he tried to swim for help and perished," Beth said.

"Does that seem likely?" Sully asked. "You're in the middle of one of the worst storms to hit the islands, your house has been hit by lightning and you swim for help? Wouldn't you try to get your family out first?"

"Well, yeah," she said.

"Mary and I were friends with the Ruby kids, as they were just a few years younger than us. There was something not right in that house. Neither of us ever believed that Peter Ruby died trying to save his family."

"Do you think he killed them and used the storm as cover to escape?" Lindsey asked. They were passing the island, and she turned to study the remnants of the burnt house and scorched lives.

"That's exactly what I think," Sully said. His voice was grim, and it gave Lindsey the shivers.

"Then why . . . ?" Beth asked, looking as disturbed as Lindsey felt.

"It was twenty-eight years ago. People don't talk about it," Sully said, correctly interpreting her expression. "Mostly because it is so horrible, but also the local businesses don't want to scare off the tourists."

"Does anyone ever go there?" Lindsey asked.

"No, the structure is too dangerous to wander around, and because of the deaths, no one has been eager to buy it and rebuild."

"That's a shame," Lindsey said. "It's a lovely spot."

"You should have seen it in the day," Sully said. "Mrs. Ruby planted climbing roses, and they all but took over the island. Mary and I used to pretend it was enchanted."

"Why did you tell us this?" Beth asked. "I mean,

I've lived here for ten years and no one has told me that story."

"Well, you two are the town librarians; if anyone should know the true history of the Ruby house, it's you two," he said. "Who knows—maybe you'll solve the mystery."

"I think that's Chief Daniels's job," Beth said.

"But thanks for telling the truth," Lindsey said. She was glad he trusted them enough to tell them the real story, but still, she felt better when the island was behind them. Maybe it was an over-active imagination on her part, but she could swear she felt malevolence pulsing off of the island and pushing against the waves that splashed against its shores.

They were silent as Sully navigated a few more islands, slowing down as he approached one that was small in size and had only one house on it. Sully cut the engine and coasted up against the wooden dock that floated out from the island. One of the pilings was carved into the shape of a seagull, thus the name Gull Island, Lindsey presumed. Rick's boat was there, signifying that he was home.

Beth handed Lindsey her portfolio and hopped onto the edge of the boat. She nimbly jumped onto the dock, taking the boat's rope with her. She swiftly tied the boat up and reached out a hand to take her artwork back from Lindsey.

Lindsey scrambled over the side and caught the

edge of the boat with her hand as the dock bobbed and weaved beneath her feet. She steadied herself and took a few steps forward, relieved when she kept her balance.

"Are you ready?" she asked Beth.

"I want to face him alone."

"But I thought you wanted backup, in case you felt the urge to put a hurt on him," Lindsey said.

"I want him to talk to me. I want him to explain this." Beth held up the page of the catalog. "And I don't think he'll talk in front of an audience."

"You're sure?"

Beth grimaced, but she looked determined. She gave Lindsey a nod and turned toward the stairs, which led from the dock up the short hill to a deck above.

"I guess we wait," Lindsey said.

Sully stepped out of the boat with two bottles of water in his hands. He gave one to Lindsey and they sat on the bobbing dock with the island to their backs and facing the shoreline they'd left behind.

"Think he'll tell her the truth?" he asked.

Lindsey took a long pull off of her water bottle and thought about Rick. From what she knew of him, he was the type of person who in his opinion never erred. Even with evidence shoved under his nose, he would be unlikely to admit to any wrong-doing.

"No," she said. She glanced up and saw Beth

striding across the deck above. To get her mind off of the coming confrontation, she said, "Are there a lot of stories about the Thumb Islands that no one else knows?"

Sully glanced at her, and she appreciated the way the sunlight brought out the red in his mahogany curls. His face bore the tanned and weathered skin of a sailor, wrinkled before its time, mostly from squinting she guessed.

"How much time do you have?" he asked. His smile lit up his bright-blue eyes, and Lindsey liked that his good humor was so genuine.

She was getting the feeling that with Sully there were no hidden agendas or dark secrets lurking within. He didn't seem to feel the need to prove his youth or stamina, not like some other men she could name. He seemed content with his life and himself, and she was surprised to find that it was a very attractive trait in a man.

She opened her mouth to answer when a scream ripped through the comfortable fabric of the day.

Sully was on his feet first, and he pounded down the dock toward the stairs. Lindsey was right behind him, trying to keep her balance as she ran on the wobbly wood. They scrambled up the stairs to the deck above. The door to the small house stood wide open. They raced forward, and Lindsey blinked when they stepped into the sudden darkness.

"Beth?" she cried. She hurried forward and

slipped on a piece of drawing paper that was lying on the wooden floor. Sully caught her by the elbow and pulled her upright.

A quick glance about the room and it was clear that something horrible had happened here. Papers were strewn everywhere. Pictures were smashed and what looked like an awards shelf was barren, with just shards on the floor below it.

"Beth!" Lindsey cried. She was beginning to feel panic surge through her.

A whimper from the back of the house sounded. Sully and Lindsey strode through the main room together toward the back. There was a small kitchenette and a short hallway that led to a bathroom and two bedrooms. A quick glance at the first room, the bedroom, proved it to be empty. In the next room, which was outfitted to be a studio with an easel, a drawing table and a large desk with a computer, they found Beth.

She was standing in the center of the room, with one hand over her mouth and her portfolio hanging limply from the other. Her eyes were huge and fixated on a corner of the room. Lindsey stepped inside and followed her gaze.

Slumped in his desk chair, with the word *LIAR* written across his forehead, sat Rick Eckman. He wore his usual grubby T-shirt, but this time it was saturated with a deep red stain. Lindsey didn't have to get any closer to know he was dead.

CHAPTER 9

A hiss escaped Sully as he stepped into the room after Lindsey. He immediately crossed over to Eckman and grabbed his wrist. It came as no surprise when he shook his head. Rick was dead.

"There's nothing we can do for him," Sully said. "Let's go call the police."

Beth looked like she would balk, but Lindsey took her portfolio out of her hand and led her outside. They waited, leaning against the deck railing while Sully used his cell phone to contact the local authorities.

The sun disappeared behind a fluffy roller of a cloud, and Lindsey felt her skin grow cold. Someone had murdered Rick Eckman. The realization sent shock waves coursing through her. She could feel Beth shivering beside her and knew she must be feeling it even more strongly.

She braced her friend with an arm around her shoulders. Beth leaned into her ever so slightly.

"It's going to be all right," she said. They were hollow words, and she knew it, but she had nothing else to offer. Beth nodded.

Sully snapped his phone shut and joined them. "I couldn't get through to the police station, so Ronnie is calling it in. It's going to be a while.

Would you rather wait down in the boat?"

Lindsey knew she would prefer that, but she left the decision up to Beth. This was her boyfriend, after all.

"I think we should stay here and watch over him," Beth said. Her voice, normally so light and cheerful, was low as if weighed down by the shock.

Sully and Lindsey nodded at one another. He leaned against the railing beside them, and they listened to the cries of a yellow warbler, obviously irritated to have strangers on his turf, as he made an indignant *cheepa-cheepa-cheepa* sound at them before taking flight with a flash of his yellow wings. Lindsey wished she could go with him.

The local police force was made up of two men and one woman who were stationed in a small brick building next to the post office on the main road that ran through Briar Creek. They had one boat that patrolled the islands, mostly during the summer months, when the resident and tourist season was at its peak.

The small, navy-blue motor boat was smacking hard against the waves as it raced toward the island. Sully pushed off of the rail where he'd been leaning and jogged down the wooden stairs to the dock below to help them tie up.

Lindsey watched from above as Chief Daniels lumbered out of the boat, followed by Officer

Plewicki. She had only met Daniels once. He was one of the two cops who'd had guns pointed at her face when the library alarm had gone off because she hadn't known the fifteen-second rule. Thanks, Ms. Cole.

The chief's uniform was snug around his generous middle, and he had a habit of hitching up his pants by the belt every few minutes, as if he spent his days in a constant tug-of-war with gravity.

Officer Plewicki, on the other hand, was a young and fit female with jet-black hair and a very pretty face. She was at least twenty years younger than Daniels, and although Lindsey didn't know her well, she was betting she was twenty times smarter, too.

They talked to Sully on the lower dock for a few minutes and then climbed up the stairs toward the house. Plewicki was in the lead, and she hurried up the stairs, leaving her boss and Sully to follow.

She crossed the deck and tipped her head to study Beth. "How are you doing, Beth?"

"Fine," Beth said, but her voice quavered with emotion.

Officer Plewicki nodded in understanding and turned to Lindsey. "Ms. Norris, I'm Officer Plewicki. I think we've met before."

"Yes, at the library," Lindsey said. "You're a fan of C. J. Box's books."

Officer Plewicki smiled at her. "Very observant."

Chief Daniels joined their group. His breath was sawing in and out of his mouth like a rusty blade through a piece of knotted wood.

"Ladies," he gasped, trying to catch his breath. "We're going to check out the house. You stay here."

With that, he turned around and headed for the open door. Officer Plewicki nodded at them and followed.

Lindsey didn't generally make snap decisions about people, but she was pretty sure that Chief Daniels was an idiot and that wasn't just because he'd pulled a gun on her previously.

Sully must have read her expression, because he said, "No, he's not the sharpest tool in the shed."

Lindsey turned to face him. "I've been getting that impression."

"He means well," Sully said. "Thankfully, Briar Creek and the islands don't generally suffer much crime. The occasional stolen bicycle or barking dog . . ."

"Until now," Beth said. "Now there's a murder."

Lindsey glanced at her friend. She was still sickly pale and wide-eyed. She wondered if Beth was going into shock.

"We don't know that yet," Lindsey said. "I mean, it could have been suicide."

Beth looked at her with a glimmer of possibility that rapidly faded. "Suicide victims don't usually stab themselves, do they?"

"Uh . . . no," Lindsey said.

"Did you see a weapon in there?" Beth asked. "Something had to have made that hole in his chest."

"It was a knife," Sully said.

Both Lindsey and Beth looked at him.

"I recognize it from my naval training," he explained. "That wound was a deep lateral slash, definitely made by a knife."

"Did either of you see a knife in there?" Beth asked. They both shook their heads.

"Maybe the police will find something," Lindsey said. Neither Sully nor Beth looked like they believed her, which was fine because she didn't believe it either.

A half hour passed before Chief Daniels and Officer Plewicki rejoined them. They both wore blue gloves and matching grim expressions.

"Well." The chief glanced around the deck as if uncertain of what to do next. "I guess we need to . . ."

"Seal off the scene," Officer Plewicki finished for him. "I'll just go down to the boat and get some crime tape. Do you want me to put a call into the medical examiner and state forensic lab while I'm down there?"

"Uh, yeah," Chief Daniels said and tugged up his waistband. "Meanwhile I'll question these folks."

"Yes, sir," Officer Plewicki said. She stripped

off her gloves as she headed down to the boat to get her supplies.

Chief Daniels studied the three of them. He seemed at a loss for where to start. He frowned and then asked, "Did you touch anything when you were inside?"

"No," they answered in unison.

"What about the door? Who opened it?" he asked. He seemed to be gaining confidence with each question.

"It was open when I got to it," Beth said. She swallowed as if her throat was tight and she was trying to loosen it.

"You were the first to enter?" he asked. He stripped off his gloves and stuffed them into his back pocket.

"Yes, I came to talk to him," Beth said. "I thought he had the door open because it was such a nice day. I called out but he didn't answer."

She stopped speaking, and Lindsey could tell she was mentally back at the moment she had crossed the threshold. The shock must have been a soul crusher. Geared up to confront the boyfriend who plagiarized her prized story and instead she found him dead.

Officer Plewicki returned and began to seal off the door with yellow plastic tape that read "Crime Scene Do Not Cross" in bold letters. The sight of it made Lindsey's stomach whoosh down to her belly. She glanced out at the idyllic day and had to shake her head. A murder here? It seemed improbable, and yet there was a body just feet away from them.

"What did you do next?"

"I knocked on the door frame," Beth said. "When he still didn't answer, I went inside. I walked into the studio and there he was."

"So, you were alone?" Chief Daniels asked. His gaze narrowed on her face.

"For a minute or two," she said.

Lindsey did not like the way the chief was looking at Beth. His gaze was speculative, as if he was assessing the truth of her statement.

"We were right behind her," Lindsey said.

The chief turned to look at her. She glanced at Sully with wide eyes.

"It's true," he said. "We heard her scream and raced up the stairs. She wasn't up there more than a minute or two by herself."

"What have you got there?" Chief Daniels asked.

Beth glanced down at the portfolio in her arms. "My artwork."

He looked at Officer Plewicki and said, "We're going to need to take that."

"But . . ." Beth stammered and clutched the black case closer to her chest.

"It'll be all right," Officer Plewicki said. "I'll take very good care of it. I promise."

Lindsey stepped close to Beth and put an arm around her shoulders.

"I know what you're thinking," Beth said.

Chief Daniels glanced at her. "And what would that be?"

"I didn't kill him," she said.

"Now why would I think that?" he asked. His tone was deceptively mild.

Lindsey heard warning bells ring in her head. "I'm sure he doesn't think that, Beth. That would be ridiculous." She knew her voice had an edge to it, but she didn't care.

"Would it?" Chief Daniels asked. He stared hard at Beth. "What was your relationship with the victim?"

"We were a couple," Beth said. "For almost five years."

"Were?" Chief Daniels asked.

"Yes, we broke up last night," she said.

"Who broke up?" he asked. "What I mean is who broke it off?"

Beth's eyes went wide as if she finally realized that the breakup between her and Rick did not help her at all and that she might as well have a big bulls-eye on her forehead.

"He broke it off," she said. "But I agreed."

"And why was that?" The chief looked smug as he pulled up his waistband again, and Lindsey had to bite back the urge to tell him to buy some suspenders.

"It was silly," she said. "It was just a misunderstanding."

"After five years, you must have been angry," Chief Daniels said. He had a glint in his eyes like a fisherman about to hook the big one.

Officer Plewicki had the grace to look down, letting Lindsey know even she didn't like the way this was going. Abruptly, Sully pushed off of the railing.

"How about we finish this at the station, Chief?" he asked. "Miss Stanley and Miss Norris have had quite a shock; besides I'm sure you need to get ready to greet the state investigators. They won't be able to find their way out here without an escort."

Chief Daniels gave Sully an annoyed look. His jowls wobbled as he bit back what he really wanted to say, in favor of a quick nod.

"Fine, but I'll want to talk to all three of you again," he said.

"Understood," Sully agreed. Wasting no time, he cupped both Lindsey's and Beth's elbows and led them to the steps.

"One more thing, Miss Stanley," the chief called after them. "Was this your first visit out here today?"

"Why . . . yes," Beth stammered.

"How about last night?" he asked, staring at her face. "Did you come out here last night?"

"No," she said. "The storm was terrible. I was home all night."

"Alone?" he asked.

"Yes, well, except for my cats," she said. "But I don't suppose they count as witnesses."

"No, I don't suppose they do," he said.

Chief Daniels turned away from them and Sully swiftly ushered them to his boat. They pushed off the island less than five minutes later.

As they headed back to the mainland, Beth sat huddled in one of the boat's chairs, hugging her knees to her chest. Lindsey sensed she was working through what had happened and gave her some time to herself.

She took the empty seat beside Sully and let out a pent-up breath. She had a bad feeling about this whole thing.

Sully must have, too, because he turned to her, and she noted the creases around his eyes were deeper, and he said, "I was wrong."

"About what?" she asked.

"Chief Daniels," he said. "He's going to take the shortest route from point A to point B and completely disregard anything that doesn't fit into his preconceived notion of what happened."

"Beth's in trouble, isn't she?" Lindsey asked in a soft voice that only he could hear.

"Yep," he said, his voice grim.

CHAPTER 10

The boat ride to the shore was not nearly as exhilarating as the one out. The sun remained hidden behind a large fat cloud, taking its warmth with it.

Lindsey felt goose bumps rise up on her arms, but she couldn't decide if it was from the chilly air or the shock of what they'd found on Gull Island. She glanced back at Beth. She'd had the sense to wear a thick sweater, and although she was pale, she didn't look cold.

She turned back to find Sully holding out a fleece to her. It was navy blue and looked as if it would hang down to her knees, but that was fine with her. She pulled it over her head and burrowed into its warmth.

He was wearing a windbreaker and didn't appear chilled at all. She wondered if sailors just got used to the frigid temperatures out on the open water.

"Thanks," she said. "Are you sure you don't need it?"

"Nah." He shook his head. "I'm good."

"Good, because I really don't want to give it back," she said. She burrowed into its warmth and was pleased to discover that her teeth stopped chattering.

She wanted to ask more questions about Chief

Daniels and what sort of trouble he would make for Beth, but she didn't want to do it in front of Beth. Besides, she was still a newcomer in Briar Creek, and even though Sully had been very nice, she wasn't sure how comfortable a townie would be when she asked pointed questions about the police chief.

They docked at the main pier, and Sully helped them both out of the boat. They headed toward his office, where he stuck his head in to let Ronnie know he was back. Then he walked them over to the Blue Anchor.

"You need to eat something," he said to Beth. "You look like you're going to fall down."

"I'm not hungry," she protested, but Sully ignored her and steered them to a corner table in Mary's café. He stopped by the kitchen, and Lindsey saw Mary step into the doorway and cast a glance their way. Her eyes looked grave, and Lindsey wondered what Sully had told her.

He came over to join them with a large pitcher of water and three glasses. He took a seat at the table and poured them each a glass. Beth ignored hers, but Lindsey was surprised to find that she was parched. She drank down a whole glass, and Sully refilled it.

Mary arrived a few minutes later with bowls of chowder and a basket of bread. As she unloaded, she took the empty seat at their table and studied Beth's face.

"Are you all right, sweetie?" she asked.

Beth's face crumpled, and she squeezed her eyes up tight. She sucked in a few deep breaths, obviously trying to pull herself together.

Mary handed her a spoon. "Eat. You'll feel better."

The order wasn't just for Beth. She gave Lindsey and Sully pointed stares as well. They all began to spoon up their chowder in slow measured scoops. Mary's chowder was more of a broth with chunks of potatoes and loads of clams. It had a mild flavor of ground black pepper to it, and even though she could have sworn she couldn't have eaten a bite, Lindsey was surprised to find herself scraping the bowl for that last bit of clam.

She felt warmed from the inside out, and her body became lethargic now that it was full and the initial shock had faded away with time and distance.

Mary, who had sat silently with them while they ate, glanced around the table as if the suspense was killing her and she just couldn't wait any longer.

"So, is it true?" she demanded.

"I'm afraid so," Sully said.

"I can't believe it," she said. "I never would have thought he'd be the type."

"The type?" Beth asked with a frown. "What do you mean?"

"You know, to run off like that," Mary said.

Now Lindsey frowned. "Mary, who are you talking about?"

"Barney Corson, of course," she said. She glanced around the table. "What? Sully said you'd been out to one of the islands and had a bit of a shock. It wasn't the Corsons?"

"No," Beth said with a shake of her head. "Why would you think that?"

"Because Barney left his wife of thirty-seven years this morning," she said. "He packed up his boat and just sailed off into the Sound."

"Oh, no, poor Alice," Beth said.

Lindsey said nothing. She had yet to meet Barney Corson and had only met Alice once or twice. She was a tiny lady who enjoyed Marion Chesney's Regency romances. Lindsey wondered what possessed a man to sail off from a life of thirty-seven years with someone. No wonder the town was abuzz with the news.

"If you're not sad about the Corsons, what did you see out there that was so shocking?" Mary asked Beth.

Sully and Lindsey exchanged a glance as if uncertain whether Beth had the stamina to answer or not.

"It was Rick," Beth said, relieving them of the burden. "He's dead."

"Oh, my God!" Mary's jaw dropped. "But who . . . how?"

"That's what Chief Daniels and Officer Plewicki are trying to figure out," Sully said.

"We went out there to talk to him about Beth's book," Lindsey said. "But when we got there, we found him . . ."

"Stabbed in the chest," Beth said. Her voice was faint and Mary looped an arm about her shoulders and gave her a fierce squeeze.

"I'm so sorry," she said. Beth nodded but seemed incapable of saying anything more.

"Do you think we should go to the station?" Lindsey asked Sully. "Chief Daniels did say he wanted to speak to us again."

"He's going to be busy with the crime scene," Sully said. "I'd say let's get you two home, and when he wants to talk to you, he can call you in."

Beth looked up from her half-eaten bowl of chowder. "I suppose I should call a lawyer."

Sully gave her a measured glance. "I think that would be wise."

CHAPTER 11

Lindsey soaked her shock-weary body in a steamy shower in the small bathroom of her third-story apartment. She and Sully had dropped Beth off at her small beach house, and then Sully had taken her home. Mercifully, it was still daylight and there was no drama unfolding at her own home. Frankly, her nerves were shot.

She left the small bathroom and wandered into her bedroom. She pulled on a pair of well-worn jeans and a chenille turtleneck sweater in a shade of ocean blue that brought out the blue in her normally hazel eyes. She toweled off her long blonde hair, letting the curls air dry.

She was restless and left her bedroom to go make a cup of tea in the kitchenette. This small but delightful kitchen was the main reason she had taken the apartment. It had a wall of windows that overlooked the ocean, with a small eating area that led into a spacious living room that boasted more windows and a small veranda that overlooked the water.

She could see the Thumb Islands off to the right. It was hard to believe she'd been out there just hours ago. She checked her phone to see if Chief Daniels had called asking to see her, but there were no messages. She wondered if she should call Beth and check on her, but she thought maybe she'd give her some time to herself to process all that had happened.

The microwave beeped, and she dunked her tea bag into the steaming water. While it steeped, she watched a seagull ride the winds coming in off of the water. He fell and rose with the ever-changing temperament of the wind, and Lindsey wondered if he did it for fun or if it was the equivalent of a bird workout to keep his wings strong.

The day, which had been so bright when it began, was becoming overcast as it closed, with a chill in the air to match. She squeezed her tea bag and added honey to the soothing chamomile. She felt the knot in her shoulders begin to ease—and then it started.

Boom. Boom. Boom. She felt her floorboards shake. She had forgotten this afternoon was practice. She took her tea and her cell phone and headed into the living room. There she grabbed her knitting bag and strode out of her apartment, closing the door behind her.

She wasn't leaving the house, so she didn't bother to lock the door. She wound her way down the stairs to the second-floor landing, where the *booms* became positively deafening, and continued on to the first floor. The door to Nancy's apartment was ajar. She didn't bother knocking because Nancy would never hear her but entered, closing the door behind her.

She crossed through the house. It was the largest of the three apartments. Nancy had a collection of delicate antiques, a small oak secretary and several spindly looking tables, interspersed with squashy sofas and armchairs upholstered in chocolate-brown suede. Oil paintings of the sea and bookshelves stuffed to bursting dominated the walls, giving the space a sense of good taste and comfortable living.

Lindsey passed through the living room, the kitchen, the dining room, down the narrow hall to the bedrooms. The very last bedroom was the master suite, where she had tucked Nancy the night before, and off of it was a glassed-in porch boasting a stunning view of the water. It was decorated with several comfy wicker chairs and lots of hanging plants.

As Lindsey pulled open the door, Nancy looked up from her seat in one of the wicker rockers and shouted, "I wondered when you'd get here!"

The screech of a guitar riff and a pounding drum solo drowned out anything Lindsey would have said in return. She sat down in the empty chair beside Nancy's and pulled a pair of earplugs out of her knitting bag.

Once she had the plugs firmly wedged in her ears, she took out her knitting. Since her sock had turned into a hat, she had transferred the project onto one circular needle. She liked how easy it was to knit the stocking stitch on the circulars. It was a simple constant knit stitch with no need to worry about purling or cabling.

Lindsey found it soothing, and it gave her a chance to think.

Her thoughts immediately strayed to Rick Eckman's murder. She wanted to talk to Nancy about it but didn't want to shout over the noise of Charlie's band. She'd wait. They usually only rehearsed for an hour because the lead singer was a bartender at Toad's Place in New Haven and had to get to work.

She wondered how Beth was doing. She paused to pull her cell phone out of her knitting bag. She wanted to see if Beth had called, but there were no messages. She put it back and resumed her knitting. She felt Nancy watching and glanced up.

Nancy was working on a hat and scarf set for a niece of hers, but she had paused and was wearing a concerned frown, so Lindsey pointed toward the ceiling and Nancy nodded. They would talk when the band was done.

Lindsey resumed knitting. The yarn moved comfortably through her fingers as she slipped her needle into a loop, threaded yarn around the tip and pulled it through the loop, moving the yarn to the other needle. It was rhythmic, and as the hat got bigger with each round, she delighted in a feeling of accomplishment.

As her fingers worked, her thoughts strayed back to the afternoon. She had never seen a dead body that was not inside a casket before. It was disturbing. The position Rick had been sitting in made her think that he hadn't expected what was coming. Had the person caught him unaware or was it someone he knew and trusted?

A knife in the chest seemed very metaphorical. She supposed she couldn't really blame Chief Daniels for considering Beth a suspect, given that they had just broken up. But Beth was a children's librarian, not a killer. Surely the chief could see that.

Thankfully, Sully had been with them and could vouch for Beth as well. Lindsey had a feeling his word meant much more to the chief than hers. Not a big surprise, considering he was a native and she was a newcomer.

Lindsey wondered when Rick had been stabbed. Had someone been to the island right before them, or had it happened the night before? She hoped for Beth's sake that the medical examiner put the time of death long before their arrival.

She felt Nancy nudge her elbow. She glanced up. Nancy was taking out her earplugs, so Lindsey did the same.

"Is it safe?" she asked.

"Looks like they've called it for the day."

Sure enough, the booming bass beat and wicked guitar riffs were no more.

"I'm glad you don't mind that Charlie's band practices here," Nancy said. "He drove my last tenant out after the first month."

"No, they're a good band," Lindsey said. "Just really loud. And they only practice on Saturday afternoons, so that's manageable. It gives me a chance to catch up on my knitting."

They were quiet for a moment. Lindsey wasn't sure how to tell her about Rick, and Nancy was plucking at the ball of yarn in her lap as if she had something to say as well.

"I . . ." they began at the same time.

"You go ahead," Nancy said.

"No, it'll keep. What were you going to say?"

"Oh, just that I'm dreadfully sorry about last night. I sleepwalk occasionally," she said. Her face was slack with sadness and her usual sparkle was subdued. "Usually it's on a night like the night . . ."

Her voice dwindled and Lindsey reached over and patted her hand. "Don't you worry. It's fine. I'm just glad everything turned out okay."

"Thank you," Nancy said. Her blue eyes sparkled again. "Now, what were you going to say when I so rudely interrupted?"

"Beth went to meet that editor today," she said.

"How did it go? Did she love her work? I knew she would."

"Er, well, not exactly," Lindsey said.

"What do you mean?" Nancy said. She looked huffy, and she shoved her knitting into the basket beside her chair. "Beth is brilliant. Surely she recognized that."

"It turns out that Rick plagiarized Beth's book, the hamster in the library story, and it's coming out in a book next fall," Lindsey said.

Nancy gasped. "No!"

"I'm afraid so," Lindsey said.

"Why that good-for-nothing, no-account . . ." Nancy began, but Lindsey interrupted. "He's dead."

Nancy shook her head as if Charlie's band was

still playing and surely she had heard Lindsey wrong.

"It's true," Lindsey said. She folded up her own knitting and slid it back into her bag. Then she told Nancy the entire story from start to finish.

When she finished, Nancy said nothing. She rose from her seat and said, "Come on, I need to process this over some peanut-butter cookies and milk."

"Good thinking," Lindsey said. Nancy was the best cookie baker in Briar Creek, and Lindsey was always happy to be on the receiving end of her oven's gifts. She shouldered her knitting bag and followed.

"What do you think is going to happen next?" Nancy asked after they had polished off a short stack of cookies each.

"Chief Daniels said he wanted to talk to each of us," Lindsey said. "So I expect to be called in sometime soon."

"What could he possibly want to ask you?" Nancy asked. "I mean, all you did was find the body."

"I wish I knew," Lindsey began but was interrupted by her phone chiming in her knitting bag. She fished it out and saw that a text from Beth had just come in.

She opened the message and her heart slammed into her throat. "Oh, no."

"What is it?"

"Beth's been arrested."

CHAPTER 12

It was hard to tell who jumped to their feet first, but Lindsey and Nancy raced for the door at the same time. Lindsey kept her bike on the side of the house and made to grab it, but then remembered that she had left it at the library the night before. Nancy took her arm and steered her toward the garage. Inside was a 1965 powder-blue Mustang with a white ragtop. It was her late husband's car, and she rarely drove it, but she must have considered this an emergency.

Lindsey hustled into the passenger seat, and with a squeal of the whitewalls, Nancy backed out of the garage and out onto the road. She spun the wheel, and they headed into town. Lindsey felt her fingers dig into the armrest as they took a curve at high speed. Afraid she was going to gouge the restored leather, Lindsey forced her fingers to uncurl.

Nancy hit the curb as she pulled into the narrow lot behind the small police station. They slammed their doors as they raced into the squat brick building that sat on the edge of the park a few buildings down from the library.

Lindsey yanked open the door to the building, and Nancy strode in, approaching the front desk with an almost military bearing.

"Officer Plewicki, I want to see Beth Stanley right now," Nancy demanded.

The pretty, dark-haired officer was staffing the desk, and she glanced up in surprise at their entrance.

"Hello," she said.

"Hi," Lindsey said. "I'm sorry; we're just concerned."

"Understood," she said. "You can call me Emma, by the way, especially you, Nancy. Who do you think you're fooling calling me Officer Plewicki? You've known me since I was in pigtails."

"I thought that would sound more official," Nancy said.

"It's not necessary," Emma said. "Beth is in the chief's office with him and a state investigator. They're just talking. I'm sure she'll be out shortly."

"So, she's not under arrest?" Lindsey asked.

"No," Emma said. "She's just being questioned. In fact, I'm glad you're here. I was about to go and pick you up in the squad car, so we can talk to you, too."

"Did you pick up Beth?" she asked.

"Yes, why?"

Lindsey looked at Nancy. "That explains it. She must have seen the car, thought the worst and texted me."

Nancy visibly sagged into the nearest chair. "Well, thank goodness."

"Can you stick around for a while?" Emma asked.

"Sure," Lindsey said. She had planned to wait for Beth anyway.

"We should have brought our knitting," Nancy said.

"I have our book club books at the library," Lindsey said. "I could run over and get them."

"*The Last Time I Saw Paris*?" Nancy's eyes lit up. "Go. I'll hold them off."

Lindsey had to smile. Nancy sounded as if she planned to fight off a sheriff's posse to get their next reading-club book.

"I'll be right back," she said. She left the police station and turned toward the library. As always, just the sight of it made her happy.

With its thick stone walls and welcoming glass front doors, she always felt as if she were going home when she walked into the Briar Creek Library. Instead of the smell of her mother's rosemary chicken, however, the library greeted her with the perfumed scent of old paper pressed between the hard covers of books on wooden shelves dusted faintly with lemon furniture polish.

As always, Lindsey felt all of her troubles ease once she was back among the familiar. Just seeing the names on the spines of the books was like calling hello to old friends. They had always

115

given her solace in their steadfastness, and she valued each and every one more than she could ever say.

Ann Marie was at the front counter and glanced up with a smile. "Don't you ever take a day off?"

"I am; I promise," Lindsey said. "I'm just picking up my crafternoon club books. Is everything going okay here?"

"All is well," Ann Marie said. "There was a woman in asking for you earlier. I put a note on your desk."

"Thanks," Lindsey said. She glanced at the clock on the wall. The library would be closing in fifteen minutes, at six p.m. "Do you need help locking up?"

"No, Ms. Cole managed to chase everyone out," Ann Marie said. "She's over in children's picking up."

"You never saw me," Lindsey said.

Ann Marie smiled. "Roger that."

Lindsey circled the circulation desk and hurried into the main workroom. Two of their part-time teen workers were organizing book trucks for shelving returned materials, and she gave them a wave as she went through the room to her office in the back.

Six copies of Lynn Sheene's book were sitting on her desk. The courier for the state's interlibrary loan service had dropped them off yesterday. Normally, the books never would have gotten here so fast, but Lindsey and Beth had a friend from grad school in the interlibrary loan office and he helped them out when he could. She stuffed them into her canvas Friends of the Library tote bag and hurried back out of the office, pausing only to grab the memo paper off of her desk from the woman who had stopped by to see her. She put it in the bag, planning to read it later. Right now, she felt the need to get back to the police station ASAP.

"Ms. Norris," a stern voice called out. It didn't sound like a greeting exactly, but still Lindsey was behooved to stop and respond. She noticed the teen workers were watching them, so she forced herself to smile.

"Hello, Ms. Cole," she said.

"Isn't it your day off?"

"It is," Lindsey agreed.

"Then why are you here?" Ms. Cole asked. Her nostrils were flared, and her eyes were wide with indignation.

For a nanosecond, Lindsey was tempted to tell her that she was checking up on her, but she knew that would be like throwing a match at a gas can. Ms. Cole was obviously having turf issues with her, and for the good of the library, she needed to be kind even if pulling out her own tooth with a pair of rusty pliers would hurt less.

"I just stopped in to pick up the books for the crafternoon club," she said.

Ms. Cole's nostrils shrank as she eyed the tote bag on her arm. "Oh."

"You seem to have everything running smoothly," Lindsey said. "Nice work."

Was it her imagination or did Ms. Cole puff up just the littlest bit?

"Well, I should hope so," Ms. Cole snapped, turning away. "If you'll excuse me, we need to start the closing procedures."

Okaaaaay. Obviously, it had been her imagination.

"Absolutely. Don't let me keep you," Lindsey called after her. "Have a lovely evening."

Ann Marie gave her a wave, and Lindsey scooted out the front door to retrieve her bike from the bike rack and head back to the police station.

She wondered how it was going for Beth. Surely they couldn't think that a woman who spent her life doing felt-board stories, puppet shows and dressing up like Eric Carle's very hungry caterpillar was a murderer. It was preposterous.

She thought back to the few moments that she'd stood on the dock with Sully. How long had they been there waiting for Beth? It had only been minutes, definitely not long enough for Beth to have stabbed Rick. She was sure of it. But if Chief Daniels wanted to push it, could she and Sully swear to an absolute knowledge of time passing? Neither of them had worn a watch.

She felt a creepy, cold-fingered tickle of unease ripple over her skin like a chilly breeze ruffling the surface of the water in the bay.

It would be too easy to blame Beth as the dumped girlfriend, she thought. Given that Beth had no witnesses other than her cats to say she was at home all night, Chief Daniels could make a case against her without even straining himself. As Sully had said, it was going to be a no-brainer for the chief to go after Beth.

The books in the tote bag banged against her side as she pushed her bike, bringing her back to the present. The weight of the books grounded her, giving her careening emotions purchase with their heft and substance. She left her bike outside the station and mounted the steps to the front door.

Nancy pushed open the door as soon as she stepped close to the entrance, as if she'd been watching for her.

"Any news?"

Nancy shook her head.

They were alone in the front room and sat on the hard wooden bench in front of the window.

"Where's Emma?" Lindsey asked.

"She went to go get Sully," Nancy said. "They want to talk to him, too."

Lindsey opened her tote bag and pulled out two copies of the book. She noticed that her palms were damp, and she wondered at her sudden case of nerves.

"Thank you," Nancy said. She looked at Lindsey and asked, "Who was it who said, *'I've never known any trouble that an hour's reading didn't assuage'*?"

"The French lawyer and political philosopher Charles de Secondat," Lindsey said.

"Brilliant," Nancy said and cracked open her book and began to read.

Lindsey opened her own copy, looking for the balm of a good story to take her mind off of the fact that she was sitting in a police station, waiting to be questioned.

She was never given the chance.

"Ms. Norris." She glanced up to find Chief Daniels at the front desk.

"Yes?" she asked.

"If you'll follow me," he said. Without waiting for her to rise, he turned and strode toward the back of the station.

Lindsey put her book back in her bag and followed. As she passed the main desk, she couldn't shake the feeling of doom that enveloped her like a shroud.

CHAPTER 13

The room was small and cramped with a scarred wooden table and two folding chairs. Chief Daniels gestured for her to take a seat. Lindsey sat in the chair that gave her a view of the door.

"Detective Trimble will be joining us shortly," Chief Daniels said. He hitched up his pants. "You want anything, a glass of water or a can of soda?"

"No, thanks, I'm fine," Lindsey said.

She saw two people cross in front of the door. She recognized Beth's black spiky hairdo, but the other person she didn't recognize. They were gone before she could call out to them.

"I'll be right back," the chief said and he exited the room.

Lindsey folded her hands on the table. There were initials carved into the distressed surface, but they were jagged and hard to make out. There was also a skull done with more finesse than the initials, but maybe that person just had better tools or more time.

There was another drawing, in black marker. It took her a moment to figure out what it was, but then she realized she was looking at the rear end of a donkey with the name Daniels spelled out in the long hair of the tail.

She couldn't help it. The assessment was so spot-on, she laughed.

"Something funny, Ms. Norris?" Chief Daniels asked as he walked back into the room with a man in a suit right behind him.

"No, sir," she said. "There's nothing funny here, not at all, not a bit."

The man in the suit watched her as she glanced away from the drawing on the table. With a frown, he came around to her side and studied the drawing in black marker, while Chief Daniels ducked out of the room to get another chair.

"I'd say that's quite an accurate rendering," he said. His voice was very matter-of-fact, and Lindsey felt her mouth pop open just the littlest bit.

He smiled at her and took the seat across the table from her. Chief Daniels returned with another chair and plunked it next to the man in the suit.

"Ms. Norris, this is Detective Trimble," he said. "He's with the state police."

The detective extended his hand across the table, and Lindsey shook hands with him. His grip was firm and warm, solid without being brutish. The cut of his suit was perfect, accentuating his broad shoulders and trim waist. His black hair was cut with military precision, and the glasses he wore gave him the look of a scholar.

Perhaps it was just his slick packaging, but

Lindsey felt like he had a lot on the ball. For the first time since she'd gotten the text from Beth saying that she was being taken to the police station, Lindsey felt herself relax just the tiniest bit.

"How are you?" Detective Trimble asked.

"I've been better," Lindsey said.

Chief Daniels sat down but had to push his chair away from the table to accommodate his girth. The metal chair scraped across the floor, making a screech that sounded like the chair was under protest.

Detective Trimble gave the chief a look and then pulled a pen and a small pad out of his suit coat pocket.

"We'll make this as quick as possible," he said to Lindsey. "We want to go over the events of the day to understand how it all unfolded. Are you ready?"

"Yes," Lindsey said.

"Was Ms. Stanley upset after her boyfriend dumped her?" Chief Daniels asked. He leaned forward in his seat and gave Lindsey a squinty-eyed glare as if he were daring her to lie to him.

Lindsey raised her eyebrows in surprise and looked helplessly at Detective Trimble. "I thought we were talking about today."

"We are," Trimble said and gave Daniels a quelling glance. "When did you and Ms. Stanley decide to go out to Mr. Eckman's island?"

"Right after lunch," she said. "After we met with Ms. Carlisle, the editor, and discovered that Rick had plagiarized Beth's work."

"Allegedly plagiarized her work," Chief Daniels cut in.

"There's nothing alleged about it," Lindsey said. "I've known Beth for years, and I know she came up with the story about the hamster ages ago. It's hers."

"Really? How is Ms. Stanley with a knife?" Chief Daniels asked.

Again, Lindsey turned to look at Trimble. He squinted his eyes as if trying to force back a headache.

"Chief Daniels, let's have a quick chat in the hall, yes?" It was posed like a question but was anything but. The chief grumbled as he followed Trimble out into the hall. He shut the door after them.

From what Lindsey could hear, the conversation that followed seemed fairly one-sided. Trimble growled, the chief but . . . but . . . butted and Trimble growled some more. When they reentered the room, Daniels was red in the face and looked like he had an aspirin lodged in his throat.

"Now, where were we?" Trimble asked. He looked as smooth as ever, and Lindsey had to admire his cool.

"Beth and I decided to go out to the island after lunch," she said. "Neither of us has a boat, so we stopped by Captain Sullivan's to see if he could take us."

Trimble jotted something down in his book and then glanced up at her. He gave her an encouraging smile. "Continue, please."

Lindsey took a deep breath and told them all the events of the day as she could remember them. Daniels glowered, looking like he wanted to bust out with questions, but he managed to contain himself. Trimble took notes and nodded at her as if what she was saying was about what he expected.

When she got to the part about Beth going up to the cabin alone, Daniels looked like he was going to pop a blood vessel. He obviously wanted to focus on Beth, but Trimble gave him a look, and he slumped back in his chair in defeat.

Finally, when there was nothing more to say, Trimble handed her his card. "I'd like you to call me if you remember anything that you think might be of interest even if it seems like nothing. All right?"

"Yes." Lindsey took the stiff white card with the state of Connecticut's seal on it and slipped it into her pocket.

There was a knock at the door, and Emma, Officer Plewicki, opened it enough to poke her head in. "Captain Sullivan is here, sirs."

"Excellent. Send him in," Trimble said.

Chief Daniels openly glared at him, and Lindsey

got the feeling that he didn't like Trimble ordering his officers about.

Trimble rose when she did. Daniels did not.

"Thank you for your cooperation, Ms. Norris," he said.

"You're welcome," she said. As she turned into the hallway, she bumped into Sully. "Oh, sorry."

"Not at all," he said and steadied her with a firm hand on her elbow.

"How are you holding up?" he asked.

"Okay," she said, but it sounded lame even to her own ears.

"I've got a question for you." He lowered his voice and leaned close so only she could hear him.

"All right," she whispered, wondering what could be so urgent. Did he know something? Was she not supposed to say something to the police? Did he suspect who the real killer was? What?

"Tell me the truth. They didn't use the rack, did they?"

His voice was teasing, and she knew he was trying to jolly her out of her nerves. She gave him a small smile.

"It's worse than that, I'm afraid." She lowered her voice, trying to make it sound ominous.

"No. Say it isn't so," he said, faking a look of horror.

"I'm afraid it's . . ." she began, but he interrupted, "No, don't say it."

"Thumbscrews," she said.

He clapped both hands to his cheeks and widened his eyes. His look of dismay was comical, and this time Lindsey felt a full-on grin break across her face.

"Captain Sullivan, if you're ready?" Chief Daniels snapped from inside the room.

"Oh, better go," Sully said with a grimace.

"Good luck," she said. Then she wiggled her thumbs at him, and he gave her a quick wink before the door shut behind him.

CHAPTER 14

Not surprisingly, sleep eluded Lindsey like a cat that did not want to be found. She tried tightening and loosening each muscle in her body from her feet to her head. It didn't work.

She got up and heated some milk. It needed chocolate; better yet, it needed to be Sully's hot chocolate.

She shuffled back to her bedroom and opened her window so she could hear the waves crashing on the beach. The air blew in cold, and she had to add another blanket to her bedding. She tossed and turned, but the bedsheets put up a pretty good fight, alternately strangling her and slipping across the bed to leave her cold.

After her breakup with her ex-fiancé, when she

had packed up her things and moved to Briar Creek, she had discovered that she was prone to insomnia. Back then she had spent the sleepless nights watching old Hollywood musicals, falling asleep to the cheeky beat of Carmen Miranda working it in her ruffles and fruit hat.

Mercifully, that phase had passed, and as she settled into her new home and job, the sleepless nights had become few and far between. Until now, at any rate, and somehow she didn't think a musical extravaganza was going to help wipe the imprint of Rick Eckman's dead body out of her mind.

She gave up the wrestling match with her covers and grabbed her bathrobe off the foot of her bed, pulling it on as she headed out to the living room. She switched on the small lamp by her leather recliner and debated whether she should read or knit. She knew if she was knitting she would be thinking, which was the main reason she couldn't sleep. She pulled her copy of *The Last Time I Saw Paris* out of her bag and opened it to page 1.

With any luck, Lynn Sheene's words would lull her to sleep before much more of the night passed. The living room was chilly, so she pulled her favorite afghan over her legs. It was one large granny square crocheted in a rainbow of colors made from her Gram's leftover skeins and hanks of yarn. Her grandmother had made it for Lindsey when she was a teenager, and Lindsey had taken it with her on every move, from leaving home to college, to apartments on her own, to her shared life with John, and now it was with her still, outlasting several boyfriends and one fiancé. It was like wrapping herself in a cinnamon-scented hug from Gram every time she used it, and she cherished that.

She yawned as she opened the book and took that as a good sign that she was beginning to relax. She was well into chapter 3 when the book slipped from her fingers and she burrowed into her chair with a soft snore.

Lindsey woke up with a crick in her neck. It took her a moment to stretch the kinks out of her back and wipe the sleep fog from her brain and remember why she was asleep in the recliner.

She reached down and scooped up the book, which had fallen to the floor. She found her bookmark wrapped up in the afghan and carefully marked her place and set the book on the table.

Today was Sunday, so the library was closed. She wished it were open so she'd have something to keep her busy. She glanced at the clock. It was past ten, so Sunday service was well under way. She supposed it was just as well. She wasn't sure she was ready to face the entire town and the rampant speculation about yesterday even in a house of worship.

She wondered how Beth was faring. She and Nancy had taken her home in the Mustang after their time at the police station. Lindsey had offered to spend the night, but Beth assured her that she'd be okay. Nancy thought she was still in shock, but they let her go after making her promise to call them if she needed them.

Lindsey felt uneasy when she thought of Beth home alone, trying to process how her world had just imploded. That decided it. She was going to bike over to Beth's house and see how she was. She'd stop by the bakery in town for coffee and muffins. No one could turn away coffee and muffins, right?

In no time, Lindsey was unlocking her bike from the porch rail on the side of the house and pushing off toward town with the wind in her hair and the smell of the sea in her nose. She loved her red Schwinn Cruiser with its whitewall tires and handy basket in the back. When she had moved to Briar Creek, she had promised herself she would be more green, as in environmentally aware, so she'd sold her car and become a bicyclist.

She had to grocery shop more frequently since her bicycle basket couldn't hold a big load, but since the small grocery store was on her way home, she had folded it into her daily routine and found that she felt very European going to the market more frequently.

It felt good to do something for the planet, and on the upside, it had taken a few unnecessary inches off of her behind. She took the winding shore road into town. It was cool today, and she was glad she'd worn her heavy windbreaker over her knit top and jeans.

She parked in front of the Briar Creek General Store. It was quiet with few customers before church let out. Lindsey locked up her bike and went inside to the back of the shop, which had a small bakery. She was not surprised to find Milton Duffy there.

He was standing with his arms over his head, palms pressed together. His right leg was raised and bent at the knee with the sole of his foot lined up against his left knee. Lindsey recognized the position as Vrksasana, or the tree pose. Milton had tried unsuccessfully to teach it to her, but Lindsey always looked like a tree that had just been cut down when she tried it, and Beth had taken to yelling, "Timber!" right before she fell.

"Lindsey," he greeted her. "Don't tell me; you were lured here by the fresh chocolate-chip muffins."

"And a steaming latte," she said. She turned to the counter and asked, "May I have two lattes and two chocolate-chip muffins, please?"

"Coming right up," the girl behind the counter answered. She looked to be somewhere in her late teens. Lindsey was sure she had seen her at the library. If she remembered right, her name was Robin, and she was an avid science fiction and fantasy fan.

"How did you like *The Hunger Games*?" she asked as the girl bagged the two muffins and handed them to her.

Robin grinned at her. "You remember me. I loved it. I'm already on the third book in the trilogy." She paused to yawn. "Sorry. I stayed up too late reading last night."

Lindsey returned her smile as she took the lattes and paid for her order. "I know the feeling."

Milton released from his pose and began to walk with her as she headed for the door. "I don't want to pry, but how is Beth?"

Lindsey knew that Milton was operating from a place of concern, so she squeezed his arm and said, "I think she's in a state of shock."

A head popped up from behind a rack of post-cards of the Thumb Islands. It was Candace Halpern, or, as Beth liked to call her, "the heli-copter." According to Beth, when authors Foster Cline and Jim Fay coined the phrase "helicopter parent" in their book *Parenting with Love and Logic*, they were talking about Candace.

Somewhere in her early forties, Candace was short and skinny and seemed to be in a perpetual state of anxiety. Probably, all of her manic energy kept her from gaining any weight. Having recently gone nose to nose with her about keeping *The Dangerous Book for Boys* in the library, Lindsey had to bite back the urge to tell her to have a muffin and calm down.

Candace had two children and was a frequent user of the library, but as far as Lindsey could tell, her kids were never allowed to be more than six inches from her person at any given time and were certainly not allowed to participate in anything that might actually be fun.

Finger painting was forbidden as the paints might have hidden toxins, books about adventures were discouraged because they might give kids bad ideas and germs were everywhere. The kids weren't allowed to touch anything until Candace had wiped it down with the antiseptic wipes she had on hand at all times. Yes, this included library books.

Lindsey could understand it if the kids were toddlers or prone to illness, but these kids were healthy eight- and nine-year-olds who could barely function on their own because Candace wouldn't let them. It was just sad.

"Well, I for one demand that you fire her," Candace said, inserting herself into the conversation.

"Excuse me," Lindsey said. She gave her a hard stare, but Candace was taking the stance of morally outraged parent and was not about to back down.

"Milton, you're on the library board," Candace said to him. "I will expect you to represent the interests of all the parents in Briar Creek and make a motion for the swift dismissal of Beth

Stanley from the library. Imagine, a murderess in contact with our children."

"Beth is not a murderess," Lindsey said through gritted teeth. "I will not fire her, nor will Milton make a motion for her dismissal."

"I heard they found his body chopped up in pieces and shoved in his freezer," Candace said. There was a hysterical delight in her voice that belied her outraged concern, and Lindsey felt her nose wrinkle with distaste.

"That would be highly inaccurate," she said. "Good day, Mrs. Halpern."

"If you won't fire her, I'll have your job," Candace threatened her.

"Now, Candace . . ." Milton began in a placating voice, but Lindsey interrupted. "If I am forced to let go of my children's librarian, one of the best in the state by the way, because of unfounded rumors and innuendo, then by all means, Mrs. Halpern, you can take my job and sh . . ."

Milton pushed Lindsey out the front door before she could finish her sentence. Catching her balance on the bike rack, she gave him an annoyed look.

"What'd you do that for?" she asked. "I was just going to say, she could take my job and shop for a new director."

"Uh-huh." Milton didn't look like he believed her not even a little bit. Smart man.

"Okay, maybe I shouldn't have blasted her, but,

oh, she was getting under my skin."

Milton nodded. "Understandable. Are you going to see Beth now?"

"Yes. I'm worried about her," Lindsey said as she put the coffee and muffins in the basket behind her seat.

"Would you give her my best?" he asked. "And tell her not to worry. Her job is safe."

"I'm sure she'll appreciate that," Lindsey said. "See you at the board meeting tomorrow?"

"Ten o'clock," he agreed. "I'll be there."

Lindsey pedaled down the shore road. The sun was warm but the air was chilly. She hoped the coffee didn't cool off too much by the time she got to Beth's house.

She refused to dwell on the narrow-minded Candace Halpern and offered up her fretting to the wind, letting it carry away her worries to parts unknown. She had found that giving up the things she couldn't change to the universe was very therapeutic. Now if the universe could just make sure that Rick's killer was caught, that would be helpful.

She followed the winding beach road until she came to the cluster of beach houses. She rang the bell on her handlebars with a flick of her thumb. She wanted to give Beth a heads-up that she was here.

Lindsey had just toed her kickstand down when Beth's door opened. She was wearing a fluffy

135

white sweater and jeans. Her black hair looked flat on one side as if she'd been lying down.

Her two cats, Slinky Malinki and Skippy John Jones, both named for cats in popular children's picture books, were pacing around her sock-clad feet as if they knew she was upset and they were trying to talk her down with lots of purrs and ankle rubs.

"I brought coffee and muffins," Lindsey said. "Are you up for company, or should I just leave the food and slowly back away?"

"No, come in, please," Beth said. "I'm driving myself crazy. Maybe you can help put on the brakes."

Lindsey hurried through the door Beth held open, being careful not to step on Slinky or Skippy as she went. She handed the food bags to Beth and hung her windbreaker on a hook in the foyer.

The door on the left led to the kitchen, but they went past that to the living room beyond. Two cushy love seats flanked a cozy fireplace that was alight with a welcoming flame behind its mesh screen, and between the small sofas was a chunky wooden coffee table, where Beth gently placed the bags Lindsey had brought.

While Beth went to retrieve plates and napkins, Lindsey held her hands out to the fire to warm them. Large windows with sheer curtains over them looked out over Beth's small backyard to the marsh beyond. While Lindsey watched, she saw an osprey circle and dive, probably catching its lunch for the day.

Slinky and Skippy both sprawled on the floor below the hearth, letting the fire melt their bones. Obviously, now that Lindsey was here, they felt their work was done.

Beth came back and handed Lindsey a plate and a napkin. "You didn't have to do this."

"I know," she said as she took the seat opposite her friend. "I wanted to."

She saw Beth's copy of *The Last Time I Saw Paris* resting facedown on the armrest. She looked to have gotten about as far as Lindsey.

"Well, I'm as ready as I'll ever be," Beth said.

"For what?" Lindsey asked.

Lindsey opened the bag and pulled out a chocolate-chip muffin and tore off a bite with her finger. She popped it into her mouth and realized how hungry she was. The muffin was moist, and the chocolate chips added a tasty surprise to the texture. She had to restrain herself from cramming the whole thing into her mouth. She took a sip of coffee and realized Beth was staring at her expectantly.

"What?" she asked.

"Aren't you here to tell me I'm on suspension?" Beth asked.

"No!" Lindsey said through a second mouthful of muffin. "Whatever made you think that?"

"Well, I just assumed, given that I'm a murder

137

suspect and all," Beth said.

"Beth, until they find the killer, technically we're all suspects, aren't we?"

"Except I was the only one dating him," Beth said.

Lindsey sighed. "Have you eaten anything?"

"No," Beth said.

"Eat first," Lindsey said. "Then we'll talk."

"But you promise you're not here to suspend me?" Beth asked.

"I swear," Lindsey said and raised her right hand, still holding a bit of muffin.

"Does a muffin swear count?" Beth asked. "Or is that the same loophole as crossing your fingers?"

"I think it's actually more legally binding," Lindsey said. "Trust me. I'd tell you if you were in trouble."

Beth heaved a huge sigh of relief, and Lindsey decided then and there that Candace Halpern would get her wish over Lindsey's dead body, or better yet, Candace's.

Beth picked up the chocolate-chip muffin Lindsey had put on her plate and relaxed against the couch. They didn't talk while they ate, and Lindsey was relieved to see the food bring a little color back to Beth's pale complexion.

"So, what now?" Beth asked.

Lindsey knew she wasn't talking about what they might do that afternoon.

"We wait," she said. "Who knows—maybe

Detective Trimble and Chief Daniels have the killer in custody already."

"You think?"

Lindsey shrugged.

Beth blew out a breath and said, "If Chief Daniels has his way, it's going to be me who gets arrested. The minute he found out that we broke up, he started thinking I was the crazy ex-girlfriend bent on revenge, and then when he found out that Rick had plagiarized my story, well, you could practically hear the cell door slamming shut in his head."

"Well, then it's a good thing the state has put Detective Trimble on the case."

"Maybe," Beth said. "What if he thinks I did it, too?"

"He seems smarter than that."

"Well, he seemed to believe me up until the plagiarism thing came out. Then, I swear, his attitude changed."

"It's unfortunate that it does give you the appearance of a solid motive, but Sully and I were there on the island with you, and we are witnesses on your behalf."

"Except for those few minutes that I was alone."

"When the medical examiner gives the time of death, I am sure it will put you in the clear. Really, Beth, don't fret. It's going to be okay."

Beth stared helplessly around her little house. "I didn't do it, Lindsey, I swear. I didn't kill Rick."

CHAPTER 15

Lindsey stayed with Beth until she fell asleep on her couch. She tucked her in on the sofa with a deep purple chenille throw and turned the gas fire off. With any luck, Beth would sleep the day away and be refreshed tomorrow. She picked up their coffee cups and cleaned up the muffin crumbs. She hoped Beth managed to eat more later.

She locked the door behind her and climbed onto her bike. It was late afternoon and she knew she should head home, but she found that she really wanted to go to the police station and see if they'd made any arrests.

She knew Beth would feel so much better if someone was arrested for killing Rick—well, someone other than her. Given his charming personality, surely there had to be someone else who had a stronger motive than plagiarism for stabbing him.

The wind was at her back on the return ride, which made the pedaling much easier. Lindsey looked out at the islands when she rode by the Look Off, a small pull-out on the shore road where the view was the best, and she saw two of Sully's tour boats out on the water. They appeared to be on their way back in.

She knew that they gave a history of the islands as they puttered around them, and she wondered when they would tell of Rick's murder or if that would become like the Ruby house, the truth of which the town would keep to itself, not wanting outsiders to know.

She turned away from the water and headed down the road into town. It was Sunday, but surely someone would be at the police station, especially with an ongoing murder investigation.

She parked her bike in front of the squat brick building. Locking it in front of the police station seemed ridiculous, but given that it was her only mode of transportation, she took the precaution anyway.

She pounded up the front steps and through the glass door. No one was at the front desk. She looked for a bell to ring, but this wasn't exactly a deli.

She glanced around the empty room and called out, "Hello?"

She heard the scrape of a chair being pushed back and the heavy tread of footsteps coming her way. The door behind the front desk opened, and Chief Daniels peered out at her over a piece of fried chicken that he was in the midst of gnawing on.

"Oh, I'm sorry to interrupt you, Chief Daniels," she said. "I was just wondering if any progress has been made on the Eckman . . . er . . . case."

"Why?" he asked. One eyebrow lifted higher

than the other, and she watched as he pulled the meat from the bone with his teeth.

"Why?" she repeated.

"Yeah, what do you care? You weren't dating him, too, were you?"

"No!" she said. "But Beth is upset, and it would ease her mind if some information has come to light about how he died."

"Don't think there's much question in the how," the chief said. He tossed the stripped chicken bone into the nearby wastebasket and wiped his fingers on the paper napkin he held in his other hand.

"Okay then, knowing when he died would also be helpful," she said. "Has the medical examiner set a time of death?"

"Now why would I tell you that?" he asked. "So you and your friend can cook up an alibi to try and stop us from arresting her for murdering her boyfriend?"

It hit her suddenly who Chief Daniels reminded her of, or, more accurately, *what*. A pig. No, that wasn't right. Pigs were cute in their own way, and she'd lay odds they were smarter. No, Chief Daniels was like a wild boar—big, loud and aggressive.

"No, that would be ridiculous since she didn't harm him," Lindsey said. She was pleased that her voice was calm, given how truly annoyed she felt. "I am merely trying to help her deal with her loss."

"Sounds to me like she lost him *before* she

stabbed him." He tossed the paper napkin into the trash.

He looked so pleased with himself. It was all Lindsey could do not to snap at him. Beth was right. He was certain she was the killer, and there would be no convincing him otherwise. It was maddening.

"If you learn anything that might help her in her time of grief, I would really appreciate it," Lindsey said. She stepped back toward the door, knowing that this was as far as this conversation was going to go.

He began to speak, but she let the door swing shut on his words. She was certain they weren't worth the oxygen being used to expel them.

She still had Detective Trimble's card. She could call him. Even if he couldn't give her information, she knew she would feel better just knowing that someone with some common sense was working on the case. Obviously, Chief Daniels certainly didn't suffer from an overabundance of it. But then, having worked at the university most of her life and now with the public at large, she had discovered common sense wasn't as common as you'd think.

She still remembered her first week staffing the reference desk at the Briar Creek Library. She was used to professors asking for the impossible, but it had never occurred to her that the general public could be equally demanding.

On one particularly grueling day, she'd been asked the proper scientific term for *boogers,* where could a person find a photograph of Leonardo da Vinci, oh, and what was the only word in the English language to end in—*mt?* It had taken some convincing to get the patron to understand that cameras came long after da Vinci had shuffled off this mortal coil and a picture of a painted portrait was the best they were going to do. She still wasn't sure the patron believed her, and neither did the one asking about boogers. *Dried nasal mucus* was as good as she could get, and apparently it was a very unsatisfying term. The only patron happy on that day was the one looking for the word *dreamt,* the only word in the English language that ends in *mt.*

She unlocked her bike and climbed on. It would be getting dark soon, so she headed out toward the beach road that would take her home. On the way there, she pedaled past the Beachfront Bed and Breakfast. She braked hard.

She had an idea. It was a long shot, but she had nothing to lose. She climbed off of her bike and locked it to the porch railing.

She was going to see if Sydney Carlisle was still in town and, if she was, whether she knew anything about who might have wanted to murder Rick Eckman. As she rang the doorbell, she fervently hoped that Sydney knew either a disgruntled editor in New York, a literary agent with a bad temper or perhaps a bitter rival author, any of whom might have had murder on his or her mind.

Jeanette Palmer answered the door. She was a tiny little bird of a lady who wore her snow-white hair in a topknot and was partial to sensible shoes and floral-print dresses. Her bed-and-breakfast had been a tourist mainstay in Briar Creek for as long as anyone could remember. She was pushing eighty, but other than the yard work, she did all the cooking and cleaning herself. Most everyone who stayed with her felt as if they were visiting their grandmother with her spotless house and homemade banana-nut bread. But Lindsey knew her secret.

Jeanette opened her mouth to speak, but Lindsey held up her hand. "No, it's not in yet."

"Dang!" Jeanette said. She swung her little fist in front of her in a gesture of disappointment, and Lindsey smiled. Jeanette was an ardent fan of J. R. Ward and her Black Dagger Brotherhood series, which was interesting primarily because it was a paranormal romance series featuring vampires that really pushed the sensual envelope. Jeanette loved it.

Her budget didn't allow for her to buy the latest hard copy, so she waited to buy the books when they were released in paperback and borrowed the hardcover from the library. She had been eagerly awaiting the latest release.

"It's due out next Tuesday, and your name is first on the list," Lindsey assured her.

"That's going to take forever to get here," Jeanette said. She sounded like a kid waiting for Christmas.

"I know," Lindsey agreed. "Why can't our favorite authors write faster?"

"Really," Jeanette humphed. "So, what brings you by then?"

"I was wondering if I could speak to a guest of yours, Sydney Carlisle," Lindsey said.

Jeanette frowned. "Do you know her?"

"We met briefly the other day."

Jeanette leaned close and whispered, "How do you like her? I've found her to be a bit of a cold fish."

"A bit," Lindsey agreed, thinking back to their disastrous lunch.

"I'll go see if she's taking visitors," Jeanette said.

"How about I come with you?" Lindsey asked. "Harder for her to refuse that way, don't you think?"

"Follow me," she agreed. They walked up the main staircase toward a hallway full of doors. The burgundy carpet was thick, the wall sconces glowed and the photographs that lined the hall didn't have a speck of dust on them. Lindsey thought Jeanette would have made a good sea captain; she certainly ran a tight ship.

They stopped at room 3. Jeanette knocked on the door and then stood back.

There was no answer so she knocked again.

"What now?" called a voice from inside. "Does peace and quiet mean nothing to you people?"

"There's someone here to see you, Ms. Carlisle," Jeanette called back.

"Tell them I'm not to be disturbed," Sydney said. The door opened a crack, and she glared out at them. "I mean really, I came here to get away from it all—not to have people knocking on my door morning, noon and night."

"Who else has knocked on your door?" Jeanette asked, sounding miffed. "You've been holed up here for three days. Now you can tell Lindsey yourself that you're too busy to talk to her." With that, she turned on her heel and strode away.

Lindsey noticed that Sydney was wearing a robe and had a towel on her head. Obviously, she had just taken a shower.

"I am so sorry to intrude," she said. "I won't take more than a minute of your time. I promise."

Sydney stared at her for a moment. Lindsey tried to look pitiful.

"All right," Sydney said reluctantly. She opened her door and gestured for Lindsey to come in. She kept one hand on the front of her towel turban where the twist began as if afraid it was going to fall off.

In marked contrast to the rest of the house,

Sydney's room looked like her Louis Vuitton luggage had upchucked its contents all over the antique furniture. Shoes were scattered across the floor, while a rainbow of blouses, skirts and pants lounged on the furnishings as if enjoying the air out.

"I need to ask you some questions," Lindsey said.

"Look, before you start," Sydney interrupted her, "I appreciate that your friend really wants her book published, but given that Rick is already publishing a book just like hers, however that came about, she really needs to go back to the drawing board. Literally."

"Actually, this isn't about that," Lindsey said. "I wanted to ask you some questions about Rick Eckman, in fact."

"What about him?" Sydney looked surprised.

"You're his editor, aren't you?" Lindsey asked.

Sydney studied her for a moment. Her hand had left the twist in the towel and several strands of pale hair stuck out. Aware of Lindsey watching her, she put her hand back and tightened her hold on the towel.

"Yes, I am," she said. She turned and began to gather her clothes, dropping them carelessly into a suitcase that was on the floor in the corner.

"What's his reputation?" Lindsey asked. "In the publishing industry, I mean."

"He's considered brilliant," Sydney said. "A real

innovator in children's picture books."

"So he's well liked?" Lindsey asked.

"I didn't say that."

"So, he isn't well liked?"

"Look, I don't know. He won't even come in off his island to meet with me," Sydney snapped as if Lindsey had given her a target at which to direct all of her anger about Rick. She spun around to face her. She looked flushed and agitated. "He's aloof, a recluse. He never comes into the city. He refuses to sign books or go on book tours. He's difficult. Why are you asking me these questions?"

"I just wondered who might want him dead," Lindsey said.

"What?" Sydney shook her head as if trying to clear her hearing. "What are you talking about?"

"You haven't heard?"

"Heard what?"

"Rick Eckman is dead," Lindsey said. "He was stabbed sometime early yesterday."

CHAPTER 16

Sydney sat down hard on the edge of the bed. Her mouth was slightly agape, and she stared at Lindsey in surprise. "Well, that's just . . . unbelievable."

"I'm sorry. I know it must be a bit of a shock," Lindsey said. "No one told you before now?"

"I was out walking the beach earlier," Sydney said. "I've been leaving my phone behind, trying to get away from the hustle and bustle. Then when I came back, I took a nap."

A guilty look passed over her face as if it was unforgivably rude of her to be resting when one of her authors had just been murdered.

"Look, I have to make some calls," Sydney said. She rose from her seat and moved to the door.

Lindsey knew that she was being dismissed. Sydney held the door open for her, giving her no choice but to go.

In the doorway, she spun around so that she was just inches from Sydney. They were about the same height, and Lindsey studied her face closely when she asked, "Do you know of anyone who wanted Rick Eckman dead?"

Sydney's eyes went wide and then narrowed shrewdly. "Only your friend, the plagiarizer."

"She didn't do it."

"We'll see, won't we?"

Lindsey got the uneasy feeling that Sydney would be making trouble for Beth. Great. In her efforts to help her friend, she may have just made a bad situation worse, much worse.

Sydney shut the door, signaling pretty clearly that the conversation was over. Lindsey turned away with a knot in her stomach the size of Texas.

She hurried down the stairs and found Jeanette waiting in the front parlor for her. "How did it go?"

"Not good."

"She's checking out tomorrow, and truthfully, she's the first guest I've been happy to see go home." In a high-pitched voice, Jeanette mimicked Sydney. " 'Mrs. Palmer, this tea isn't sweet enough. Mrs. Palmer, I need at least three pillows to elevate my head. Mrs. Palmer, can't you quiet the ocean down? I'm trying to sleep.' Good riddance, I say."

"She does seem a bit high maintenance," Lindsey agreed.

"What did you want to see her about?"

"She is Rick Eckman's editor," Lindsey said. "I thought she might know of someone who wanted him dead."

"Any luck with that?"

"Not really, although it sounds as if he was as popular in New York as he was here."

"Which means not very," Jeanette said. "Can I get you a cup of tea before you go? It's getting cold out there."

"Thank you but no," Lindsey said. "I'd better get home."

"Give Beth my best," Jeanette said. "It'll be all right. You'll see."

Lindsey left with a wave and walked down the steps to her bike. It was fully dark now. She switched on her blinking bike light. In case any motorists happened by, they would be able to see her. She also dug her helmet out of the bottom of the rear basket. She wasn't always great about wearing it, but given that it was dark and she was more at risk for getting into an accident, she figured she'd play it safe. She supposed seeing Rick's body had given her a new awareness of how swiftly things can change.

The wind blowing in from the water had turned bitter. It would be a chilly ride home. Hopefully, it would clear her head and give her a chance to think.

She wished she knew who Sydney was going to call: Rick's agent or the publisher's public-relations people? Rick had won some of the most prestigious awards in children's literature, including a Caldecott, and they were going to have to address his violent death even if it was with a "no comment" for now.

Monday arrived with a streak of sunshine that snuck its way through Lindsey's curtains and shined on her eyelids, refusing to be ignored. She had talked to Beth the night before and had actually managed to sleep, but she was pretty sure her body and brain would happily lap up twelve more hours of slumber.

She glanced at the antique clock on her night-stand. If she was going to be presentable for the ten o'clock board meeting, she had best get it in gear.

She flipped on the Weather Channel on her flatscreen television in the living room while she went to the kitchen to make some coffee. As the perky morning weathercasters talked about the United States, she waited for the "Local on the 8s." At 7:08 on the dot, the local forecast began scrolling across the screen.

It read cloudy and cold with a chance of more rain. She glanced at the window to verify the brilliant sunlight and turned back at the television. Hmm.

She'd wear opaque stockings under her wool skirt and a cotton blouse under her matching wool jacket. When in doubt, it was always best to layer.

She didn't want to fuss with drying her long blonde hair, so she combed it back from her face and plaited it in one thick braid that hung down her back. She could have put it up, but she always tried to buck the librarian stereotype of hair buns and sensible shoes, which is why she chose her high-heeled Mary Jane pumps to complete the look.

She put the rest of her coffee in a travel mug, grabbed an apple and her umbrella and headed out the door.

At the bottom of the stairs, she remembered she should have worn sneakers to bike in but a glance at her watch told her she was out of time.

She put her things in the basket and arranged her skirt on the narrow bike seat. She pushed off and headed down the narrow gravel drive toward the street. There were no cars coming so she shot across the road without stopping.

The day was brisk, and she could feel the cold air sting her cheeks and the tips of her ears and nose. She turned onto the main road and caught sight of Beth on her bike up ahead. Lindsey dug deep and put on some speed in an effort to catch up. Given that Beth was barely pedaling, it didn't take long.

"Beth, good morning!"

Beth turned to look at her. Her eyes were red and swollen as if she'd been crying. Lindsey felt her heart pinch at the sight. The poor thing was the picture of misery.

"Hi, Lindsey." Her voice was toneless as if it took all she had to muster a greeting, never mind add any emotion to it.

They pulled to a stop in front of the library together. They both locked their bikes onto the rack and headed for the staff entrance.

"You know, if you need to take some time off, that would be fine," Lindsey said.

"No. I can't stand to be inside my own head anymore," Beth said. "I'd rather be here, where I can keep busy."

"All right," Lindsey said as she led the way into the building, switching off the alarm as she went.

"But if you change your mind, just let me know."

"Thanks," Beth said. As if Lindsey's kindness was going to be her undoing, she hurried into her office, which was in the back corner of the building in the children's department.

Lindsey switched on the lights in the main workroom and strode toward her office. She flipped on her desk lamp and opened the blinds, filling the small room with light. She was fortunate to have large windows dominating one side of the room that afforded her a lovely view of the park and the bay.

She put her umbrella and purse in the lower right-hand drawer of her ancient wooden desk and took a seat in her black swivel chair. She turned on her computer, and while she waited for it to boot up, she took long fortifying sips of her coffee. She left her apple on her desk for later.

The library would be opening shortly, and she needed to get the meeting room ready for the library board. She had to print out copies of the agenda and have coffee, tea, water and snacks available. She refused to think about how the meeting would go if Candace Halpern had been contacting board members and insisting they let Beth go. She had a good board. She had to trust that they wouldn't be swayed by "the helicopter."

With a glance at the clock, she left her office and headed to the meeting room. It was situated at the front of the building. It had windows that overlooked the grassy side yard of the building. Lindsey had often thought she should offer it up as a good spot for a community garden, but she imagined that might push Ms. Cole right over the edge. Besides, it might be something to think about after the coming winter loosened its icy grip. Planning a garden would be a nice distraction from shoveling snow.

A large glass table dominated the room, and seven padded chairs on casters circled it as if awaiting a meal. There was a small cabinet along the back wall, which is where Lindsey stored the board's snacks and beverages. She flicked on the lights and began to set up.

The lights in the main part of the library turned on automatically, and Lindsey poked her head out the door to be sure her staff had all arrived and were preparing to open. She could see Beth at the children's desk, Ms. Cole was tending the circulation desk, two of their senior volunteers were wheeling a book truck to the book drop to empty the night's haul, and Jessica Gallo, another part-time library assistant, was staffing the reference desk. All was calm on the library front.

Milton was the first to arrive for the board meeting. Always early, he offered to finish brewing the coffee while Lindsey went to print the agenda.

On her way to the office, she said hello to Ms. Cole and was greeted with a grunt of unhappiness.

The lemon looked to have her full pucker on today. Given the weekend she had just had, Lindsey was not in the mood.

She stopped short and spun on Ms. Cole. "Is there a problem?"

Ms. Cole raised her eyebrows in surprise and her lips thinned. "Of course not."

"Then I would appreciate a civil greeting in the morning," Lindsey said. "And I'm sure the rest of the staff would as well."

Ms. Cole stared at her without blinking and then turned back to her computer without saying a word. For a nanosecond, Lindsey was overcome with a sudden and violent urge to howl like a dog at the moon. Luckily, it passed.

"I will assume from your silence that you agree," Lindsey said. Feeling validated that she'd gotten the last word, again, she continued on to her office to pick up her notebook and paperwork for the meeting.

When she got back to the room, four of the five board members were in attendance, as was Herb Gunderson the liaison from the mayor's office. The fifth board member, Doug Dowd was away on a cruise, so the group had agreed to go on without him.

Milton had taken his seat as chairman at the head of the table. Lindsey handed out the copies of the agenda while he called the meeting to order. The agenda was called to be approved by Lydia

Wilcox, a retired teacher, and was seconded by Earl Longren, who owned the general store, and Carole Towles. As they moved on to the first items, Lindsey glanced out the window and saw Sydney Carlisle in a small white compact car with a rental sticker on the back, stopped at the stop sign in front of the library.

Sydney's pale hair was again up in a twist, and she was talking on her cell phone while she sat there. She looked every bit the New Yorker, which explained the rental car. Most New Yorkers didn't bother to own cars since they really served no purpose in the city. An older couple was in the crosswalk making their way to the library, and Sydney honked at them when they didn't move fast enough.

As they gave her outraged looks and picked up their pace, Sydney squealed past them, leaving behind some skid marks and blue exhaust.

"Lindsey?" Milton said her name, and she turned toward him. From the way everyone was looking at her, she thought he'd probably called her name more than once.

"Sorry," she said. "I was just worried that car was going to hit two of our patrons."

"Tourists," Lydia said. "Can't live with them; can't shoot them."

Earl laughed, and Lydia grinned. Herb, the mayor's liaison officer looked ready to chastise them, but Milton turned to Lindsey and said,

"We're ready for your report."

Lindsey shuffled the papers in her lap. She passed out copies of her monthly library report and then glanced at the bullet points on her own copy. She was more than a little relieved that she'd gotten this done early last week.

"Okay then," she began. "Let's start with our circulation and program statistics, and I have some suggestions from our patrons to share . . ."

The door to the meeting room was abruptly flung open, and in strode a buxom woman in a tight skirt and silk blouse with a cameraman tailing behind her.

"Mrs. Norse," the reporter spoke into her microphone. "I have a few questions for you."

She strode right up to Lydia Wilcox and shoved the mic in her face. Lydia was pushing seventy, had silver hair and reading glasses and dressed in what Lindsey thought of as Connecticut genteel; in other words, she looked like Kate Hepburn in her later years in tailored slacks and turtlenecks with a sweater tied over her shoulders.

Lydia had taught high school English for thirty-five years. She was smart, sassy and did not suffer fools gladly.

"If you want to be taken seriously as a journalist," she said as she gave the young woman a scathing once-over, "you should do more with the pair on your face and less with the pair on your chest."

The girl tilted her head like a dog hearing a high-pitched whistle. She didn't get it.

"I'm not Mrs. Norse," Lydia snapped. "There is no Mrs. Norse; rather, it is Ms. Norris."

"But you look like a librarian," the reporter insisted.

Lydia huffed, giving the girl a disgusted look.

"I motion that we adjourn the meeting until we figure out what Miss . . ." Milton paused and stared at the reporter until she smiled and gave her name. "Oh, I'm Kili, like the fruit but with an *l* instead of a *w*, Peters."

"What Ms. Peters wants," Milton said. He spoke so politely, you'd have to know him very well to know he was irritated. Lindsey was pleased that she could tell.

"I'm Ms. Norris," Lindsey said as she rose from her seat. "How can I help you?"

"You're awfully young to be a librarian," Kili said.

"You don't go to libraries very much, do you?" Carole asked. Like Milton, you wouldn't be able to tell Carole was irked, unless you knew her. By the flash of Carole's light-green eyes, Lindsey hoped Kili was wearing flame-retardant clothing.

"Never," Kili said.

"What a surprise," Carole replied.

Lindsey heard Lydia snort behind her but didn't dare look at her for fear she'd burst out laughing, too.

"We're on a time crunch here, Kili," the cameraman said.

"Oh, right," she said. "Start rolling; we'll edit later."

"Fine," he said. A red light went on above the camera lens, which was pointed at Lindsey and Kili.

"This is Kili Peters reporting from Briar Creek. I'm here with the town librarian Lindsey Norse, er, Norris. Ms. Norris, what are your thoughts on your employee Beth Stanley?"

"Excuse me?" Lindsey asked.

"Did you have any idea she would become the suspect in the murder of her former lover Rick Eckman?"

"Suspect?"

"Do you have any plans to put her on suspension? A violent criminal working in the sanctity of a library, after all, would put the public at risk, wouldn't it?"

"Are you insane?" Lindsey asked.

"Is that a risk you're prepared to take?"

Now the mic was thrust into Lindsey's face, and she had to curb the urge to wrestle Kili to the ground and stomp on her mic until it was just useless bits of plastic and wires.

"I think you need to leave now," Lindsey said.

She took Kili by the elbow and forcibly pushed her through the meeting-room door. The cameraman was forced to back up or be stepped on.

But Kili wasn't done yet. She wrenched her arm out of Lindsey's grasp and approached a young mother with her toddler.

"Ma'am, are you prepared to have a murder suspect reading to your baby?" she asked and thrust the mic into the woman's face.

"What?" The woman pulled her child away from Kili.

"The children's librarian, Beth Stanley, is suspected of murdering her fiancé, and the library isn't going to do anything to stop her from having access to your precious babies. How does that make you feel?"

"Well, I . . ." the mother looked at Lindsey in confusion. "Is this true?"

"No," Lindsey said. "It's a gross misrepresentation of anything even resembling the truth."

"Then you didn't spend all day at the police station on Saturday being questioned about your friend's role in the murder of the famous children's book author Rick Eckman?"

Lindsey felt a growl start down low and deep. Who had told her all of this? She glanced up and saw Ms. Cole watching from the circulation desk with a very self-satisfied smile.

"Milton, could you escort Ms. Peters and her cameraman out?"

"You can't do this," Kili protested. "The public has a right to know."

"You know, you seem to be lacking the proper

paperwork for filming in a municipal building," Lindsey said. "How unfortunate."

"If you'll follow me, please." Milton gripped her elbow in a viselike grip, and Kili was forced to scurry on tippy-toes to keep up with him.

Once the door shut behind them, Lindsey turned back to the board, still standing with their mouths agape, and said, "If you'll excuse me."

She noted that the mother with the child had left the building in Kili's wake, which made Lindsey so mad she could have chewed nails.

She found Beth in her office packing up a brown cardboard box full of her things. The box screamed "quitting" and tuned out all other thoughts in Lindsey's head.

"Beth, don't . . ." Lindsey began, but Beth interrupted her with a shake of her head.

"It's better this way," she said. "If I quit, then you don't have to fire me. It'll look better when I search for another job."

"You're not quitting, and I'm not firing you!" Lindsey said. "This is ridiculous."

Beth just stared at her. "This isn't going to go away."

"You're the best children's librarian in the state," Lindsey protested. "I won't let you just walk away from all you've done here. You've developed an early years literacy program that has become the national model."

Beth opened her mouth to protest, but Milton

appeared in the doorway and cut her off. "Lindsey is right. There is no way Briar Creek is going to let you go."

Lindsey turned and gave him a grateful smile. She knew if they ganged up on her, Beth would buckle.

"That being said," Milton continued, "I do think you should take some time off."

Lindsey opened her mouth to disagree. She didn't like the idea of Beth being alone and unoccupied.

Milton held up his hand and said, "You have suffered a terrible loss. Even though you and Rick had parted ways, you still spent five years with him. Finding him like you did, well, you can't just ignore it or all of the emotion that comes with it. If you do, it'll just bite you in the backside when you're not looking."

"I know." Beth's head sagged, and Milton crossed the room and looped an arm about her shoulders.

"I have the number of a friend of mine who specializes in grief. He got me through the worst of losing Anna, and I want you to call him," Milton said. "Come on, I'll take you home."

"Thanks, Milton," Lindsey said. She stepped forward and took Beth's hands in hers. "I'll call you later."

She watched them leave through the back door and hurried back to the meeting room. Carole was the only one left, and she was busily cleaning up the snacks and drinks.

"Since Milton adjourned the meeting, we figured we'd better postpone until next week to deal with all of this."

"Sounds good. I'll send out an email to confirm," Lindsey said as she sank into a chair. It was funny how none of her classes in library science had prepared her for this sort of thing, dead bodies, staff under suspicion, crazed reporters. Really, they needed to consider expanding the curriculum.

After a couple of deep breaths, she got up from her chair and started to help Carole clean. A knock at the door brought her attention around. The lemon was standing there, looking even more pleased than before, and Lindsey knew it was because she considered Lindsey's reign as director to be crashing and burning in the current chaos.

"Ms. Norris, you have a room full of mothers and babies waiting for story time."

"Excuse me?" Lindsey asked.

"Story time," Ms. Cole said. "Should I tell them that Ms. Stanley has walked out and there will be no story time today?"

"No," Lindsey said.

She looked at Carole, who smiled at her encouragingly.

"You can do it, Lindsey," she said. "This is what public librarianship is all about."

Lindsey glanced back at Ms. Cole, who looked annoyingly triumphant. For a moment, she considered having Ms. Cole do story time, but she didn't want to be responsible for any psychological damage done to the babies.

"Please tell them I'll be right there," Lindsey said.

Carole nodded approvingly. "Good for you."

"Well, it's not like I have a choice, do I?"

CHAPTER 17

"You might have mentioned that one of the Wilson twins always sits in your lap," Lindsey said.

"Oh, well, generally it's the one who has just been productive in his diaper. Usually, you can smell him coming," Beth said. "I've found it's best to mouth breathe during the stories."

Lindsey lifted the ice pack off of the bump on her forehead and gave Beth another hard stare. "Again, information I could have used."

Beth ducked her head, and Lindsey was pleased to see a smile twitch her lips. They were crashed on the love seats in front of Beth's fireplace, sharing a meatball sub and a bottle of red wine. She had stopped by on her way home to check on Beth, and she was happy if her disastrous story time gave her friend something to smile about.

"So, I'm still not sure how you smacked your head on the puppet theater," Beth said.

"It was the hokey pokey. The heel on my shoe broke in the middle of putting my right foot in, and to avoid flattening little Emma Jacobs, I had to twist my body, which made my forehead connect with the corner of the puppet theater."

Now Beth's shoulders were shaking. Encouraged, Lindsey continued, "Of course, when the puppet theater went down, we were all worried that it was going to take the entire picture book section with it. Milton took one for the team there and dove in front of it."

"Was he okay?" Beth asked.

"He was gored in the behind by your unicorn puppet, but thankfully, only his dignity was left to bleed out as the horn is squishy."

"Oh, well, um, thanks for covering," Beth said around what were obviously choked-back spasms of laughter.

"Huh." Lindsey grunted, swigged some wine, replaced her ice pack and said, "Remind me to give you a raise."

"Don't worry, I will," Beth said. In a quieter voice, she said, "The news is coming on."

"Do you think that's wise?"

"Better to know than not," Beth said.

"All right." Lindsey struggled up to a seated position. She reached for her half of the meatball sub, while Beth turned on the flat-screen TV that hung on the opposite wall. They both turned in their seats to watch.

"Do we know what station that Kili person worked for?"

"The same as Charlene," Beth said.

Charlene was Violet La Rue's daughter and one of their crafternoon book club members when her schedule as an anchorperson for the local news station allowed.

The television came to life with Charlene's coanchor, Ty Ferguson, who looked like his hair had been shaped with wax, speaking.

"We're now joined live by our own Kili Peters in Briar Creek. Kili?"

"Good evening, Ty." Kili spoke into her hand-held mic. "I'm standing outside the Blue Anchor with Chief J. R. Daniels, who is leading the investigation in the murder of esteemed children's book author and Thumb Islands resident, Rick Eckman. Have you made an arrest yet, Chief?"

Out of the corner of her eye, Lindsey saw Beth sit up straighter in her seat, and she knew Beth was hoping for news that would clear her. Lindsey held her breath.

As Kili tipped the mic toward Chief Daniels, he hitched up his pants and tilted his head back to stare into the camera. He lowered one eyebrow in a studied pose, and said, "No, but we have a pretty good idea of who wanted the victim dead."

"Oh, really?" Kili asked. "Do you expect to be making an arrest soon then?"

"I'd say within the next twenty-four hours," he said.

"Well, I'm sure the residents of Briar Creek will be sleeping easier tonight, knowing that you're on the case," Kili twittered. "I know I would."

She gave him a flirty hair toss, and the chief's shirt puffed up until Lindsey feared he was in danger of popping a few buttons.

"Believe me, little lady, this perp isn't going to know what hit her," he said.

Lindsey and Beth exchanged an alarmed look. He said *her,* as in he thought the killer was a woman. That couldn't be good.

"Excuse me," Detective Trimble said as he muscled his way into the interview. "I think the chief is speaking prematurely. This case is still under investigation, and as such, we have no comment at this time."

The chief flushed an unhealthy shade of red and looked ready to argue, but Trimble grabbed his arm and yanked him away from the buxom Ms. Peters, who signed off looking annoyed to have had her interview preempted by the detective.

"Well, thank goodness someone working the investigation has a brain," Lindsey said.

"I have a feeling I'd be in jail now if it weren't for Detective Trimble," Beth said. She sounded scared, and Lindsey couldn't blame her. There wasn't a lot standing between her and a locked cell.

"I'm sure Detective Trimble won't let that happen," she said. She hoped she sounded more convincing than she felt. She grabbed the remote and clicked off the television before any more cheery news could ruin their evening.

"I just feel so helpless," Beth said. "I realize now how little I knew about Rick. He kept me at arm's length and I let him. Now he's gone, and I'll never really know him."

"Beth, he stole your story idea, submitted it as his own and it's going to be published," Lindsey said. "Not to speak ill of the dead, but I think it's safe to say he wasn't a nice person. Are you really sorry you didn't know him better?"

Beth blew out a breath and took a sip of wine. "Maybe if I'd known him better, I'd know why he did what he did."

"Because he's a lying cheat?" Lindsey asked.

"Maybe, or maybe he had writer's block and was feeling desperate," Beth said.

"Do you think you're the only person he's done this to?"

"What do you mean?"

Lindsey considered her words carefully. "Don't you think it's possible that he's plagiarized before?"

"But he won a Caldecott," Beth said. "Don't you think he would have been sued?"

Lindsey shrugged. "I was thinking of giving Sydney Carlisle a call."

"Why?"

"She said Rick was a recluse, refused to go on book tours and do other author promotion. She said he wouldn't even come off island to meet with her, but I wonder if she could get me in touch with his agent, and then I could ask him or her some questions," Lindsey said.

"No, actually, Rick recently fired his agent," Beth said. "If I remember right, this was his fifth agent in five years."

"Doubtful that they'd talk to me then, huh?"

"Yeah," Beth agreed. "Maybe we should leave this to the police."

"We can if that's what you want, but we've established contact with Sydney, and I certainly don't think we'd be doing any harm by asking."

"Yeah, we've met her, but I didn't get the feeling that she had the warm fuzzies for us," Beth said. "Don't forget she thinks I was passing off Rick's idea as my own."

"She was just misinformed," Lindsey said. "I think it's worth a stab."

"So to speak," Beth said dryly.

Lindsey cringed. "Sorry."

"It's all right," Beth said. "You know, he had no family."

"No, I didn't know." Lindsey watched while Beth nibbled at the outer crust of her sub. She was picking at it like a grackle pecked at a bread crumb.

"He was a ward of the state," Beth said. "He spent his childhood in foster care and then got a scholarship to the New London School of Design. He always said he'd have been a criminal if it weren't for his love of art."

Lindsey thought of how he'd plagiarized Beth's story and thought he hadn't gotten that far away from being a criminal after all, but she refrained from pointing that out.

"If we hadn't broken up, I'd have been the one arranging his funeral," she said. "Now who's going to do it? Who are they going to release his body to?"

Lindsey had no answer for her. The body of a murder victim with no family was out of her realm of experience. The best she could do was offer to call someone.

"I'll talk to Detective Trimble," she said. "I'm sure he can tell us what the process is."

"I want to make sure he's laid to rest in Briar Creek Cemetery," Beth said. "I know he wasn't a native, but he lived here for five years, and he really loved his island."

"Milton can probably make sure of that," Lindsey said. "Maybe Sydney can tell us who his lawyer was. If he left a will, he may have stated what he wants done with his body. That would make it a lot easier."

"Good idea," Beth said. "Lindsey, I know this wasn't the library career you had in mind. I know your heart belongs to those ancient papers you spent your twenties archiving, but I have to tell you, I am really glad you're here."

"Me, too," Lindsey said, surprised by how much she meant it. "Me, too."

CHAPTER 18

Lindsey picked up the photograph of her family, taken last Thanksgiving at her parents' house, from where it resided on the corner of her desk. She studied the four of them while she mulled over what Beth had told her yesterday about Rick.

She had always been close to her parents. A book lover from childhood, she had been well suited to be the daughter of academics. She couldn't imagine not exchanging daily e-mails with them or missing her weekly call home. Her brother, Jack, was the rambunctious one; brilliant but adventurous, he had always looked to escape the small college town of their childhood.

Even now, Lindsey could hardly keep up with him, and last she'd heard, about a month ago, he was off to study snow monkeys in Japan. She loved him dearly, but he'd always made her feel pale in comparison. Her fair skin and blonde hair when measured against his olive complexion and black hair just never seemed to have much oomph. The only feature they shared was their mother's hazel eyes.

Where she loved the comfort of the familiar, surrounding herself with the same environment she'd grown up with, he longed to see every corner of the globe, live out of a bag and wake up in a new time zone every day. They were as different as night and day, but still, she couldn't imagine her world without Jack and her parents, and she couldn't help but feel sorry for the lost little boy Rick had been, shuffled from foster family to foster family but never really belonging.

A knock on the door broke Lindsey out of her reverie. Violet La Rue, wearing her usual brightly colored flowing caftan, strode into the office.

"Hi, Lindsey. I just brought a hot dish over to Beth's." Violet sat down on the other side of Lindsey's desk. "She looks terrible. I don't think she's slept in days."

"There's a lot of that going around," Lindsey said.

"What's wrong?" Violet asked. "Other than your story time."

"You heard about that?"

"Please, you were the talk of the Blue Anchor last night. That knot on your head is a lovely shade of purple, by the way." Violet's lips twitched, and Lindsey knew she was teasing her.

"I tried to accessorize it." Lindsey gestured at

174

her purple sweater, which she'd put on over a pair of charcoal gray slacks and black suede boots.

"Very nice," Violet said. "Anyway, since I got a message from Nancy that our crafternoon has been canceled for this week, I thought I would offer up my services to fill in and do Beth's story time until she comes back."

"Oh, Violet, really?" Lindsey asked. "That would mean so much to Beth and to our regulars."

Violet waved a graceful hand. "I'm happy to help for as long as you need me."

Another knock sounded at the door, and they both looked to find Ms. Cole standing there, looking more puckered than usual.

"A detective is here to see you," she said.

"My cue to go," Violet said, and she rose from her seat with a wave to Lindsey. "Good luck."

"Thanks," Lindsey said. She rose, too.

As Violet left in a swirl of color, Detective Trimble entered. Ms. Cole stood in the doorway, obviously hoping to be invited to join them.

"Thank you, Ms. Cole," she said.

Ms. Cole gave her a dour look and shut the door behind her.

"Sorry to disturb you," Detective Trimble said.

"Not at all," Lindsey said.

He took the seat Violet had just vacated, and Lindsey resumed her seat.

"What can I do for you?"

"Well, I've been going over your statement," he

said. "I have some questions about the time frame of events."

Another knock sounded at the door, but before Lindsey could answer, the door swung open and in stepped Chief Daniels.

"Well, now isn't this cozy?" he asked as he strode into the room and sat in the last remaining chair. "I must have misplaced my memo about this meeting."

Lindsey glanced at Trimble. He looked completely at ease, so she felt herself relax. If he wasn't going to let Daniels get to him, then neither was she.

"You must have," Trimble agreed. "Ms. Norris and I were just going over the time frame of the day."

Lindsey had to wonder why they felt the need to revisit the day's events. What more could they know now that would make this information important? Then it hit her. "You know the time of death, don't you?"

Trimble studied her for a moment while Chief Daniels said, "Well, that hardly seems the point. And even if we did . . ."

"Yes, we know the approximate time of death," Trimble said.

"Well, that's wonderful, then you know that Beth couldn't possibly . . . oh, no," she stammered to a halt. "It's bad, isn't it?"

Chief Daniels opened his mouth, but Trimble silenced him with a hand. "It makes it very possible for your friend to have committed the murder."

Lindsey felt as if an icy hand was clutching her insides and squeezing hard. "She didn't."

Daniels made a snort of disbelief and crossed his arms over his chest. Trimble ignored him, but Lindsey had to resist the urge to kick him.

"Help us prove it," Trimble said. "Let's go over the day again. We'll be talking to Captain Sullivan, too."

"Okay, well, it started at the Blue Anchor," Lindsey said. "We were meeting Sydney Carlisle for an early lunch."

"And then," Chief Daniels prompted her, sounding irritated.

Lindsey shook her head. "Well, we went for a walk while I told her about the book Rick plagiarized."

"Supposedly plagiarized," Chief Daniels countered. "There is no proof that he stole Ms. Stanley's work."

"No proof?" Lindsey snapped. "He took everything. The main character, the plot and what would have been the start to a career."

"Prove it," Daniels said.

Lindsey felt her jaw spasm, she was clenching it so hard.

"Let's stay on task, shall we?" Trimble asked. "We aren't here to decide a plagiarism case; we're trying to solve a murder."

Lindsey took a deep breath. He was right. "After

I showed Beth the catalog page, we decided to go out and see Rick to ask him about it."

"And what time was that?"

"I'm not sure. Ronnie was working the desk at Sully's office. She might have a better idea. I know we had to wait quite a while for Sully to come in with the taxi. He was out picking up the Ginowskis."

"Once Sullivan arrived, how long did it take you to get to Mr. Eckman's island?"

"A little less than an hour," Lindsey said. "I was so busy looking at the scenery, I don't know that I'm the best judge of time passing."

"How about your friend's portfolio?" Chief Daniels asked. "Are you a good judge of that?"

"What do you mean?"

"Rick Eckman was stabbed. Your friend was carrying that big bulky case. It would have been easy for her to conceal a knife in there."

"You think Beth had a weapon?" she asked.

Chief Daniels stared at her and then said, "Yep. Woman scorned and all that. It's the oldest story in the book. Broad gets dumped and stabs the man. The end."

"Did you just say *broad?*" Lindsey asked. She wasn't sure, but she could feel her eyeballs practically bulging out of their sockets. "What decade are you living in exactly?"

"Now, everyone, let's just calm down," Detective Trimble said.

"I will not calm down," Lindsey said. "This troglodyte needs to catch up to a few thousand years of evolution, come out of his cave and get a clue. Now this interview is over. If you have any more questions for me, you can contact my attorney."

"Do you really want to play it that way?" Detective Trimble asked.

Lindsey tipped her head at Chief Daniels. "I don't think I have a choice. I won't help you railroad my friend just because he's too lazy to perform a real inquiry."

"Hey!" Chief Daniels jumped to his feet in protest. His fists knotted up, and Lindsey stood up to face him.

If he took a swing at her, she'd have him locked up in his own jail so fast he'd have whiplash.

He seemed to see the resolve on her face because he uncurled his fists and shoved his hands into his pockets.

"I'll be in touch," Trimble said as he rose and pushed Chief Daniels toward the door, none too gently.

"I don't doubt it," Lindsey said.

Once they left the library, she sank into her seat. She was so angry she was shaking. She didn't doubt that Detective Trimble was trying to do a solid investigation of Rick's murder, but Chief Daniels had already made up his mind that it was Beth, and he was going to do everything he could to skew the case that way.

Had she really told them to contact her attorney? Oh, dear. She supposed she could call her father and have him give the family lawyer a heads-up, but she didn't want to worry her parents. They'd been in a state over her for the past year.

The grim reality of what she had to do settled in her chest like a stone. Without dwelling on it, she picked up the phone and dialed the number she hadn't called in over six months, although she still knew it by heart.

"Hello?" The voice on the other end sounded achingly familiar.

"Hi, John. It's Lindsey," she said.

"Lindsey." His voice wrapped around her name with ribbons of regret and longing. It caught her off guard.

"I'm sorry to call you out of the blue," she said.

"No, don't be," he said. He cleared his throat.

There was an awkward pause, but Lindsey took a deep breath and forged ahead. She would treat this just as a business call. She would push aside the memories of this man as her best friend, her partner, the person with whom she'd thought she'd spend her life. No big deal, really.

"I need a favor," she said.

"Anything."

"Can you recommend a good criminal defense attorney?" she asked. "It's for a friend."

Silence greeted her request, and then he said, "The best is Kerry Sharpe."

"Excellent," she said. She could almost hear his brain buzzing with questions. She tried to lighten the conversation. "I always figured knowing a law professor would come in handy one day."

"Lindsey, we need to . . ." John began, but she cut him off, "Thank you so much, John. Take care of yourself."

"Lindsey . . ." he began but she hung up.

She replaced the phone on its receiver and let out a breath. There—that hadn't been so bad. Yeah, right. Then why did she feel as if someone had snuck up and kicked her in the pants when she wasn't looking?

She did a Google search on Kerry Sharpe and found the number for his New Haven office. She would pass this on to Beth later today as a just-in-case.

In the meantime, she was going to see what else she could find out about Rick Eckman. Beth had said she didn't feel as if she knew him as well as she should have after five years. Sydney Carlisle had called him a recluse, but he had to have a past. Everyone did.

She figured she'd start with his books. She left her office and headed for the picture books. He would be filed by his last name in the *E* section. Because the children's area was geared toward kids, obviously, the shelving was all low to the ground, giving kids access to the books.

Lindsey crouched and went past *Go, Dog. Go!*

by P. D. Eastman, a classic, until she reached Eckman. They had several copies of Rick's books. She grabbed one and checked the back-cover flap. Oddly, there was no author picture. The bio was short, stating that Rick was an award-winning author who lived in the Northeast. That was it.

Lindsey checked another book, but it had the same bio. She flipped to the front to see what the acknowledgments said. They were cryptically brief, too. *For my editor, S. C., and my agent, T. R. Thanks.*

Lindsey snapped the book shut and put it back on the shelf. None of this was helpful. She really didn't want to pester Beth, but if they were going to steer Chief Daniels in a different direction, they needed more information.

She wanted to talk to Sydney again, and Rick's former agent, too. She wondered if Detective Trimble had already done so. Of course, he would have access to Rick's house and all of his personal files so he may be working through a list of people in Rick's life, and quite probably he was finding someone with a stronger motive for murder than Beth.

Still, Lindsey would feel better if she talked to someone who knew Rick, either on a personal or professional level. Then, if Beth needed to retain an attorney, she'd have some information to give them.

Lindsey glanced out the window. It was mid-afternoon. The sky was blue, the air still. Maybe she would just go take a walk along the pier and see if anyone was around.

She grabbed her purse and left her office. Ms. Cole was in the workroom, bossing their teen pages around.

"No, no, no," she said. "How many times do I have to tell you that in fine sorting, you go all the way through the Cutter number? So, obviously, 743.27 L293 comes before 743.27 R731."

The young man looked miserable, and Lindsey had no doubt he was mortified to be dressed down in front of the other page.

"Hi, Perry," Lindsey said as she joined their group. "I see Ms. Cole is teaching you the finer points of the Dewey decimal system."

"Yes, ma'am," Perry said. He looked as if he were bracing for her to yell at him, too.

"It's a little tricky, but once you get the hang of it, it makes a lot of sense. Heather has been working for us for a long time, so if you get confused just ask her," Lindsey said. "Right, Heather?"

Heather blushed and nodded.

"Excellent," Lindsey said. "It's always nice to have a mentor. Oh, and Perry, the artwork you did for the bulletin board in the children's area is fantastic. I meant to tell you that earlier. I had no idea you were so talented."

"Uh . . . thanks," Perry stammered.

"Well, I'd best let you get back to shelving," Lindsey said. "I'm sure you have them up to speed now, don't you, Ms. Cole?"

"There's more to learn." Ms. Cole glared at her with her eyebrows forming a dagger's point in between her eyes.

Lindsey had no doubt that she had just deprived her of her afternoon's plaything. Too bad. She wouldn't tolerate bullying on her staff.

"True, there's always more to learn, but just like you can't eat a five-course meal in one bite, you can't learn an entire job in twenty minutes. Why don't you two take this cart out and start shelving?" Lindsey asked.

"Yes, ma'am," they said together and practically ran from the workroom in their haste to get away.

"Am I in charge of the pages?" Ms. Cole asked.

At least that's what Lindsey thought she said. It was hard to make out her words as she was talking between clenched teeth.

"Absolutely," Lindsey said. "And I'm sure they're as fond of you as you are of them."

That left Ms. Cole staring at her in confusion, but Lindsey didn't linger. She wanted to get going before the chief or the detective or the reporter or anyone else came looking for her.

Ann Marie was working the front desk. Lindsey gave her a big smile and said, "I'm taking some personal time for an appointment. I'll be back in a bit."

"Okay," Ann Marie called after her. "See you later."

Lindsey gave her a weak smile and kept going.

The door swung shut behind her, and she shouldered her bag and headed for the pier. The lunch crush had dissipated from the Blue Anchor, and Mary was seated at one of their outside tables, enjoying the mid-afternoon lull. She was reading her copy of *The Last Time I Saw Paris* and soaking up a little sunshine while she ate a late lunch.

"Hi, Mary."

"Hey there." Mary glanced up from her plate of cheese fries. "How's tricks?"

"They've been better," Lindsey said. "Beth has taken some time off, and I am really getting annoyed with Chief Daniels."

"I heard he's decided she's the murderer," Mary said. "What an idiot. How is she holding up?"

"As well as can be expected," Lindsey said. "At least Violet is going to sub in for her story times."

"Yeah, that's a nice knot on your head," Mary said. Lindsey sighed and Mary continued, "Don't take it too hard; story time just isn't your gift."

"You can say that again."

"Story time just isn't . . ." Mary began but Lindsey cut her off, "I get it."

Lindsey glanced down the pier to see if the water taxi was in. The sun glinted off of its bright canopy, and she felt like this was confirmation that her crazy idea was a good one.

"Is Sully kicking around?" she asked.

Mary lifted a brow and studied her for a second. "He just finished lunch. Why?"

"Oh, no reason, really," Lindsey said. "Hey, I'm going to stretch my legs. I'll be back."

"Uh-huh." Mary gave her a dubious look, and Lindsey knew full well that she'd be asking her brother what this was about later. That was fine with Lindsey. She just didn't have time to explain right now.

She waved and hurried off toward the boat office on the other side of the pier. The rough-hewn planks, worn from years of sun and sea, were uneven beneath her feet, and she was glad she had on a pair of low-heeled boots.

She saw Sully, sitting on a bench outside the office. He was reading the sports page of the newspaper, which looked fragile in his large, square hands. The sun glinted off of his mahogany hair, making the red more pronounced. He was what her mother would have called a dangerously attractive man, the kind of man a woman made bad decisions over.

Luckily, she had spoken to John today. With the bitter taste of that breakup still in her mouth, it was easy to shake off Sully's good looks and focus on the task at hand.

"Good afternoon, Captain," she said.

He glanced over the top of the paper at her, and

she admired the way his bright blue eyes crinkled in the corners. She shook her head—okay, maybe it wasn't quite so easy to ignore his good looks.

"Hi, Lindsey," he said. "What brings you out from the book stacks?"

"The weather," she said. "Isn't it a lovely day?"

"Very," he agreed. He was silent, watching her, and she had a feeling she didn't fool him, not even a little bit.

"I thought it would be a great day for a boat ride," she said. "Do you have a small boat that I could rent just for an hour or two?"

"No," he said.

She raised her eyebrows. "Why not?"

"They're all out," he said.

She glanced at the pier. It did seem to be empty of boats, except for the taxi.

"Could I rent the water taxi?" she asked.

"No," he said. "But if you need to go somewhere, I can take you."

Lindsey toed the rough plank at her feet while she considered. She didn't know Sully that well, but she liked the way he had handled that first day out at Rick's, and he had been wonderful when Nancy had been so vulnerable, and he did make a mean cup of cocoa. She believed he was okay, but then it wasn't like she had a lot of choices.

"Well?" he asked. "Have you decided?"

"Decided what?"

"Whether you trust me or not?"

"Yes," she said. Their eyes met, and his crinkled in the corners again when he grinned at her.

"So, we're off to Gull Island?" he asked.

"Yes," she said. "And it goes without saying that we tell no one."

"Then why say it?" he asked as he stood. He folded the paper and tucked it under one arm.

"I'm a librarian," she said. "Very detail oriented."

"Can't argue with that."

He poked his head into the office, and she heard him tell Ronnie he was taking a fare out to the islands. She didn't hear Ronnie's response, but it must have been okay, because he shut the door and led her down the pier to the boat.

As if by unspoken agreement, they spoke little on the trip out to the island. and Lindsey let her mind wander over the events of the past few days. Rick was dead, Beth was a suspect and the more questions she asked, the fewer answers she seemed to have.

"What are you hoping to find out there that the police missed?" Sully asked.

They were passing the Ruby house, and Lindsey glanced at the burnt-out hull of the cottage that remained. A shiver traveled down her spine as she thought of the poor family left behind.

"I don't know," she said. "Something that will prove Beth didn't do it."

"Pretty tall order," he said.

Didn't she know it. They traveled the rest of the

way in companionable silence. Lindsey marveled at the way Sully navigated the islands. She figured he must know every rock and narrow channel by heart.

She had once known her hometown like that. The college town in New Hampshire, where her parents were still professors, had been the perfect place for Lindsey and her older brother, Jack, to run wild. It had been a wonderful childhood, and there were days she still missed the simplicity of it all. Days like today, when the world seemed shockingly harsh and cruel.

Sully navigated around Rick's island. They both sat up in their seats as if expecting to find the police camped out on the dock. It was empty except for Rick's boat, which was in the same spot as the day they had found him.

Sully pulled up alongside the narrow wooden jetty, and Lindsey scrambled out, grabbing the rope as she went. She looped the rope around the metal tie-down on the dock's edge. Sully jumped out after her and nodded with approval at her rope skills.

"You'll make a sailor yet," he said.

Together they made their way along the bobbing dock up the stairs to the deck above. The crime-scene tape still blocked off the entrance. Lindsey had been hoping it would be gone. Now she felt as if she really were doing something illegal as opposed to just nosy.

Sully went first and turned the knob on the door. It was locked. Darn it. She didn't want to break in, and she certainly couldn't ask Sully to do it for her. She glanced around the house to see if any windows were open, but it appeared to be sealed up tighter than a vault, which she supposed was only natural, given that the police had been the last ones on the island.

"I'm sorry to have wasted your time," she said.

Sully glanced at her. "You're not packing it in already, are you?"

"Well, we can't break the door down," she said.

"No, but we can scout for a key," he countered.

"Good idea."

"I've been known to have a few," he said.

He started examining the rocks by the door. Lindsey checked under the doormat and the empty flowerpots. Nothing.

She stepped back and studied the exterior of the house. It was a gray shingled cape house with blue shutters. She wondered if Rick had ever bothered to lock the doors. Maybe the police had locked it up, and there weren't even keys for it.

The same thought seemed to occur to Sully as he stepped back and stood beside her, staring at the house as if willing it to tell him where the key was.

Lindsey thought about her parents' house. They never locked the doors unless they were traveling. There was no need. Everyone knew everyone, and as a kid she'd been well aware that if she did something bad on one side of town, her mother would already know about it long before she got home.

Her parents had gone on a cruise just last year, and her father had locked the door to the house when they left. Well, neither of them was in the habit of carrying a house key, so when they came home, they couldn't get in and had to wake the neighbor who'd been taking in their mail.

From then on, her father had put an emergency key on the corner of the door frame above the back door.

Lindsey stepped forward and checked the narrow ledge over the main door. No luck. She tried the windows, too.

Again, nothing.

"I'm going to try the back," she said.

Sully said nothing, but she felt him behind her as she followed a well-worn path around the side of the house to the back door. A picnic table and a barbeque filled the small patch of dried grass.

She tried the back door just to see, but it was locked. They began checking the logical places, and finally, tucked in a seashell to the left of the door, Sully found a key.

"Success," he said and he stepped toward the door.

The lock was in the center of the doorknob, and Lindsey held her breath until they were sure the key fit. Sully turned it, and they heard the soft *ka-thunk* of the lock disengaging.

He turned the knob and pushed open the door. He made to step inside, but Lindsey grabbed his arm. "Let's try not to touch anything."

He nodded and together they stepped into the house.

CHAPTER 19

Lindsey was surprised by how much she didn't remember from her previous visit to Rick's house. The back door opened up into the kitchenette. It was done in white paneling with white appliances. The only bit of color came from the brown-granite countertops and pale-blue curtains that hung over the window that was above the steel sink.

The kitchen looked untouched, but as they left it to enter the main room, Lindsey was abruptly reminded of the destruction they had found on their first visit. Drawing papers with half-done sketches were still strewn about but now bore the trample marks of even more pairs of feet. Obviously, cleanup was not a part of the investigator's procedure.

She glanced around the room. There were no photographs, no books or knickknacks, nothing that gave a sense of who had lived here.

She walked down the short hallway toward the bedroom. The lone twin bed was neatly made, just as it had been when they were here before. Again, there were no photographs or silly tchotchkes or even the odd collection of troll dolls, nothing that signified someone other than a monk might have slept here.

Sully had followed her into the room. He went to the nightstand and used the corner of his shirt to pull out the top drawer.

"Interesting," he said.

"What did you find?" Lindsey had opened the closet and was examining the shockingly neat clothing, shocking mostly because she had not really considered Rick a tidy person in his grubby jeans and sweatshirts. Still, here they were all hung up on hangers by color no less.

"A box of jujubes and a gentlemen's magazine," he said.

"A what magazine?" Lindsey asked. Sully wiggled his eyebrows at her and Lindsey felt her face get hot.

"Oh," she said. "Well, nothing here then. Moving on." She closed the closet door and hurried from the room.

She was pretty sure she heard Sully stifle a laugh but she didn't dare turn around to see. The only room left was the studio. Lindsey took a deep breath before stepping back into the room, which had been the scene of Rick's grisly death.

Although she hadn't remembered much of the house from their first visit, she could see Rick's dead body in her mind as clearly as if it was still there.

She stopped a few steps into the room. Sully drew up behind her and she felt his hand on her arm, giving her support and comfort. She was grateful.

This room was even more of a mess than the main room. The chair they had found Rick in was gone and she assumed the police had taken it for forensic tests. Lindsey noticed his computer was gone, too.

The easel and drawing table were littered with artwork. A floor-to-ceiling steel shelving unit was full of supplies, paints, brushes and canvases. A large steel flat file filled a corner, and Lindsey opened the drawers to find Rick's work neatly organized and preserved.

She flipped through some of the sketches, knowing she shouldn't be touching them, but still she had to see if there was evidence of the book he had stolen from Beth. She recognized several sketches from his other published works but there was nothing that resembled the hamster from his latest book. Hmm.

The sketches for the book that had won him the most awards were in the bottom drawer. She studied them, noting how his style had changed over the years from vivid colors and minimalist drawings to very detailed renderings. Was it the evolution of an artist or the scattered collection of a man who stole from others?

Sully was searching the desk. She heard him grunt a few times, and when she shut the flat file, she went to join him. He was closing the last drawer, and he blew out a breath.

"Is it just me, or is there more personal information scrawled on the bathroom walls at the Blue Anchor than we're finding here?" he asked.

"It isn't you," she said. "If I didn't know who lived here, I'd think it was just a furnished vacation rental."

"Oh, it's a rental," Sully said.

"What? Beth said Rick owned this place," Lindsey said. "Or at least, I thought she did. I just assumed he did."

"Well, after five years with the money he was making you'd think he would buy it, but as far as I know, it's been a rental property going on fifteen years now, the last five of which were Rick."

"Interesting," she said. "I wonder why he let Beth think he owned it."

"Well, it's more impressive than being a renter."

"I suppose," she said.

"Are we done?" he asked.

"Yes, I think so," she said.

They made their way through the house, back through the small kitchen and into the yard. Sully locked the door and replaced the key in its shell.

They circled the house and headed down to the dock. Lindsey felt her shoulders relax as she stepped into the boat. She hadn't known she was that tense.

Sully pushed off the dock and fired up the engine. The trip back to Briar Creek seemed shorter than the one out to Gull Island. Gone was her hope of finding a clue as to who Rick Eckman had in his life, aside from Beth, who might want him dead.

Lindsey knew it was ridiculous. She wasn't an investigator or a detective, but she couldn't help feeling like a failure. Of course, it wasn't going to be that easy to find someone with a grudge against Rick, but she had hoped.

They were pulling into the main pier when she had a thought. If Rick had rented the house for five years, surely the person who had rented it to him would know him a little bit.

"Do you know who rented Gull Island to Rick?" she asked.

Sully cut the engine and turned the boat so that it glided perfectly alongside the pier. Lindsey grabbed the rope and scrambled out.

As Sully climbed out beside her and helped tie it up, he said, "I vaguely remember that a family owned it when I was a kid, but I don't remember the name. Cheri Downs runs the local real estate office and makes it her business to know every property in the area."

"Thanks," Lindsey said. They were kneeling on the pier next to the boat tie, and Lindsey was sure she could smell the sun and salt on his skin. His blue eyes were on her face as if trying to figure out what she was thinking.

She looked away. She liked Captain Mike Sullivan, probably more than she should, but she just wasn't ready to entertain that sort of feeling for anyone yet.

He rose to his feet and offered her a hand up. Lindsey took it, ignoring the warm calluses that enfolded her fingers so gently but firmly.

"Well, I'd better get back to the library before they think I've ditched for the day," she said. "What do I owe you?"

"Nothing." He shook his head. "I was as curious as you to check out that house. I can hardly charge you for appeasing my own curiosity."

"Are you sure?" she asked.

"Very," he said.

"Well, thank you," she said. "I'll be sure you're first to get the latest Charlie Huston."

"So, I get my Harlan Coben and my Charlie Huston? Nice." He grinned. "I appreciate that."

"I'm just glad you're so well-read," she teased him. "It gives me plenty of authors to bribe you with."

"Or you could just ask me," he said.

They stared at one another for a moment, and Lindsey felt her face grow warm. With an awkward wave, she turned and hurried back down the pier. There was no sign of Mary sitting outside the café. She reached into her pocket and pulled out her cell phone to check the time. She'd been gone a little over two hours. She could only imagine what Ms. Cole was going to say about that. She put on some speed and dashed toward the library.

Lindsey had just gotten back to her office, under the disapproving glare of the lemon, when her office phone began to ring.

"Briar Creek Library, this is Lindsey Norris; how can I help you?"

"Is that murderess Beth Stanley going to be allowed to continue doing story times?" The voice was high pitched and squeaky with outrage.

Lindsey lowered her head and squeezed her temples with her right hand while holding the receiver to her ear with her left.

"Excuse me?" she asked.

"I am a parent in this community, and I want reassurance that our children will not be put in harm's way. You will be firing her, won't you?"

"I'm sorry, Ms., what is your name?" Lindsey asked. She glanced up and saw Ms. Cole watching her through the open door. She spun her chair to face the wall.

"That's not relevant," huffed the voice in the phone. "I'm a taxpayer in this town, and I demand that you fire that woman."

Lindsey hated the taxpayer line. Really? Did

these people think just because they paid a nickel into the general fund they had the right to boss the town's employees around? Besides, Beth owned property in the town and paid taxes; did that make her self-employed? Lindsey had to bite back the nasty comment and force herself to keep a civil tone.

"Well," the high-pitched complainer continued, "are you going to protect our children from that killer? She could turn on one of them. Is that a risk you're prepared to take?"

"What did you say?"

"Is that a risk you're prepared to take?"

Lindsey had heard that question before from the same shrill source. It registered in her brain like a dissonant chord.

"I was unaware that you lived here in Briar Creek, Kili," she said.

"I don't know what you're talking about."

"Oh, come on. I know it's you, Kili. Quit trying to be the concerned parent. You don't live here, and you don't have kids. You're fishing for a story."

"Well, can you blame me? That librarian of yours is being very rude and not answering her phone."

"How unhelpful of her," she said, but Kili ignored her sarcasm.

"How did you figure it out?" Kili's voice was in full pout now.

"The parents here love Beth," she said. "They are clamoring for her return. No one believes she's a killer."

"I know," Kili said. "I can't get anyone on tape to diss her. It's very annoying."

Obviously, Kili had not stumbled across Candace Halpern yet. Lindsey felt no need to enlighten her about the one disgruntled parent and decided to encourage her in another direction.

"Maybe you should work another angle," Lindsey said.

"What could be better than beloved children's librarian slays lover?"

"How about beloved children's librarian is persecuted by the media?"

"Nah; it doesn't have the same titillation factor."

Lindsey resisted the urge to comment that Kili would know all about titillation factors, but just barely. "Well, try to come up with something, because what you're doing now isn't working."

"Fine, whatever," Kili snapped. "I'll be in touch."

With a click the phone went dead.

Lindsey replaced the receiver in disgust. Poor Beth, to be caught in the sights of that one. She wondered if she could get Charlene to call her off. Then again, that might just make it worse. She wouldn't be surprised if Kili was hoping to take Charlene's job one day, and this might only goad her into causing more trouble for Beth.

She grabbed the local phone directory off of the shelf behind her desk. She scanned the yellow pages of the real estate agencies until she saw Cheri Downs's ad. It was big, taking up a quarter of the page, and it showed a pretty woman with bobbed blonde hair and a big smile.

Lindsey dialed the number listed. On the third ring, a no-nonsense female voice answered, "This is Cheri."

She sounded as if she were speaking from a distance, so Lindsey figured she was on her cell phone.

"Hi, Cheri, this is Lindsey Norris, and I'm calling about the island property Rick Eckman was renting."

There was silence on the other end, and Lindsey wondered if her cell phone had cut out.

"What did you want to know?"

Cheri sounded cautious, and Lindsey wondered if she was getting a lot of calls about the property, or perhaps the police had been asking questions, too. Lindsey figured she'd have to pose as someone interested in the property.

"I don't want to be ghoulish, but I was wondering if the current owners would be looking to rent it out again," she said.

"Are you interested?" Cheri asked.

"I might be if the price is right. Who are the owners?"

"I'm sorry, I'm not at liberty to give that information out. Can I have your contact information so I can get back to you?"

"Sure, I'm Lindsey Norris . . ." she began, but Cheri interrupted. "Wait. Aren't you the librarian?"

"Yes," she said. She really shouldn't have been surprised that in a town this small Cheri knew her name.

"Weren't you one of the ones who found him?" Cheri continued.

"Yes," she said.

"Pardon me, but I find it highly unlikely that you could be interested in renting a place that would require such a long inland commute every day, especially when you were there when a dead body was discovered."

Cheri was one smart cookie.

"All right," Lindsey admitted. "I'm not. I am, however, interested in anything I can find out about Rick Eckman."

"Why?"

"Because my children's librarian is considered a suspect in his death, and I know she didn't do it."

"I wish I could help you, but I can't," Cheri said. "I never really had any dealings with the man. He paid his rent on time, took reasonably good care of the place and pretty much kept to himself."

"Do you have any idea where he was before he came to the island?" Lindsey asked.

"I would, but the police came in with a warrant

and took all of my records on that property," she said. "I can't do anything with it until this mess is sorted out."

"Well, thanks, Cheri," Lindsey said. "You've been a help."

She hung up, and Ann Marie poked her head in the doorway. "Time to close up, unless you're planning to spend the night."

Lindsey glanced at the clock. Quitting time already? Where had the day gone?

"Thanks, Ann Marie. I'll be right there," Lindsey said, and she began to shut down her computer and grab her things. She wanted to know who owned Rick's island, and there was only one person she could think of who would know besides the real estate agent. Milton.

CHAPTER 20

Milton lived in the oldest house in town. It sat on a sweep of lawn just a few houses down from the town park.

The summer rosebushes that surrounded it were bloomless now that winter's chill was on its way, but the ivy that climbed up the chimney was thick as it hugged the stone close.

Lindsey walked up the cobbled walkway. The sun had set, and the purple hush of twilight was spreading over the town like a thick, fluffy blanket.

The lights were on in Milton's house, which she took as a good sign. She glanced at the small wooden plaque beside the front door, which had the number 1659 painted on it. Milton's house was a two-story, old stone house with a steeply pitched shingle roof, interrupted by two dormer windows that stuck out like bushy eyebrows. It was twenty years too young to be the oldest stone house in New England, as the Henry Whitfield State Museum, in Guilford, beat it out.

Milton and his wife had refurbished the old house, ripping out the nasty carpet someone had put over the original hardwood floors and having custom-made windows that resembled the originals but were energy efficient installed.

The front door was painted a cheerful blue, and Lindsey knocked three times and waited. She could hear the muted sounds of music, but no one answered.

She knocked again, and this time she heard Milton call, "It's open!"

She turned the knob and pushed open the door. She stepped into a little alcove with a staircase that led to the second floor and a small hallway leading around to the rest of the house.

"Hello? Milton, it's Lindsey," she called.

"I'm here in the study. Come on back."

She followed his voice down the short hall and

into the dining room. The kitchen was just beyond that, and the living room and parlor were to the left. She turned to the right and entered the narrow door that led to the study.

She caught the mellowing scent of jasmine incense and found Milton in the middle of his study, dressed in flowing cotton clothes and in the yoga position she knew as downward-facing dog.

"What a pleasant surprise," Milton said. "I'm just finishing my evening routine. I'll be right with you."

"Don't rush," Lindsey said. "I can wait."

She left him and crossed the room to the cushy chairs in front of the fireplace. She picked up a *Prevention* magazine and was soon happily absorbed in an article about superfoods. She was definitely going to have to start eating more blue-berries.

Milton joined her shortly with a towel around his neck and a water bottle in hand.

"Lindsey, this is a lovely surprise," he said. "I was just about to make some green tea; care for some?"

"If it's no trouble, that would be lovely. Thank you," she said.

"None at all," he said. "I'll be right back."

Lindsey continued reading her article. There was something very serene about Milton's house, and she thought this was the most relaxed she'd been since the murder.

Milton returned bearing a tea tray. A Willow Ware teapot with matching cups and saucers, along with dessert plates heaped with shortbread, crackers, Brie and grapes, filled the tray. He set it down on the coffee table between their chairs and poured the tea.

"Oh, Milton, this looks wonderful," Lindsey said. "You shouldn't have gone to any trouble."

"It wasn't," he said. "It's pretty easy to dump food on a plate. Besides, I know you just got off work and haven't had a chance to eat. My late wife, Anna, would never forgive me if I didn't feed a guest who was hungry."

Lindsey smiled. In a world full of cranky, selfish people, Milton stood out as a person who was good all the way down to his bones.

He handed her a cup, and she helped herself to sugar and milk. She felt her stomach clench, and she realized she was hungry, starving in fact. She couldn't remember the last time she had eaten.

They munched quietly. Milton seemed in no more of a hurry to get to the purpose of her visit than she was, but finally, when her belly felt full and her food and tea were gone, she knew it was time.

"So," she said uncertain of how to begin. "How are you?"

Milton grinned at her. "Much better now that I've eaten. It's always easier to converse after some sustenance, isn't it?"

"Yes," she agreed, thinking he was very wise. "I hope I am not being pushy, but I'm curious if you can tell me anything about who owns the island where Rick Eckman lived?"

Milton pursed his lips. He seemed to be lost in thought for a moment, and Lindsey wondered if he had forgotten that Rick didn't own the house on the island.

"It's been a rental for a long time," Milton said. "Let me see. Before Mr. Eckman, it was rented by a New York family, but they were only here in the summers. What was their name?"

Lindsey listened while Milton worked through it.

"The Schad family. Yes, and before them it was the Jacobs. They were fun. They liked to throw parties. And before them, well, the family who owns it lived there. What was their name?"

He sipped the last of his tea. "Oh, I remember now, the Brodericks. They haven't been in town for at least ten years."

"Do you know where they are now?" Lindsey asked.

"I imagine I could find out, but first I have to ask—why?"

"I'm trying to track down anyone who knows anything about Rick Eckman before he took up residence in Briar Creek," Lindsey said. "It's to help Beth."

"Are you trying to find someone from his past

who may have had a motive to kill him?" Milton asked.

"You read me like a book," Lindsey said.

Milton grinned at the wordplay. "Does Beth have any ideas? She knew him best."

"Beth is discovering that she didn't know him as well as she thought," Lindsey said. "And honestly, I think it's too difficult for her to talk about."

"Of course," Milton said. His voice resonated with the hollow sound of someone all too familiar with grieving. "I think I have some contact information at the Historical Society office. I can get that to you tomorrow morning, if you like."

"That would be such a help," Lindsey said. "Thank you."

"Happy to do what I can," Milton said. "Now, I have a personal question for you."

"You do?" Lindsey asked. For some reason, she dreaded that it would be about her and Sully, which was ridiculous because there was no her and Sully. She hardly knew the man.

But Milton surprised her. He held up an ornate wooden box and asked, "Do you play chess?"

"I do."

"Care for a game?" he asked. He sounded so hopeful that Lindsey couldn't have refused him even if she wanted to, which she did not.

"Absolutely."

The next morning Lindsey dragged herself out

of bed, feeling mentally wiped out. Milton had walloped her at not one but two games of chess. She was going to have to brush up on her skills. She had gotten him to agree to consider starting a chess club at the library. She loved the idea of having spontaneous chess games happening. She already knew exactly where she was going to set up the chessboards.

The bike ride into work woke her up, as the brisk October air pinched her cheeks like an affectionate auntie. She entered through the back door, happy to be the first one to arrive. She started a fresh pot of coffee and put out the newspaper as soon as she scanned the headlines.

She checked her voice mail to ensure that no one had called in sick. There was one database-salesman call, but she deleted the message, as her library budget was too small for a legal-reference database better suited to an academic or urban public library.

"Morning, Lindsey," Jessica called on her way through the workroom. She stopped to pour herself a cup of coffee and then headed out to the main library to prepare for opening.

Lindsey glanced out her door and saw that Ms. Cole was already setting up the cash register at the circulation desk. For a moment, Lindsey had the feeling that the place ran like a well-oiled machine, but then she glanced toward the children's area. It seemed empty without Beth cavorting around in one of her character costumes getting ready for story time.

She was thrilled that Violet would fill in for Beth, but she wanted her friend back. She wanted their crafternoon club back, and she wanted to be rid of this ever-present feeling of anxiety that had enfolded her since they'd found Rick's body. The only way to do it was to clear Beth's name, and to do that, the police were going to have to find the real killer. If Chief Daniels wasn't going to look further than Beth, well, then Lindsey would.

Newly resolved, she plunged into her e-mails, answering the ones from the library board members about the abrupt end of the last meeting and when to schedule the next one. She had a few from parents wanting to know when Miss Beth would be back and another suggesting that the library put out a dish of mints on the front desk as a welcoming touch for patrons. Lindsey forwarded that one on to Bill Sint, the president of the Friends of the Library, as it seemed like something they would want to do.

She tried not to glance at the clock, but at ten-thirty and ten thirty-three and ten thirty-five, she knew she was fighting a losing battle. Now she was worried about Milton. Why hadn't he called? He was usually so prompt.

She got up and went to check on the library. She was feeling restless and wanted to be in motion. Jessica was working the reference desk.

She and their regular patron Polly Carter were hip deep in recipe books, looking for a book Polly had seen last year that had a red cover and cost twenty-four dollars and ninety-nine cents. She was very frustrated when both Jessica and Lindsey gave her blank stares as to what the book could be called or who might have written it.

Lindsey was relieved when Ms. Cole came to tell her that she had a phone call.

She hurried back to her office, picking up her receiver and answering, "Briar Creek Library, this is Lindsey."

"Lindsey." It was Milton. "I have the contact information for you, but it's not good."

"What do you mean?" Lindsey asked.

"Mr. Broderick passed away last year, and Mrs. Broderick is in an assisted-care facility in Kingston," he said. "They don't have any children, so it's just her."

"Do you think she'd be willing to talk to me?"

"She might, but it may not matter," he said. "She has Alzheimer's disease."

"Oh."

"I don't know how much she knows about the house on the island or how much she would remember about who they rented it to," he said.

"Well, I have to try," Lindsey said. "Go ahead and give me the information."

She snatched up a pen and scribbled the address on her pink message pad. After thanking Milton, she hung up and pondered what to do next. She desperately wanted to go to the home now and talk to Mrs. Broderick, but she'd taken too much time from work the day before. She'd have to go after hours.

A knock on the door drew her attention around. It was Beth.

"I'm going out of my mind," she said. She crossed the room and plopped down in the seat across from Lindsey's desk. "I finished reading our crafternoon book; I'm done with the sweater I was knitting; I've caught up on all of the little house chores I'd been putting off. Yesterday, I seriously debated cleaning my oven. I need to come back to work."

Lindsey looked at the circles under her friend's eyes. They were so dark they looked like inky thumbprints had been pressed onto the skin.

"You need to lay off the caffeine and get some sleep."

"Right now I just need to be distracted," Beth said. "So I can't brood about it."

It went without saying that "it" was Rick's murder.

"Have the police been in touch with you?"

"A few times since that first day," she said. "But it's always the same questions."

She sounded tired down to her roots and looked wilted as well. Lindsey knew if it was her, she'd want to be working, too.

"Violet has volunteered to take your story times, and I said yes, as I really don't think the kids need me to do another one," Lindsey said.

A small smile lifted the corner of Beth's mouth. "I don't know if I have the energy for story time, so that's probably for the best, but could I work on my collection? I've been meaning to weed the nonfiction books. There are some dusty books that haven't been checked out in all the years I've been here."

"That sounds excellent," Lindsey said. "I've missed you. It'll be nice to have you back."

"It'll be good to be back," Beth said. "If you need me, I'll be in my office pulling up the circulation stats on my books."

Lindsey watched Beth leave. She seemed to be walking with a little bit more of a spring in her step. She was going to be okay. Well, if they could just prove she hadn't murdered Rick Eckman.

"What's she doing here?" Ms. Cole appeared in Lindsey's doorway. Her thick brows were drawn into a frown, which connected them in the middle and gave her a rather forbidding unibrow.

"She's back," Lindsey said. "She's going to be working on her collection. Problem?"

Ms. Cole must have picked up on the warning note in Lindsey's voice, because she opened her mouth and closed it, turned on her stout heel and strode away.

For some reason this made Lindsey feel as if she

had won the battle, if not the war.

The rest of the day passed mercifully quietly. Patrons came in, and patrons went out. Books came home, and books went out. The computers stayed busy but didn't have a long queue. Lindsey felt as if things just might get back to normal.

She looked up the assisted-care facility where Mrs. Broderick was living and realized she was going to need a car. She knew Nancy would probably let her borrow her car, but the fancy Mustang made her nervous. If anything happened to it, she'd never forgive herself. For the first time, she doubted the wisdom of selling her own car.

She left her office and found Jessica at the reference desk. Mrs. Carter had long since departed with a list of possible titles, and Jessica was reading through the fiction reviews in *Publishers Weekly* and marking the ones she wanted to buy for the library.

Jessica was a part-time library assistant. She was somewhere in her late forties, her brown hair just beginning to be taken over by gray. She was married to her college sweetheart and had spent her twenties and thirties being a wife and mom; now her kids were gone, and her time was consumed with earning her master's degree in library science, which Lindsey encouraged even though she knew it meant they would probably lose Jessica to a larger library.

"Hey, Jessica, I have a question for you,"

Lindsey said as she approached the desk.

"Shoot." Jessica glanced up from the magazine and gave Lindsey her full attention.

"Can you recommend a car-rental place in the area? I have to run an errand this evening that is farther than I'm willing to ride my bike."

Jessica pursed her lips. "Briar Creek is really too small to have its own. Probably you'd have to call a rental office in one of the larger neighboring towns and see if they'd be willing to pick you up. Unless . . ."

She picked up the phone and dialed.

"I have an idea," she said to Lindsey. Then she turned back to the phone. "Bruce? Hi, it's Jessica Gallo."

There was a pause and then she continued. "Yeah, it's running fine, thanks. Hey, do you remember that loaner you let me borrow? Do you still have it?"

There was another pause. "Uh-huh. Well, I have a friend who needs a car; could she borrow it?"

Jessica looked at Lindsey. "When do you need it?"

"Just for this evening," Lindsey said.

Jessica repeated the information into the phone.

"Do you have a valid driver's license?" she asked.

"Yes," Lindsey said.

She waited while Jessica concluded the call.

When Jessica hung up, she looked at Lindsey and said, "Bruce, the mechanic with the shop on Tyler Street, will let you borrow his loaner for the evening for twenty-five dollars."

"Really?" Lindsey asked. "That's great."

"Don't thank me until you've seen it." Jessica chuckled. "It's not pretty, but it runs great, and Bruce is a solid guy. He never overcharges."

"Thanks. You're a lifesaver."

Jessica flushed with pleasure and grinned. "Aw, pshaw."

Lindsey headed back to her office, feeling relieved that her first obstacle had been cleared. Now if she could get in to see Mrs. Broderick and even more importantly get her to remember anything about Rick. That would be key.

To say the loaner was not pretty was an understatement. It was a 1970s olive-green Buick Century with a white top. Lindsey felt like she was driving her living-room couch, but despite its looks, the engine purred and it glided over potholes in the road like butter on toast.

Lindsey drove through town and turned onto the road that would lead to the highway. It felt good to be driving again, and she turned on the radio; an oldies station seemed most appropriate. The music surrounded her, and she rolled down the window just a little, letting the cold night air seep in while she turned on the heater, enjoying the feel of the two air currents swirling around her.

She followed the directions she'd printed from the assisted-care facility's website, taking I-95 east past several exits until she reached Kingston. It was full dark now, and the streetlights lit her way like hovering fireflies as she drove over rolling hills lined with tall trees that were becoming skeletons of their springtime selves as their leaves fell, leaving them bare.

The road she followed led up a hill to an old stone mansion set back on a large rolling lawn. A small visitor's parking lot fronted the building, the only indication that this wasn't a private residence.

Lindsey parked in the lot. She had a moment of wondering what the heck she was doing here, but then she thought about Beth and how forlorn she'd looked and Chief Daniels's unwavering belief that she had stabbed Rick, and Lindsey knew she had to at least try to find out more about Rick's past. With his charming personality, there had to be someone else who wanted him dead.

The doors to the old house had been retrofitted to accommodate automatic sliding-glass doors. Lindsey stepped on the mat and walked through to a plush lobby full of plants and soft carpeting.

She stopped at the registration desk and asked the woman in the pink scrubs behind the desk where she could find Mrs. Broderick.

"Oh, are you family?" the woman asked.

"Cousins," Lindsey said. "I just recently heard about her decline."

"Oh, yes, I'm sorry," the woman said. Her name tag read "Trudi." "Adele is just the sweetest woman. We all adore her. Sign here, please."

Lindsey signed in as Leigh DeWay. No need to alert anyone that she'd been here, after all. Trudi handed her a visitor's badge and directed her to the fourth floor, room 421.

There were only two elevators, both in service, so she opted for the stairs. They wound up through the old building until Lindsey reached the fourth-floor landing. She followed the room numbers until she got to Adele Broderick's.

She took a deep breath and knocked on the door. There was silence, so she waited before knocking again. This time the door opened and a stout, dark-haired woman with big brown eyes peered out at her. Her face was lined with wrinkles, and her dark hair seemed to absorb light, letting Lindsey know it was a dye job and that she was probably well into her seventies.

There was a confused look on the woman's face as if she'd been expecting someone else. Then it cleared, and she grabbed Lindsey by the hand and pulled her into the tiny apartment.

The room was decked out in old-lady chic, which meant lots of brocade and doilies and fragile, glass knickknacks.

"I'm so glad you made it," Adele said. She was

wearing tennis shoes and a navy-blue track suit. "I was afraid you'd miss the beginning."

"Mrs. Broderick, I'm Lindsey Norris," she began, but the older woman pushed her down onto the couch and sat beside her. She picked up the remote and began to channel surf.

"Mrs. Broderick? Is my mother-in-law here?"

"Huh?" Lindsey felt mildly panicked that she was inadvertently messing with this poor woman's head.

Then Mrs. Broderick swatted her arm and laughed. "You're teasing me. I really thought you were going to miss the opening of the show, Sis."

"Show?" Lindsey asked. "Of what?"

"You're so funny," she said. "As if you don't know."

She flipped through the cable channels until the familiar perky theme to *I Dream of Jeannie* came on. Then she got up and started to dance in a fair imitation of a belly dancer.

"Come on, Sis; don't be a party pooper." Mrs. Broderick pulled her up, and Lindsey found herself in the awkward position of having to pretend to be Adele Broderick's sister or risk upsetting her. Oh, brother. She moved her arms and jiggled her hips just to keep her new friend happy.

Finally, when the opening music stopped, Mrs. Broderick collapsed onto the sofa in a fit of the giggles. Lindsey sat cautiously beside her.

"That was fun, Mrs. . . . er . . . Adele," Lindsey said.

Why, oh why, had she thought this was a good idea? This sweet old lady was obviously a few slices short of a loaf, and here she was trying to pump her for information. Lindsey figured she'd best get while the getting was good.

"We should sneak into the kitchen and get some ice cream," Adele said. "Mama and Daddy are asleep. They'd never know."

"Oh, I don't think so," Lindsey said. "I'm trying to maintain my figure."

Adele frowned at her. "Well, I want ice cream, and if you don't come with me, I'm going to tell Mama that you were kissing Cletus Beauregard under the bleachers at the Friday night football game."

"I did not," Lindsey protested.

"Yes, you did," Adele argued. "Molly and I saw you!" She made kissing noises at her, and Lindsey felt like she suddenly had the pesky little sister she'd never wanted.

"That's just mean," Lindsey protested.

Adele grinned at her. "Oh, come on."

She popped off of the couch, but instead of going to her own kitchenette, she went out the door of her apartment, giving Lindsey no choice but to follow.

They passed a few of the residents on their way. Some were in wheelchairs, some were using walkers and all were elderly. Adele smiled and waved at all of them, and Lindsey wondered if she had been a cheerleader in her youth; she was just so perky.

Adele led the way into an empty cafeteria. It was full of round tables with linens and center-pieces, looking more like a restaurant than an assisted-care dining hall. The kitchen doors were closed, but Adele pushed her way through, putting her finger over her pursed lips at Lindsey to indicate that she should be quiet.

The dark kitchen was a maze of stainless steel, and Adele led the way to the back, where the freezers were. Lindsey had a sneaky suspicion that Adele had done this before. She opened the Sub-Zero and turned to Lindsey and said, "We have Italian ices. Do you want lemon or raspberry?"

Suddenly the lights popped on overhead, and Lindsey whirled around to the door. A large, forbidding looking man dressed all in blue scrubs was glaring at them.

Adele poked her head out of the freezer and grinned. "Frank, I'm having lemon. What do you want?"

"Raspberry," he growled.

Lindsey blinked at him, and Adele elbowed her. "Well?"

"Lemon," Lindsey said. Adele snatched the three small cups out of the freezer and shoved one at Lindsey. She shut the door, and as they passed by Frank, she handed him the raspberry with a wink.

"Don't tell," Adele said.

Frank's frown turned into a grin as he winked back at her. Adele took Lindsey's hand and led her back to her apartment. The show had started, and they made themselves comfortable while Jeannie blinked her way in and out of trouble.

At a commercial break, Lindsey felt it was time to come clean.

"Adele, Mrs. Broderick, I'm not your sister," she said.

Adele tipped her head and studied Lindsey but said nothing.

"My name is Lindsey Norris, and I'm a librarian in Briar Creek. You own one of the Thumb Islands, Gull Island, and you were renting it to a young man named Rick Eckman. Does any of this sound familiar?"

Adele kept watching her and then said, "The cottage."

Lindsey assumed that meant she had some memory of her summer place, so she forged on. "I was wondering if you remember anything about Mr. Eckman. Did you meet him? Do you know where he was before he rented your island?"

Adele blinked at her again, and Lindsey was afraid she'd lost her. Then she said, "There's no Eckman."

"What do you mean?"

Adele got up and went over to a small writing desk in the corner. She opened a drawer in the bottom and looked through some papers and then brought back what looked like a contract. It was a rental agreement from five years before for the house on the island, only the name wasn't Rick Eckman; it was Ernie Shadegg.

Lindsey felt her heart pound in her chest. What did this mean? Was Rick's name really Ernie? She looked at Adele, and a million questions bubbled to her lips, but the show had come back on, and Adele was watching the Major try to extricate himself from some help of Jeannie's that had gone terribly awry.

Lindsey finished watching the show, mulling over what she had learned. When Adele would nudge her with an elbow at a particularly funny part, Lindsey would grin, but she really had no idea what was going on.

When the show was over, she asked Adele if she could keep the rental paper, and she nodded. "Come back next week, and we'll snitch some red velvet cake."

"Thanks, Adele," Lindsey said. "I will."

She gave the tiny woman a gentle hug and waved as she went down the hall. She would be back to visit her new friend. There was something about the elderly lady that Lindsey liked.

She parked the Buick in the driveway to Bruce's

garage and put the key in the drop box. It was late and very dark as she made her way home on her bike. She wished she'd known she would be out this late; she would have worn a heavier coat. She pedaled harder, trying to warm up.

She locked up her bike on the side of the house and crossed the wide front porch to the main door, which was unlocked. As soon as she stepped into the foyer, Nancy's door was yanked open, and out stuck two gray heads as Nancy and Violet peered at her.

"Where have you been?"

"Do you have any idea how worried we've been?"

"You could at least call, you know." That was Mary, who had joined them.

"Yeah, what they said." Beth popped up behind the others.

"Lindsey, it's so nice to see you again." Another person pushed forward through the others and Lindsey was delighted to see Charlene, Violet's daughter, appear.

She gave her a quick hug and said, "What are you doing out here? Don't you have to be on the evening news?"

"I took the week off," she said. "We all needed it. Martin wants to weatherize the cabin, and the kids were happy to miss a few days of school."

Charlene was tall and thin like her mother, with the same striking features, lovely dark skin and a generous smile.

"Well, I for one am glad you're here," Lindsey said. "I need your expertise."

"Should we bring the couch and chairs out here then?" Nancy asked with a wink.

Lindsey shook her head. "Sorry. I've just learned the most extraordinary bit of information."

"Well, what are you waiting for?" Violet asked as she ushered them all back into Nancy's. "Come in."

Nancy brought out a silver pot of hot chocolate and several mugs along with a matching silver tray weighed down with homemade cookies. Tonight they were butterscotch bars. Lindsey took two and sighed. She loved living here.

While Violet poured the cocoa, they each found seats around the room. Lindsey claimed one of the wing chairs by the fireplace. When she took a sip of her hot chocolate, she remembered sitting here with Sully. She knew it hadn't been that long ago, but given the events of the past few days, it felt as if it were months ago.

"Beth, will it bother you to talk about Rick?" Lindsey asked. "I don't want to discuss him if it will upset you."

"No." Beth shook her head. "In fact, we were just talking about him before you arrived. I'm sad for him, and I'm sorry someone killed him. He didn't deserve that, but I'm getting a little tired of being suspect number one. I have to face the fact that someone wanted him dead, and they really don't care if I get blamed or not."

"Good," Lindsey said. "Because I have some questions for you, and I doubt if it will be easy."

"Before you start," Mary said, "can I make one request?"

"Sure," Lindsey said.

"The next time you take off for parts unknown, do you suppose you could tell one of us?" she asked. "There is a murderer out there, you know."

"I'm sorry," Lindsey said. "Were you worried?"

"Yes!" the other women answered in unison, with varying levels of exasperation.

She knew it was terrible of her, but Lindsey couldn't help but feel oddly pleased. She was amazed that in such a short time, Briar Creek had become her home, with people who really cared about her. It felt good.

"So, why did you want my advice?" Charlene asked.

"Well, you started out as an investigative reporter, right?"

Charlene nodded.

"Okay, well, I went to see the woman who owns the island that Rick has been renting."

"Renting?" Beth asked. "He told me he owned it."

"No, that island has been in the Broderick family for years," Mary said.

"I thought Mrs. Broderick was in Kingston in an assisted-care facility," Nancy said.

"Alzheimer's, I heard," Violet said.

"She is," Lindsey said. "And she's quite a character. She thought I was her sister and had me help her raid the kitchen, but she also gave me this."

Lindsey handed the paper to Beth first, as she was the most directly affected.

"I don't understand," Beth said. "This is for some guy named Ernie Shadegg."

Lindsey waited while she put it together. It didn't take long. Beth had always been a quick study.

"Are you telling me that *Rick* wasn't Rick's real name?" she asked.

"Not according to Adele Broderick," Lindsey said. "She had that agreement in her desk, and it's dated five years ago. That's when Rick moved there, isn't it?"

Beth blew out a breath as if she'd just sustained a body blow she hadn't seen coming.

"I'm sorry," Lindsey said. It felt so inadequate. "This must be a stunner."

"You know, he never talked about his past. I thought it was because he'd had a rough childhood, being bounced from foster home to foster home. I had no idea that he had a different name."

"But why did he have a different name?" Violet asked.

"Maybe he was running from the law," Nancy said.

"Maybe he plagiarized someone else's work and was in hiding," Beth said bitterly.

Mary reached over and looped an arm around Beth's shoulder. Beth leaned into her as if trying to absorb some warmth or strength.

"So, what do we do next?" Lindsey asked Charlene. "I want to know where he was before he came to Briar Creek. I want to know if he made enemies, ones who may have found him here."

"May I see the rental papers?" she asked. Beth handed them over, and Charlene read through them. "He listed his previous residence as an apartment in New London. If it was a rental, you might be able to interview the landlord and see if he or she remembers him."

"What about having his DNA traced?" Nancy asked.

"Oh, I like that," Violet said. "Beth, do you have any of his hair lying around?"

Beth looked from Violet to Charlene. "She's kidding, right?"

" 'Fraid not," Charlene said. "Those two have never missed an episode of *CSI*."

"The one set in Vegas, not all those silly spin-offs." Violet sniffed as if that made it more legitimate.

"I bet Grissom could figure out who murdered Rick," Nancy said.

"Yeah, probably off of a partial fingerprint on a half-eaten donut," Violet agreed.

"You are aware that he's not real," Charlene said. "He's an actor, like you, Mom."

"I know, but it makes me feel better to think that he's actually out there fighting crime."

Charlene rolled her eyes so far back in her head Lindsey was afraid they might get stuck.

"Well, since Grissom isn't here and we're stuck with Chief Daniels, I think we should follow up on this," Lindsey said. "I'm going to drive over there tomorrow and see what I can find out."

"Drive?" Mary asked. "Why don't you just call? Surely they can tell you over the phone if they remember him or not."

"I want to be sure. I want to show his picture and make sure Rick and Ernie are the same person. Besides, I think I'll get more information if I go in person," Lindsey said.

"I'm going with you," Beth said. Everyone turned to look at her. "What?" she asked.

"Do you think that's wise?" Mary asked. "I mean you have no idea who this Ernie Shadegg was. He could have been, well, if he was hiding out on an island, he could have been a really bad man."

"As opposed to the sweetheart of a guy who ripped off my work?" Beth asked.

"I see your point," Mary agreed.

"It's probably not going to be fun," Beth said. "But I have to know. I have to know who I was really dating for the past five years."

CHAPTER 21

Road trips required a couple of things: a well-balanced diet of caffeine, salt and sugar and an excellent selection of tunes—oh, and directions.

Beth was in charge of the tunes and the navigation, and she had done well, selecting the Beatles' number-one hits and a perky 1980s compilation that included the B-52s and the Go-Go's. She'd also printed out directions from MapQuest and had them neatly stapled and sitting in her lap. Ever the prepared librarian.

Lindsey was in charge of renting the loaner from Bruce and acquiring the snacks. She went with two piping-hot coffees from Dunkin' Donuts with a mixed box of Munchkins and a bag of Cheetos from the Cumberland Farms, the convenience store on the edge of town.

Lindsey surveyed the bench seat of the Buick they shared and nodded. "I think we're good. Ready?"

Beth pulled out a roll of Tums and said, "As I'll ever be."

The drive to New London was a little more than an hour eastbound on I-95. They crossed over the multilane bridge that spanned the Connecticut River, and Lindsey noted that the trees that had been so vibrant with color just weeks before were slowly being laid bare by the coming winter.

"I'm afraid of what I'm going to find out," Beth said.

Lindsey reached out and lowered the volume on the updated car stereo, making Paul McCartney's voice quiet background noise.

"You know that's natural, right?" she asked. "I mean, you've just discovered that the man you were dating had another name, probably a whole other life that you knew nothing about. Of course, you're freaked out."

"What if he was married?" Beth asked. "That would make me the other woman."

Lindsey looked at her balefully. "No, I've met 'the other woman,' and you are not her."

"But if . . ." Beth began but Lindsey took her right hand off the wheel and held it up to silence her.

"No. An 'other woman' is a woman who knows the man she is sleeping with is already involved and she sleeps with him anyway. She cares only for herself; otherwise, she would refuse him until he did the right thing and left the woman he is engaged to first. I mean, really, is that asking so much? A little dignity? *A little respect?*"

Beth looked at her with wide eyes, and Lindsey sighed.

"Sorry. I spoke to John yesterday. I think I'm still cranky."

"You spoke to him?" Beth echoed. "But you said you'd eat arsenic pie before you ever spoke to him again."

"Yeah, well, that was before I needed a recommendation for the best criminal defense attorney in the area."

"You called him for me?" Beth asked. Lindsey glanced at her quickly and noted her gray eyes were damp.

"Do not start," Lindsey said. "It was no big deal, really."

"What else did he say?" Beth asked.

"Nothing," she said. "I got a name and then I hung up on him. I don't think you're going to need it, but I wanted to be prepared."

"Thanks, Lindsey, you're the best."

They passed through East Lyme, and then the highway split. Lindsey continued east on I-95, instead of veering north onto I-395, which would have led them upstate and eventually into Massachusetts.

Twenty minutes later, New London was in sight. Lindsey turned off the highway before the bridge that would take them over the Thames River. Beth directed her along the surface streets until they ended up on Granite Street in the Post Hill Historic District.

Lindsey had spoken to Rick's, or rather Ernie's, old landlady that morning. Ernie had rented a studio apartment in Eloise Sinclair's 1920s art deco building, and she did remember him. Lindsey had asked if they could come by to talk to her, and the woman had seemed to think that Lindsey was interested in renting an apartment from her. Lindsey didn't disabuse her of that notion.

They had agreed to meet at ten-thirty. Glancing at her cell phone, she could see they were five minutes early. She found parking, and they locked the Buick, then made their way up the walkway to the brick building that loomed over them.

The front door had lace curtains hanging in the window, making it impossible to see inside. Lindsey pushed the buzzer by the door that read "Property Manager." The rest of the apartments were listed by number only. No names.

"Yeah," a gruff voice sounded through the intercom.

"Hi, I'm Lindsey Norris. I have an appointment with Eloise."

"You're early," the voice snapped.

"Sorry," Lindsey said. "I can come back in three minutes, if you'd like."

A heavy sigh transmitted through the box. "Don't bother. You're here; you might as well come in. My door is the last one on the left on the first floor."

They heard the large front door click as it was automatically unlocked.

"Well, she sounds like a charmer," Lindsey said

as she held the door open for Beth.

"A snake charmer, maybe," Beth muttered as she stepped into the foyer.

Hardwood floors gleamed and the walls were painted butter yellow with white trim. They passed three other apartments until they came to the one at the end.

They stopped in front of the door, and Lindsey raised her fist to knock. The door opened before her knuckles connected. A plume of smoke wafted out the door, and in its wake a short, stubby blonde woman, wearing a Hello Kitty nightgown and fuzzy slippers, appeared.

Probably somewhere in her fifties, her blonde hair was limp and hung around her face, and there was a coffee stain down the front of her nightie.

She looked Lindsey and Beth up and down. "Ernie sent you?"

"Sort of," Lindsey said, going for vague.

"He didn't happen to send his last month's rent with you, did he?" The woman took a drag off of the cigarette in her hand before stubbing it out in the ashtray she clutched in her other hand.

"Uh, no," Lindsey said. She had to resist the urge to step back.

"Pity," the woman said. Her voice was a rough, tobacco-encrusted growl. "I'm Eloise. Are you two a couple?"

Beth and Lindsey looked at each other.

"I don't care," Eloise said. "I'm just asking so I know if you want a one-bedroom or a two-bedroom."

"Actually, we're here to ask about Ernie," Beth said. "I need to know if this is him."

She fished out two photos from her purse; both were of Rick Eckman. Lindsey noticed her fingers were shaking as she held the photos out to Eloise.

Eloise took them and squinted at them. "Aw, hell, I can't see these. Let me get my glasses."

She shuffled back into her apartment. Lindsey and Beth followed. The apartment had the same hardwood floors but was painted a soft blue. A large television was on in the corner, tuned to the Food Network. The furniture was worn but clean; in fact, the small space was surprisingly neat, and a fat pillar candle was burning as if to cover the smell of the cigarette smoke.

As she reached for her reading glasses, which sat in a case on top of a pile of books on her coffee table, Eloise waved for them to have a seat. Beth and Lindsey sat together on the edge of the beige corduroy sofa.

Eloise slipped on her glasses and studied the photographs. "I don't know. It's been five years."

"Please. It's very important," Beth said.

Eloise switched to the second photograph. She bit her lip and then gave a slow nod. "The haircut is different, but yeah, that's him. I'd know that self-satisfied smirk anywhere."

She took off her glasses and handed the photographs back to Beth. Beth put them back in her purse and zipped it shut. The devastation on her face told Lindsey more clearly than words that Beth had been hoping that Rick hadn't been Ernie, that their five years together hadn't been one big lie. No such luck.

"Why are you asking if that's him?" Eloise asked. She sounded suspicious. "I thought he sent you. Oh, no; don't tell me he owes you rent, too."

Lindsey wondered how much she should say. Obviously, Eloise didn't know that Rick Eckman was Ernie Shadegg and that he had just been murdered. Was it really her place to tell her all of this?

"No, nothing like that," Beth said. "It's a personal matter."

"Oh," Eloise said, and then her eyes widened and she said "Oh" again in a way that seemed to have much more meaning.

"What do you mean by that?" Beth asked.

"By what?" Eloise asked.

"Oh," Beth repeated, the way Eloise had said it.

"Nothing," Eloise said too quickly. Then her gaze grew sly. "But which one of you is it?"

"Is what?" Lindsey asked.

"Well, the one who's going to have his baby, of course."

"Oh, gross," Lindsey said.

"Hey!" Beth protested.

"Sorry," Lindsey said. "But do I look like some-one's baby mama?"

Eloise studied her. "No, you're too uptight looking." She said this as if it were a bad thing. "Then why are you two looking for him?"

"It's complicated," Beth said.

Eloise sat back and fired up another Pall Mall. "I've got time," she said.

Lindsey and Beth exchanged a look. They weren't going to get out of here with any information unless they ponied up some of their own. Lindsey nodded, letting Beth take the lead since it was her personal business they'd be disclosing.

Beth gave an annotated version. She did admit that she'd been dating Rick, but she didn't mention that he'd stolen her work and passed it off as his own.

"We can't think of anyone who wanted Rick, I mean Ernie, dead, so we thought maybe it would be someone from his past."

Eloise considered her through a plume of smoke. "Ernie was a putz. He was always late with the rent, and he liked to chat up the pretty residents, as if any of them wanted to be with an unemployed loser like him."

"Did he have any enemies?" Lindsey asked.

"None come to mind," Eloise said. "You know, I have a box of his junk down in the basement. He fled the night before I was going to have him tossed for nonpayment, and he took only his clothes, most of his artwork and his supplies. I gathered up the bits and pieces of what he didn't take. I was going to hold it until he came back to pay his rent, but he never came back for it. I meant to pitch it, but . . ."

Eloise shrugged, and Lindsey took that to mean that she had never gotten around to it.

"Well, you might as well take it," Eloise said. "I don't think he had any other family."

"No, he was a foster child," Beth said. "But I wouldn't feel right taking his things since we broke up."

Lindsey glanced at her quickly and said, "But we'd be happy to take it back and give it to the police if you think there might be something of interest in there."

"No idea," Eloise said as she stubbed out her cigarette. "Either you take it, or I'll toss it in the Dumpster, up to you."

The box sat on the backseat of the Buick on the ride home. Standard-issue brown cardboard, sealed with silver duct tape. It had a musty odor that clung to it as if the basement had wanted to climb out into the light with it.

"I still don't want anything that belonged to Ernie Shadegg," Beth said. "I don't know him. He's not the man I dated."

"No," Lindsey agreed. "I'm sorry that Rick lied to you. I can't imagine how that must feel."

"Like the entire relationship was a sham," Beth

238

said. "You know, even though I knew he had stolen my work, I kept thinking there had to be a mistake, but there wasn't. It was all a lie, even when he said he cared about me."

"No," Lindsey disagreed. "That was probably the only time he was telling the truth."

Beth shrugged. "It doesn't matter anymore."

"Yes, it does," Lindsey said. "Because until we know who killed him, you are the prime suspect, and I don't think Chief Daniels will look further than the end of his nose when it comes to solving this murder."

"Would you mind if I napped?" Beth asked. "Suddenly, I am just feeling overwhelmed."

"Go ahead," Lindsey said. "It's at least an hour until we're home."

"Thanks." Beth wedged herself between the edge of her seat and the door. In a matter of minutes her breathing had evened out and she was asleep.

Lindsey glanced in the rearview mirror at the box. She wondered what secrets about Ernie Shadegg it contained. Yes, she would take it to the police station but only after she had her own little look-see.

She dropped off Beth and headed to her own house. She would return the car in the morning after she dropped off the box at the police station. Feeling as if she'd duly rationalized the situation, Lindsey parked the car and hefted the box out of the backseat and headed into the house.

Several years' worth of dust coated the front of her shirt and her hands when she put the box down on her table. She brushed it off and washed her hands while she made a cup of chamomile tea.

She stared at the box while she debated what to do. Was Ernie Shadegg's life any of her business? Well, for that matter, was Rick Eckman's life any of her business? Other than the fact that he'd been dating her friend, no, not really. Did she have a right to go through his personal effects?

She cradled her tea in her hands and blew across the top of the mug. She thought about her dad. He was a researcher, and she knew he sometimes bent the rules to get the answers he needed. She put down her mug and grabbed a steak knife and carefully slit the tape. She pried apart the edges and peered inside.

It wasn't as if she'd been expecting gold coins or a pearl-encrusted tiara like this was a treasure chest she'd found at the bottom of the sea, but the wadded-up papers that were stuffed inside the box were a bit of a letdown.

Sketches, some charcoal, some pen and ink, and a few pastels had been tossed into the box without any regard for preserving them. It pained Lindsey's archivist soul, and she suspected Eloise had done the packing as the faintest stink of cigarette smoke tainted a few of the papers.

A portrait of a girl's face caught and held Lindsey's attention. As she studied it, she had to acknowledge that despite his loathsome personality, Rick—or Ernie, or whatever his real name was—had been a talented artist.

The girl's face was rounded, her eyes wide and her lips parted as if she expected to be kissed at any moment. She looked vaguely familiar, with blonde ringlets and a perky nose, and Lindsey wondered if it was someone she knew in Briar Creek, but that would be impossible since these pieces were from before Rick's time here.

She put the artwork aside and dug deeper into the box. There were several sketch pads and a few syllabuses from school. There were also some art supplies, broken pieces of charcoal and a few worn-out paintbrushes. Blue ribbons from art shows and award certificates made up another layer in the box. Beyond those, at the very bottom, was a photo album. The edges were moldy, and it smelled as if it had absorbed the very essence of Eloise's basement.

Lindsey put the album aside. It was time to eat something other than junk, so she made herself a spinach salad with hard-boiled eggs and mushrooms with a drizzle of raspberry vinaigrette to give it some zip.

She repacked the art and the supplies while she ate and pondered why Rick had changed his name? Had he just wanted to start fresh? Had he been trying to leave someone or something behind? Who or what?

She rinsed her bowl and placed it in the dishwasher. Although it was early evening, with the sun just beginning to set, she decided she would peruse the album from the comfort of her bed.

She put on her pajamas and climbed into bed, bracing herself against the chill of the sheets. She hadn't switched from cotton to flannel sheets yet, and the first five minutes of warming up the bed were always the worst.

She rested the album on a towel, so as not to grime up her bedspread. The album looked to be about twenty years old, and it was stuffed full of photographs. She could pick out Rick's distinctive features, the thatch of dark hair, the glasses and the smirk.

Even now, knowing that someone had murdered him, Lindsey found it difficult to identify what Beth had seen in him. A yawn caught up to her, and Lindsey tried to shake it off, but it was no use. She was dead-dog tired, and whatever secrets she might learn from Rick's personal things would just have to wait until morning.

She wrapped the album in the towel and put it on the floor. She switched off her light and burrowed low under her covers. She was asleep before the second yawn overtook her.

Lindsey's eyes popped open. Someone was in her apartment. She knew it as surely as she knew the plots of her favorite comfort books. These were the books she reached for when she needed to be soothed by the familiar old friends who chased away what Holly Golightly called the "mean reds" in Truman Capote's *Breakfast at Tiffany's*. The mean reds being the feeling that something bad was about to happen. Lindsey knew exactly what Holly meant. As she listened and heard the sound of footsteps in her apartment, she was hit with a bad case of the mean reds.

The creak of the old wooden floorboards called out a hoarse warning, and Lindsey felt her heart pound in her throat. Why would someone be in her place? She wondered if it was Nancy, but there was no storm tonight, and Nancy had always been very respectful of her privacy. Then she thought it might be Beth. Maybe she couldn't sleep, maybe she had changed her mind about looking through Rick's things or maybe she was just having a hard time reconciling what they'd learned today. But surely Beth would have called first.

One thing was for certain—Lindsey did not feel like lying in her bed, cowering in fear from the unknown. She pushed her covers back, and let her feet slide to the floor below. The fluffy area rug cushioned the sound of her steps as she slowly crept forward.

Her door was ajar, and she pressed herself against the back of it. Her apartment was dark except for the night-light in the kitchen, which gave off a soft orb of blue light. She could see a person move in front of the light. The person was average in height and build and appeared to be dressed all in black, from a stocking cap and turtleneck all the way down to a pair of gloves. Lindsey felt her breathing become shallow and her heart thumped hard in her chest as fear clutched her in a hard grip.

The black cloak of anonymity made Lindsey feel even more violated. Not being able to identify who was in her apartment made the feeling of vulnerability so much more acute.

She snatched her cell phone off the dresser and quietly flipped it open. She knew that dialing 911 would connect her to a dispatcher the next town over. She needed someone here now! She needed someone to chase the bad guy out of her home. Someone close by—Charlie! Nancy's nephew, downstairs! She quickly scrolled through her contacts until she found his number. She fleetingly thought about texting him, but what if he didn't get the message? She needed to talk to him to let him know this was urgent. She prayed he was home in his apartment and not out playing a gig somewhere.

The phone rang four times. She was about to give up when a very groggy voice answered.

"Hello?"

Chapter 22

"Charlie," she whispered.

"Hello?" Charlie answered. "Who is this? Megan, is that you?"

Lindsey couldn't help but notice the hopeful note in his voice. She did not have time to contend with his romantic exploits at the moment.

"Charlie, it's Lindsey, from upstairs," she whispered. "There's someone in my apartment."

"What? Who is this? I can't hear you," he said. Now he sounded grumpy.

"Lindsey," she hissed louder. "Someone is in my apartment. I need you to call me back and scare them off. Now!"

The sound of the footsteps stopped, and Lindsey caught her breath. The intruder must have heard her. She peered around the door. The shadowy black figure was standing by the kitchen table. In a blink the intruder snatched up the box of Ernie's things and made for the door. Oh, hell, no!

Lindsey bolted out of the bedroom in pursuit. She planned to turn that box over to the police. She had no intention of letting someone make off with it.

The intruder heard her coming from behind and turned to glance over his shoulder. He saw

Lindsey, and he yanked open the front door. He hit the landing at a jog, with the box tucked under his arm.

The cold air outside her apartment was like a slap in the face, and Lindsey welcomed it as she pounded down the stairs after the burglar, not caring that she was shoeless.

There was a bang, followed by some cursing, and she arrived on the second-floor landing in time to see Charlie flat on the floor with the stranger sprawled on top of him. As Lindsey charged forward, the burglar grabbed a work boot of Charlie's and threw it squarely at Lindsey. She dodged, but not in time, and the hard sole of the boot clipped her on the shin.

"Ouch!" She hobbled forward, but the assailant had already snatched up the box and bolted down the stairs.

Lindsey tried to catch him, but once she reached the front door without shoes, she knew there was no way she could run over the gravel driveway in bare feet.

She stomped her foot in frustration, and then turned and hurried back up the stairs to where Charlie sat. His jet-black hair stood on end, and he looked as though the wind had been soundly knocked out of him.

"Are you okay?" she asked. She knelt beside him, and he blinked at her.

"You're the one who called me, right?"

"Yeah, sorry," she said. "I just wanted you to call me back to scare off that burglar. I didn't want you to get hurt."

"I'm fine," he said, sitting up. "Just not awake yet. So, who the heck was that, and why was he in your apartment at three o'clock in the morning?"

"I wish I knew," Lindsey said.

"He didn't hurt you, did he?" He frowned.

"No, he just took a box of things that I had other plans for," she said.

A cold draft in the hallway caught her by the back of the neck and shuddered through her. The lace curtains on the window rippled, and she realized the burglar must have come through the second-story window.

Who had been in her apartment? Why had he taken the box of Ernie Shadegg's things? It couldn't be coincidence. Someone didn't want her digging into Rick's past. And the only person it could be was the murderer.

"Are you all right?" Charlie asked. "You look pale."

"I'm fine," Lindsey lied. "Come on, let's get you up."

She held out a hand and helped Charlie to his feet.

"I'm going to lock the dead bolt on the front door," she said. "You don't think Nancy will mind, do you?"

"Heck no," he said. "But don't you think you should call the police?"

"Uh, I don't really see the need," she said. "I think we managed to scare him off. I'll stop by in the morning and fill out a report then."

Charlie studied her. His brown eyes narrowed, and he looked older than his twenty-four years. "Remind me to invite you to my weekly poker game. You're a terrible liar."

"I'm sure I don't know what you mean," Lindsey said. She blinked her eyes in feigned innocence.

"Uh-huh. I get that you don't want to tell me what's going on, and that's fine," he said. "We all have personal stuff. But make sure that you're playing it safe."

"I am," Lindsey said. She figured it wasn't really a lie since she had no idea whether she was safe or not.

"Fine." He didn't look like he believed her. "I'll go down and lock the door. You go up to bed and check all your windows and doors before you go to sleep."

Lindsey opened her mouth to protest, but he cut her off by holding up his hand.

"This is not debatable. I'll keep my cell phone handy in case you need me," he said. Then he trudged down the stairs with a muttered good-night tossed over his shoulder like a chewed-up apple core.

Lindsey felt bad about lying, but she didn't really want to deal with Chief Daniels in the wee hours of the morning when there was really nothing he could do.

She climbed up the stairs to her place, where the door still stood ajar. She locked the dead bolt behind her and checked all of the windows, although she had to wonder who would be foolish enough to climb three stories to get in here. Then again, who would break into her apartment in the first place?

But had they really had to break in? She tried to remember if she had locked the door the night before. She didn't think she had. Briar Creek was such a peaceful place. She knew she had gotten lax about locking her door. Well, she figured she was cured of that. She never wanted to find a person lurking in her apartment again. Ever.

Sleep was going to be impossible. She made herself a cup of cocoa and noted that it was nowhere near as good as Sully's. Still, hopefully it would chase the chill out of her bones. She climbed back into bed with her mug and grabbed the photo album off of the floor. At least the burglar hadn't gotten it.

It was from Ernie's young life. It must have been put together by one of his foster mothers. There were a couple of pictures of him as a baby and then some grade school shots. High school showed him as the scruffy, rebellious artist, dressed all in black.

Throughout the years, he posed with different sets of people. Older couples with strained smiles and younger couples who looked overwhelmed with not just him but several more children in the picture as well.

There was one picture of him as a young boy. Lindsey guessed him to be about age nine. A middle-aged couple posed with him, and they looked delighted. It was the only photo where Ernie wore a smile, a genuine lit-up-from-within smile. Beside the picture was a newspaper clipping, yellowed with age. It stated that Liz and Calvin Shadegg had been killed in a car accident, leaving behind their newly adopted son. With no other family able to take him, Ernie would be sent back into the foster-care system.

A weight like a stone lodged in Lindsey's chest. She had not liked Rick Eckman. She didn't like his narcissism or the way he had treated Beth. She had never understood what Beth saw in him, but now she knew. Beth had seen in him that little boy who lost everything. And in typical Beth fashion, she had thought she could make up for all those years of sadness.

Lindsey sighed. She couldn't help but feel badly for the boy who had never seemed to get a break.

She flipped through more quickly until she

reached the college years. There were loads of pictures of him winning awards, most of which had been in the box that had been taken.

She took a long sip of her hot cocoa. Her thoughts drifted back to the box. This had not been a random burglary. Someone had found out that she had gone to his old address and gotten his box of things. She had told Eloise that she planned to turn the box into the police. But the intruder must have wanted to stop her, but why?

Again, she reasoned, it had to be Rick's murderer. She wrapped her hands around her mug as the shivers overtook her. A murderer had been in her apartment. The realization was not a calming one. But what did the killer expect the police to find in that box that would give him away? The only conclusion Lindsey could draw was that he had to be from Ernie's past.

She tried to remember the items in the box. The sketch of the girl was the first thing that came to mind, but there had been no name, nothing to give her a clue as to who it could have been, and she could only speculate as to what in that box would be important enough for someone to try and steal it back.

Lindsey returned to the album. Her only hope was that there might be a clue in here. She continued to flip through his college years.

There were pictures of more artwork, shows and awards. A few clippings from the school newspaper showed him to be one of the promising young artists of his class.

There weren't many pictures of him with friends. Lindsey wasn't surprised; judging by his people skills, she imagined that making friends had not come easily to him.

It was toward the back that she found it. Wedged between the pages of more artwork and awards was a five-by-seven photo of a group of kids in an art room. Ernie was in the center. He had his arm wrapped around a very pretty girl with light-brown hair, who had her hand covering her mouth as if stifling a giggle. On his other side stood a brunette; she did not have the same sparkle as the other girl but was gazing at him with an intensity that bespoke longing or loathing—it was hard for Lindsey to tell which. There were several other teens in the background, but it was the three in front that held Lindsey's attention.

She studied the two women in the photo. The darker brunette looked familiar. Lindsey recognized the angle of her head and the bluntness of her gaze. It was Sydney, the editor. She was sure of it, which meant that Sydney had known Rick in more than a professional capacity. She had known him as Ernie.

Lindsey sat back and shut the album. She could not believe it was a coincidence that Sydney had been staying in Briar Creek, had gone to school with Ernie and just happened to be in town when he got murdered, even if he was living under a new name.

She wondered if she should tell Chief Daniels and Detective Trimble. Maybe she should wait. It was possible that she was wrong and that this wasn't Sydney, even though every instinct told her that it was. She'd call Sydney in the morning and let her know what she'd found and then see what Sydney had to say for herself.

The library opened with its usual hustle and bustle. Violet came in to do Beth's story time, which was a good thing because Beth still looked pasty and fragile, and Lindsey doubted she had the stamina to entertain twenty squirming crawlers.

Lindsey waited until the staff was immersed in their work, and then she closed her office door. With any luck, no one would come looking for her for at least a half hour.

She typed in the URL for Rick's publisher's website and then selected its contact-us hyperlink. It listed a main number for Caterpillar Press in New York City. She took out her cell phone and dialed it. She had been hoping to find Sydney's direct number listed on the website, but no such luck.

The main operator connected her to Sydney's line, which, after a few rings, switched over to voice mail. Lindsey considered leaving a message, but she doubted Sydney would actually call her back. She decided to get sneaky, and she called the main number again. This time she asked to be connected to Sydney's assistant.

The phone was answered after three rings. A strained voice answered. "Hello, Sydney Carlisle's office. This is Tina speaking."

"Hi, Tina. I'm Lindsey Norris. I was wondering if I could speak with Sydney." There. That sounded right, as if she and Sydney were on a first-name basis but not overly chummy.

Silence greeted her request. Uh-oh. She wondered if Sydney was standing beside Tina and giving her the slashing motion across her throat indicating that she wanted no calls from Lindsey. The silence continued, and Lindsey wondered if they'd been disconnected.

"Hello?" she said. "Tina, are you there?"

"I'm sorry," Tina said. Her voice cracked. "It's just that I'm finding this very difficult."

"What is it?" Lindsey asked. She sat up straight, knowing by the young woman's tone that something was very, very wrong.

"Sydney is dead," Tina said.

Chapter 23

"What?" Lindsey asked. She was sure she must have heard her wrong.

"She fell from the train platform this morning on her way to work and was hit by . . . ugh." Unable to go on, Tina broke down into sobs.

"I am so sorry," Lindsey said. She felt as if she'd just been punched in the gut. Sydney was dead? How could this be?

"I just don't understand what's happening," Tina sobbed. "First Sydney's top author is stabbed, and then she's killed in a freak accident. It's just so wrong."

"Yes, definitely wrong," Lindsey muttered as she tried to process the tragic news.

"I have another call coming in," Tina said. She took a deep breath as if bracing herself to give more bad news. "Information about her service should be announced as soon as her family has it planned."

"Thank you," Lindsey said. "Again, I am so sorry."

Tina mumbled something that sounded like good-bye before the line went dead.

Lindsey slumped back in her chair. She didn't know what to think. She had just spoken to the woman a few days ago, and now she was dead. She closed her phone and put it back in her purse.

She had planned to take the photo album over to the police on her lunch hour. She opened the drawer where she had stuffed it and pulled it out. She flipped through until she got to the photo. With shaky hands she studied the picture. Maybe she had been wrong. Maybe the girl in the photo wasn't Sydney. But no, she was Sydney, several years younger, but there was no mistaking her.

Lindsey knew she needed to tell Beth, but she wasn't sure how to go about it. By mid-morning, she had yet to come up with an idea, but she realized she couldn't put it off any longer.

She found Beth sitting at the desk in the children's area. Violet was with her, changing out of her Little Red Hen costume. Several children were talking to the mechanical parrot, Fernando, while others were hip deep in the treasure box outfitting themselves as a pirate, a princess and a banana.

"How did it go?" Lindsey asked Violet.

"Very well. No one cried or pooped his or her pants. I call that a success," Violet said.

"Not exactly Broadway, is it?" Lindsey asked.

"Are you kidding? Broadway is a snap compared to this," Violet returned. "Kids are the most honest audience an actor can have. They let you know if you stink, and they make you work for it."

"Don't I know it," Lindsey said dryly, and Violet chuckled. Then she leaned close and whispered,

"But I'm worried about Beth. She's not herself."

"I know," Lindsey said. "This is going to take a while, I'm afraid, especially since they don't have the killer in custody yet."

"Huh," Violet grunted, letting Lindsey know she was not happy about that.

"Thanks again for doing this, Violet," she said. "I'm going to see if I can get Beth to step out for some fresh air."

"Good idea." Violet went to hang up her costume, and Lindsey approached the desk.

"Beth, how are you?" she asked.

Beth glanced up at her, and her gray eyes were shadowed with sadness. She didn't look as if she was feeling very functional.

"Come on," Lindsey said. "Let's go for a walk."

Beth snatched a tissue out of the holder on her desk and followed Lindsey to the door.

"I'm sorry. I know I probably should just go home, but I feel better at work," Beth said. She had grabbed her jacket off of the back of her chair, and she bundled up in it now to buffer the offshore breeze that chilled their bones after the sleepy, sunny warmth of the library.

Lindsey pulled the sleeves of her sweater down. They crossed the street to the park and took a seat on a vacant bench. They stared silently out at the water for a few minutes until Lindsey figured she couldn't stall any longer.

She had brought the photo with her and now

she quietly handed it to Beth. "This is a picture of Rick with some other people. Tell me if you recognize anyone else."

Beth took a deep breath and studied the picture. She was quiet for so long that Lindsey thought maybe she was wrong, maybe it wasn't Sydney.

"That's her, isn't it?" Beth asked. She tapped the picture with her forefinger. She was pointing to Sydney. "That's Sydney, the editor who was here."

"That's what I think, too," Lindsey said.

"So, she went to school with Rick?" Beth asked. "Huh. Rick never told me that."

Lindsey turned to gaze out at the water. She saw a seagull swoop down toward the water and then ride an air current back up into the sky.

"And now Sydney is dead, too," Lindsey said.

Beth's head snapped in her direction. "What?"

"I just got off the phone with her assistant," Lindsey said. "She fell off of the platform this morning at the train station and was killed by an oncoming train."

Beth put her hand to her throat. "Oh, how awful."

"I can't help thinking that the two deaths are connected," Lindsey said. "Look at the way she is watching him in the picture."

They both leaned forward and studied Sydney's face. Intense emotion was etched into her every feature as she gazed at Ernie. Whatever her feelings may have been about him, they were anything but ambivalent.

"Do you think she's been carrying a torch for him all these years?" Beth asked. "Maybe it just got to be too much for her. Maybe she came out here to confront him."

Lindsey nodded slowly. "I was thinking that myself. Maybe Sydney is the killer."

"And then killed herself?" Beth asked. "In a murder-suicide?"

Lindsey shrugged. "Maybe."

"We need to take this to Chief Daniels and Detective Trimble," Beth said. "They should know these two deaths are connected."

"We *think* they're connected," Lindsey said. "We could be wrong."

Beth raised one eyebrow higher than the other and gave her a look that said more clearly than words "Yeah, right." Lindsey smiled. It was nice to see a glimmer of the old Beth back.

"My only problem with that is then I would have to tell Chief Daniels that someone broke into my apartment this morning," Lindsey said.

Beth gasped. "And you're just telling me this now? What happened? What did they take? Are you all right?"

"I'm fine," she said. "Charlie helped me to chase him out."

"You could have been killed," Beth said. "Why didn't you call me?"

"It was three o'clock in the morning."

"So? Who held your hand the first time you got your eyebrows threaded?"

"You."

"And who was the one who left a flaming bag of dog poop on John's doorstep when he cheated on you?"

"You."

"All right, then; who do you need to call when you're being robbed in the middle of the night?"

"You. Okay?"

"No, the police—then call me," she said.

"All right, I get it."

"Good."

"The more important issue is that whoever broke into my apartment made off with the box of Ernie's belongings," Lindsey said. "I don't really want to explain that to Chief Daniels, especially since he seems fixated upon you as the main suspect. He might think I was hanging onto it because it held evidence about you. Of course without it, I can't prove that, never mind explain why someone else would want to steal it."

"Why would someone want to steal it?" Beth asked. "It was just a moldy old box of junk."

"That's all I saw, but maybe there was something of value that I missed," Lindsey said. "Look, I think this picture was taken at his art school, and I was thinking we should go to the school and see if anyone remembers him and Sydney and find out what they have to say. Maybe we'll uncover proof of some unrequited-love situation that will back up our murder-suicide theory."

"Since it's my bacon in the skillet, count me in," Beth said.

"Excellent. Let's go now."

"What about the lemon?"

"What about her?"

"Don't you think she's going to get testy and report your absences to the board?"

"You mean she'll start saying, 'Mr. Tupper never took this many days off' or 'Mr. Tupper was here every day and night. He never needed to eat or sleep,' " Lindsey said. "And that would be different from every other day how?"

Beth laughed and then said with a sigh, "I think she was in love with him."

Lindsey nodded. "That makes sense. When I first started, I almost expected to find a shrine to him in the broom cupboard. I think she must have said 'Mr. Tupper this' or 'Mr. Tupper that' at least fifty times on my first day."

"She cried at his good-bye party," Beth said. "I found her at her desk curled up in a heap, sobbing."

"Do you think he knew?" Lindsey asked.

"No. He was a bit of an absent-minded professor," Beth said. "Plus, he was happily married."

"Well, that makes me feel badly for the lemon," Lindsey said.

"Don't worry; once she opens her mouth, it'll wear off," Beth said with a shake of her head.

Together they rose from the bench and headed back across the park to the library. Lindsey's conscience raised its head, and she felt a twinge of guilt that they weren't beating feet right to the police department, but then again, they were only waiting an afternoon to ask a few more questions. What could possibly happen in a few hours?

CHAPTER 24

Lindsey called in both Jessica and Ann Marie to cover for them for the afternoon. Being part-time help, the women were both eager to pick up extra hours before the upcoming holidays.

Lindsey's budget only allotted so many part-time hours per year, and she knew she had banked a nice amount to give them coverage for vacations, illness and emergencies. They hadn't used many, so she figured she could count today as an emergency. After all, if Beth was taken in for murder, they'd be short a children's librarian, and she did not have enough hours put aside to cover that. Feeling much better after her rationalization, Lindsey and Beth took the Buick and headed east on I-95 to visit Rick's alma mater.

Beth ignored her big coffee and wedged her

262

head between the seat and the door. Lindsey remembered this pose from their infamous spring-break trip back when they were in grad school. Beth was supposed to be their navigator on that trip while Lindsey drove, and instead she fell asleep, and they wound up in New Orleans instead of Panama City.

"You're going to fall asleep, aren't you?"

"Who me? No," Beth said. Her eyes were already at half-mast, and her voice was a sleepy slur. She looked pie-eyed tired, and Lindsey wondered how long it had been since she'd slept through the night.

"Go ahead," she said. "I don't need a navigator for this trip."

"Thank God," Beth said. Her eyes shut, and she was snoring softly before Lindsey merged into the highway traffic.

The drive to New London seemed shorter this time. The college Rick had attended was on a fifty-acre campus on the shore in the heart of the town. Known for its art and design program, the New London School of Design took only select students with strong arts backgrounds. Rick must have shown tremendous potential if he had gotten a full ride there.

Lindsey roused Beth when she turned onto the exit for the school. Beth stretched and yawned, looking better for the nap.

They parked in the main lot several rows from

the walkways that led to the campus. A large bulletin board and directory stood at the edge of the lot, and they paused to study it.

"Where should we start?" Beth asked. "Registrar's office?"

"I don't think they'll be able to tell us much more than the fact that he was enrolled here ten years ago, which we already know," Lindsey said.

Beth looked away from the board and studied the campus. It was a small school with less than a thousand undergraduates. There were several large, three-story redbrick buildings that appeared to be classrooms. Beyond that was a cluster of houses that looked to be student housing. They were various shapes and sizes, but they were all painted white with black shutters. They seemed to be a couple of centuries old, as if they were here before the school had been founded.

"Do you know what Rick's major was?" Lindsey asked.

"Traditional art."

"Let's start with the dean of that school," Lindsey said. "Maybe that person will remember him."

They checked the board and found that the dean of arts' office was located in the farthest brick building. A brisk wind was blowing in off of Long Island Sound, and Lindsey pulled the collar of her jacket up around her neck to keep warm.

Students were scattered along the walkways,

and Lindsey was reminded of how much she had loved her college years, particularly graduate school with Beth.

"Doesn't it seem like we were just this age?" Beth asked.

"I was just thinking that," Lindsey said. "You know, I found a gray hair the other day. I almost broke the sound barrier rushing to the pharmacy to get some dye."

Beth snorted. "Oh, please! You're a blonde—no one can see gray hair up there. Now, you get one down under, and then you can panic."

Lindsey laughed. It was nice to see Beth's sunny-side-up personality was making a slow return.

The black tackboard directory in the building's lobby listed all of the deans' offices as being on the third floor. The dean of arts was named T. Cushion and was in office 332.

Beth found the elevator, but it looked older than the building itself. They decided to take the stairs. Lindsey was grateful that she'd given up her car and started bicycling in Briar Creek. A year ago this climb up three levels would have left her wheezing.

Groups of students came barreling down the stairs, and they were forced to hug the wall or risk being pushed back down by the surge. Once the students passed, they resumed climbing, stopping at the top to catch their breath.

Beth started down the hall. Her chin was set with grim determination, and Lindsey wasn't sure if she was dreading the upcoming encounter or eagerly anticipating it. Probably a little bit of both.

They paused in front of room 332. Lindsey rapped on the door and called, "Professor Cushion?"

There was no answer, and they exchanged a look. Beth checked the hours posting beside the door. It said the professor was open for office hours at this time.

Lindsey tried the doorknob. It turned, so she pushed it open.

She stepped into the room, but stopped short, leaving Beth to plow into her back with a grunt.

"Ouch! What's the holdup?"

Lindsey knew she should look away, but found that, no, she really couldn't.

Standing in the center of the room on a table in all of his naked glory was one of the most handsome men she had ever seen.

"Oh my," Beth said faintly from behind her.

Several heads turned their way, and it was then that Lindsey noticed the five easels and artists set up around the man, obviously sketching him.

The male model, who had his profile to them, seemed to sense the intrusion because he turned to face them.

"May I help you?" he asked.

Lindsey locked her eyes onto his and forced

herself to keep them there. "We're, uh, looking for Professor Cushion."

"You've found him," he said.

"Oh, is he here?" Lindsey glanced around the room, relieved to be able to look away. She noticed Beth did not, and she jabbed her with a sharp elbow to the ribs.

"Huh," she grunted and looked away.

"I'm Professor Cushion," the model said.

Lindsey whipped her head back in his direction and stared at the part in his shoulder-length, thick black hair. "Really?"

"Yes," he said. "Here, everyone, let's break for today. We'll resume tomorrow."

"Oh, we don't want to interrupt . . ." Lindsey's voice trailed off as he grabbed a robe and covered himself. He hopped off of the table and strode toward them.

"No, it's fine. My leg was beginning to cramp."

"But you're their professor," Lindsey said. The words flew out before she could stop them.

"Meaning they shouldn't see me naked?" he asked.

"Well, it just seems . . ."

"Inappropriate?" he supplied.

"Well, yeah," Lindsey said.

"Why didn't I have any professors like you when I was in school?" Beth asked. Her voice came out breathy, and her eyes were a bit glazed.

Professor Cushion threw back his head and laughed. It was a good laugh, deep and resonant and pure. Lindsey found herself warming to him even though she questioned his judgment for disrobing in front of his students.

"This is an advanced class in the study of the human form. Everyone in here will be the model at some point in the semester. I figure I can't ask the students to do something I won't do myself," he said.

Beth looked at him with shining admiration, and Lindsey figured she'd best steer them back to the matter at hand.

"Professor Cushion," Lindsey began, but he interrupted, "Call me Tim."

"Tim, I'm Lindsey Norris, and this is my friend Beth Stanley. We're here hoping to ask some questions about a former student in the art program, and we're wondering if you can help us."

"I'll certainly try," he said. "Come on, let's go to my office, where we can sit."

He led them through another door to a cubbyhole of an office. It was full of books and half-done paintings, and the smell of oil paints and turpentine perfumed the air. An easel was set up by a window with a half-done portrait on it. Even to Lindsey's untrained eye, she could see that he had talent.

There was no desk in the room. A laptop sat on the windowsill, and there was a couch and two comfy armchairs wedged in the corner. Lindsey and Beth took the couch, while Tim sat on the chair.

"Can I get you anything? Coffee? Water?"

"No, thank you," Lindsey said.

"Very nice of you to offer, though," Beth added.

"So, you have questions about a student?" he asked. "You know I can't give out personal information."

"It's a matriculated student," Lindsey said. "In fact, he graduated about ten years ago."

"What's his name?" he asked.

"Ernie Shadegg," Beth said.

Tim sat back against the couch as if he'd been pushed. "I haven't heard that name in a while."

Lindsey studied him. She guessed him to be about their age. He obviously had an advanced degree to be teaching on a college campus.

"Did you go to school with him?" Beth asked.

"No, I did my undergraduate work in Philadelphia and my later degrees in New York City, but Mr. Shadegg is a legend at this school. I think he won just about every award ever given."

"Really?" Lindsey hoped she sounded like she didn't already know that. "Any word on what he is doing now?"

"Ah, so that's why you've come," Tim said. He smiled. It was a good smile that reached his eyes and made him even handsomer, if that was possible. "You're interested in the legend."

"Legend?" Beth repeated. She ran a hand

through the short spikes of her hair, giving away her state of nervousness. Lindsey wondered if it was the handsome Professor Cushion making her nervous or if she was worried about what they'd find out. Lindsey was willing to bet it was a little bit of both, with the professor tipping her into a fine case of the jitters.

"It was before my time," Tim said. "I've only been here about three years, but I've heard all about Ernie from other faculty."

"What was their take on him?" Lindsey asked. "Was he well liked?"

"I wouldn't say that," Tim said. He leaned forward and rested his elbows on his knees. His robe gaped open and both Lindsey and Beth averted their eyes. "Oh, sorry about that. Here, I'll change, and then we can finish our conversation."

He rose and strode over to the corner of the room, where a neat pile of clothing was folded. As they watched, he dropped his robe, giving them a good shot of his backside. They exchanged a glance and turned away, staring at the opposite wall.

Lindsey could feel Beth's shoulder shaking against hers, and she knew she was fighting off a sudden fit of the giggles. Lindsey pressed her lips together for fear that she was going to lose it as well.

"Get a grip," she murmured out of the side of her mouth.

"I'm trying," Beth said, but it was engulfed in muted laughter, which made Lindsey snort out her nose as she tried not to crack up as well.

"There," Tim said as he rejoined them. "Now I feel like I can have a grown-up conversation."

They turned back to face him. He was looking at them with one eyebrow raised as if he knew quite well that they'd been laughing at him.

"I'm sorry," Beth said. Her voice still held a trace of amusement. "We're librarians, so the naked people we see are generally not as good looking as you."

"Librarians see naked people?" Tim asked. His dark-brown eyes were alight with curiosity as he used an elastic band to secure his long hair at the nape of his neck.

"Well, mostly naked. I do believe Mr. Bagwell was wearing his shirt and shoes," Beth said.

"And he had his book bag," Lindsey said.

"It was a cold day outside," Beth agreed. "He might have caught a chill otherwise."

"But why was he naked?" Tim asked.

"He just forgot," Lindsey said with a shrug.

"His underwear?"

"And pants," Beth added. "Apparently, he was so eager to return his DVDs, so as not to get a fine, he just plain forgot."

"I had no idea libraries were so rich with characters," Tim said. "I should bring my sketchpad and camp out."

"When you work with the public, you see all sorts of things," Lindsey said.

"Like Johnny, the transvestite with the broken heel," Beth said. "Poor thing, he never could get a date with that hobbling walk of his."

Tim's eyebrows lifted up on his forehead. "You're teasing me."

"Nope," they said together.

"Don't forget about poor Karen," Lindsey said. "She's a regular who flosses her teeth with her hair. It's a nervous habit."

Tim looked at them as if he was trying to decide if they were messing with him or not.

"Now back to Ernie Shadegg," Lindsey said. "What can you tell us about him?"

"Like I said, it was before my time here, but I got the feeling he had been a star student, loads of awards and accolades. Everyone expected really big things out of him. Word had it, he had tried to break into illustrating but had been unsuccessful."

"Was he teaching at the school? Is that why he was still in the area?" Beth asked.

"No, I'm not sure why he was still here, other than he was still the big man on campus, and according to the people who knew him, he was arrogant enough to really like that."

"So, what happened to him?" Lindsey asked.

"About five years ago, he just disappeared."

"Without a trace?"

Tim nodded. "Thus, the legend."

Lindsey and Beth looked at each other. They, of course, knew what had happened to Ernie. He had moved to the Thumb Islands under the name Rick Eckman and gone on to be a renowned children's book author.

If being the big man on campus had been so important to him, it was hard for Lindsey to believe that he'd walk away from the bragging rights of his success. Unless, of course, there was a reason that he couldn't brag, like maybe he had launched his new persona Rick Eckman with plagiarized work.

"Is there anyone at the school who might still remember him?" Beth asked.

"There are a few people on staff who knew him," he said. "I'm sure they'd be happy to talk to you. But now it's my turn to ask a question. Why are two librarians interested in a former student who disappeared years ago?"

CHAPTER 25

Lindsey and Beth exchanged yet another look. Lindsey was going to leave it up to Beth. He had been her boyfriend, after all.

"We think we know where he's been for the past five years," she said. "In fact, we're sure of it. He's been living under the assumed name Rick

Eckman on an island off of Briar Creek. It's about an hour down the shore from here."

"Really?" he asked. "That's extraordinary. In this day of computers, you'd think it'd be impossible to disappear."

Lindsey pulled the school photo out of her purse. "Can you tell if this picture was taken here?"

Tim studied it for a moment and said, "Wow, this is disturbing."

"Because it was taken on campus?" Lindsey asked.

"Well, that, and because I know two of the people in the picture with him," he said. He shook his head and flipped over the photograph. "How old is this?"

"Almost ten years, I think," Lindsey said. "It looks as if he was still a student."

"I never knew that he and Sydney were a couple," Tim said. "Man, they look so young."

"He and Sydney were a couple?" Beth asked. "I assumed he was dating the one that he has his arm around."

"Yes, that's Sydney Carlisle," Tim said. "She's very active in the alumni association. A power-house of an editor in New York; she brings in a lot of money."

"I think you're mistaken," Lindsey said. She rose from the couch and looked over his shoulder. "Sydney is the one off on the right with the weird look on her face."

"No, that's Astrid Blunt," Tim said. "I'm sure of it."

"Who?" Beth and Lindsey asked together.

"Professor Blunt," Tim said, with more than a trace of dislike flavoring his words. "She's a professor here, has been for years."

"But . . ." Beth began, but Lindsey cut her off. "Do you think you could tell us where to find her?"

Tim checked his watch. "I have just enough time before my next class."

They followed him out of his office and back down the stairs to the art rooms below.

Tim stopped and tried a door at the end of the hall, but it was locked. He frowned and checked his watch again. "She should be here. She's supposed to have a class right now."

"This can't be good," Beth said. Her eyes searched the cavernous hallway as if expecting the woman they knew as Sydney but who was actually Astrid to leap out from any corner.

Lindsey blew out a breath. She met Beth's gaze and realized she was coming to the same conclusion that she had. Astrid had come to Briar Creek and posed as Sydney Carlisle. The question was why? What had she hoped to gain?

Lindsey thought about the picture. Rick, or rather Ernie, had his arm around Sydney Carlisle. They looked to be the picture of a young, happy couple. But something must have happened for

Ernie to change his name to Rick and completely disappear from his alma mater. The fact that Sydney went on to be a successful children's book editor, Rick's editor in fact, and then Rick suddenly changed his name and won a Caldecott made Lindsey suspect that the two of them had done something irrevocable. Something that would cause someone to hate them so much that he or she would murder them. Lindsey felt a shiver run down her spine.

"We think Astrid killed Rick Eckman—your Ernie Shadegg—and Sydney Carlisle as well," Lindsey said.

"Sydney?" Tim asked. "What do you mean?"

"Sydney is dead," Lindsey said. "She was killed in a train accident."

"That we're not so sure was an accident," Beth said.

"No! Meek, little Astrid?" he asked. He shook his head and said, "No, I just can't see it."

"The photograph," Beth said. "Where's the photo?"

"Oh, nuts. I left it up in my office," Tim said.

"She can't get her hands on that. It's evidence," Beth said. Her voice had risen to a frantic pitch.

"It's okay," Tim said. He put his hand on her arm in reassurance, but Beth was so jittery, she jumped at the contact. "I'll jog up and get it."

He turned and took the stairs two at a time. Lindsey and Beth moved across the hall, away from Astrid's classroom. Students were milling around the locked door, obviously wondering why they hadn't heard that their class had been canceled. Lindsey wondered why Astrid wasn't here. If they were right and she had killed Ernie and Sydney, had she gone into hiding? She hated to admit it, but a small part of her was relieved not to have to face the woman. The whole situation was beginning to give her the creeps.

Other classes were starting now, and students were moving through the halls. Most carried heavy black art portfolios as well as backpacks. They all looked freshly scrubbed and innocent, with their lives ahead of them, the path uncharted.

Lindsey thought she'd feel envious of their freedom but was surprised that, instead, she was looking forward to her life in Briar Creek. She was settled, and she was happy about it.

She glanced up the stairs, hoping to see Tim returning. But there was no sign of him. She turned to suggest to Beth that they go upstairs when the noisy chatter of the students was interrupted by a sharp bang and a second later by a scream.

Everyone froze in place. It was Beth who moved first, dashing toward the stairs, yelling at students to get out of the building. As students poured toward the exits, Lindsey and Beth fought their way back up to Tim's office.

An apple-cheeked student stood in the doorway.

Her hand was pressed over her mouth, and her eyes were huge.

Beth reached her first. "Are you okay?"

The girl pointed into the office. "Professor Cushion."

Lindsey pushed around them and stumbled into the room. Tim was lying on the floor. A red rose of blood was blooming on his shoulder. Lindsey grabbed the bathrobe he'd been wearing earlier and stuffed it against the wound, trying to staunch the flow.

"Tim, can you hear me?" she asked.

His face was taut, and his eyes were glazed. He started to shiver, and Lindsey suspected he was going into shock.

"Call an ambulance!" she yelled at Beth, but Beth already had her phone to her ear and was giving information to the emergency dispatcher.

An ambulance with two EMTs arrived within minutes. They took Tim's vitals and whisked him out of the building on a stretcher as if they were in a race against death. This did not comfort Lindsey, as she suspected that was exactly the race they were in.

It was only after Tim was taken away, and the campus police were clearing the building, that Lindsey thought to look for the photo they had left behind, but the table where Tim had put it was bare.

"Please tell me it isn't our fault that Tim Cushion was shot."

"How is that our fault?" Lindsey asked.

"We show him a photo, he identifies someone we thought was someone else and then winds up shot," Beth said. Her voice held a note of hysteria. "This Astrid person is here. She's following us. She knows what we're doing, and she's going to kill anyone we come into contact with. We have to tell the police."

Lindsey grabbed Beth's shoulders and forced her to look at her. "Beth, Tim is going to be okay. Now we have to calm down and think."

"I can't think," Beth protested. "Lindsey, I'm scared."

Lindsey nodded. She was, too. "The campus police told us it would just be a few minutes before they interview us," she said. "We just have to wait a few more minutes, and then we can tell them everything. It's going to be okay. You'll see."

They were standing outside the arts building, which had been cordoned off by yellow "Crime Scene Do Not Cross" tape, amid a swarm of students. The day had become overcast and cold, and Lindsey shivered in her hooded sweatshirt and wished she'd worn a warmer jacket.

The police had questioned the young woman who had found Professor Cushion and were now moving through the crowd asking whether anyone had seen or heard anything suspicious. The head of campus security had asked Lindsey and Beth to wait, as the police wanted to conduct a lengthier interview with them, so they stood cooling their heels, literally, while they waited for him to get to them.

"I'm freezing," Beth said. "Do you suppose we could run to the car, so I could get my coat?"

"I don't see why not," Lindsey said. "It looks like this is going to take a while."

They headed down the walkway to the Buick. It was easy to spot with its white top and olive body, and Lindsey longed to climb in and crank the heater. She unlocked the passenger door so that Beth could retrieve her jacket.

Once she'd locked the car again, they turned back to the building. The crowd was finally showing signs of thinning. They'd only gone a few steps when a woman wearing a New London School of Design sweatshirt stepped out from behind the directory.

With her brown hair in a ponytail and her face scrubbed clean of makeup, it took Lindsey a second to place her. It was a second too long.

"Sydney," Beth breathed from beside her.

"No," Lindsey said. "Astrid. Astrid Blunt."

CHAPTER 26

"Move back to the car," Astrid ordered. "And don't do anything stupid. As you know, I will use this."

She pointed a small handgun out of her sleeve, and Lindsey assumed it was the same gun she'd used to shoot Tim.

Together, she and Beth backtracked to the car.

With shaky hands, Lindsey unlocked the doors. She had the irrational thought that she should be able to overpower Astrid and wrestle her to the ground, but the lethal-looking weapon the other woman carried made her pause. What if an innocent bystander got hurt? She couldn't risk it.

"You drive," Astrid said to Lindsey. "And I want your hands where I can see them, at ten and two on the wheel."

Lindsey slid into the driver's seat. Beth went to get into the back, but Astrid stopped her, pushing her forward.

"Oh, no, I want you in front with your hands on the dashboard."

Astrid climbed into the backseat and leaned over the bench seat, so her head was solidly in between Lindsey's and Beth's. There would be no whispered plan to get rid of her.

Beth was pitched forward at an awkward angle

with her hands on the dash. Lindsey turned the key, and the engine purred to life.

"Turn on the heater," Astrid ordered. "It's freezing out there."

Lindsey did as she was told and then asked, "Where do you want to go?"

"Briar Creek," Astrid said. Her voice sounded smug. "Back where it all began."

Lindsey put the car in reverse and slowly backed out of the parking lot. She was hoping the head of security would see her and stop them. But no matter how slowly she drove, no one paid them any attention. With a sigh, she pulled out onto the main road and headed for the highway.

She had a feeling this was one road trip that was not going to end well.

She was just merging onto the highway when Beth looked over her shoulder at Astrid, and in a voice that trembled, she asked, "Why? Why did you kill him?"

"I'm assuming you mean Ernie, or rather Rick, as you knew him?" Astrid asked. Her voice was irritated as if she found Beth's question tiresome.

Lindsey glanced in the rearview mirror to see Astrid's face. One eyebrow was raised and her lips curled into a sneer.

"I would think you, of all people, would thank me," she said.

"Thank you?" Beth choked. "He was my boyfriend and you killed him. Why would I thank you?"

"Oh, please, you dumped him before I killed him. Obviously, you were over him."

Beth was making choked sputtering noises, so Lindsey figured she'd better intervene and draw the attention away from Beth.

She intentionally moved her hands on the wheel, dipping the right one down and out of sight. She felt the hard metal tip of the handgun press into her right temple.

"Ten and two," Astrid repeated.

"Sorry," Lindsey said. She returned her hands to their original positions.

"No matter what he did, he didn't deserve to die," Beth said.

Lindsey had to navigate the Buick in between a tractor-trailer truck and a Mercedes, so she couldn't see Astrid's expression, but she could hear the tone of her voice clearly enough, and it was scathing.

"You don't know anything," Astrid said. "What are you, a children's librarian with aspirations to write a children's book? Big deal."

"It is to me," Beth said. "I've worked for years on my story."

"And your boyfriend stole it," Astrid said. "Boo hoo. I'm so sad for you."

Beth looked ready to snap, but Lindsey turned her head and caught her eye. She gave a slight shake of her head, and Beth took a deep breath in a visible effort to calm down.

"Try sinking yourself into a debt hole so deep you can't find a way out," Astrid said. "That's what I did with student loans so I could have the über-art-school education."

"How does that . . ." Beth began but Astrid cut her off, "Shut up. I'm not finished."

Astrid took a deep breath and continued. "Then imagine falling in love with the most talented boy at the school, a boy who makes you think you're his everything, only to walk in on him in bed with the school's pretty girl."

"So, Ernie cheated on you?" Lindsey asked. "That happens to everyone at some point or another. You don't paint *LIAR* on their forehead and gut them like a fish."

"Well, maybe if we did, they'd be less likely to cheat," Astrid snapped.

Lindsey had a quick vision of John, her ex, tied up and mortally wounded. It didn't comfort and it did nothing to make the betrayal less.

"It's no solution," she said.

"Oh, what do you know? Besides, he did more than cheat on me," Astrid said. "He messed with my heart and my mind. After I caught him, he begged me to come back, said it had all been a drunken mistake and that I was his muse and he couldn't work without me. I believed him and I was powerless to resist. I loved him with everything I had."

"So, you took him back," Beth said.

"Again and again and again," Astrid said.

Lindsey caught the expression of self-loathing that passed over Astrid's face.

"We were living together," she said. "I was working days as a waitress and then working on my picture books at night. He didn't have a job because, well, it would hamper his creativity."

Beth's mouth turned down in one corner, and Lindsey wondered if she had heard this same rationale from Rick.

"Then one day I came home and he was gone," Astrid said.

"So you killed him because he left you?" Beth asked.

"No," Astrid said. Her voice made it clear that she thought Beth was dumber than a sack of hammers. "I killed him because when he left he took all of my work with him."

Beth's eyes went wide.

"Yeah, the Caldecott that he won as Rick Eckman, that should have been mine. He took everything, every scrap of art that I had produced. He even took the computer I used to archive my work."

"Oh, my God," Beth muttered.

"You didn't think you were the first, did you?"

"I thought maybe he did it because he had writer's block," Beth said. "I thought maybe he was panicking about his reputation."

"Tell me, did he seem to be clearing out his

belongings in his cabin?" Astrid asked.

"I don't know," Beth said. "I was rarely allowed on his island. In fact, I had only been there twice before the day we found his body."

"Whoa, sister, and I thought I was pathetic." Astrid sneered. "You really were taken for a ride."

"How did you find him?" Lindsey asked. "He'd been hiding on that island for five years."

"Well, it took some doing," Astrid said. "First, I was completely broke, so when an offer to work at the school came up, I took it. Then one day the alumni association was having a big to-do, and I heard Sydney's name come up. I knew if Ernie had kept in touch with anyone, it would be her. He always had a thing for her.

"When I confronted her, she denied it. But I was able to find out that she had gone on to be a children's book editor, and from there it was just a matter of tracing all of her clients. When Ernie won the Caldecott for a book that was so obviously a rip-off of mine, I threatened Sydney to tell me where he was, but of course she wouldn't. She couldn't have me suing her best author, after all. He had her so convinced that I was just a crazy stalker. She didn't believe me when I told her the work was mine."

"What you said to me in the Blue Anchor that day, 'Surely you're not suggesting he stole his idea from her. Why would he? No one would ever believe it,' " Lindsey quoted. "That was what Sydney said to you, wasn't it?"

Astrid gave a bitter laugh. "Verbatim. Once I took care of Ernie, I knew I had to get rid of her. I knew the police would contact the real Sydney in New York. I knew it wouldn't take much for her to put together that I had finally found Ernie and given him exactly what he deserved. I couldn't risk it. Of course, I didn't count on you two figuring out who he was before he was Rick Eckman."

"You were the one who broke into my apartment," Lindsey said. "You were trying to recover his things."

"I couldn't risk anyone linking him back to me. I found out where he was about a year ago. Once I decided I was going to confront him, I spent the next year wiping out any trace of a personal connection between Ernie and me. The few faculty who knew about us have since retired, and the students, well, like Sydney, most have gone on to fabulous careers where they certainly don't remember meek little Astrid," Astrid said, her voice dripping with bitterness. Then she cocked her head to the side and considered Lindsey. "In a way, I was trying to save your life. You found the last link between us. I really wish you hadn't gotten the photo album."

"I'm sort of wishing that myself now," Lindsey said. Astrid met her gaze in the rearview mirror and gave her a small smile that seemed more like the baring of teeth from a feral animal. It sent a chill from the nape of Lindsey's neck all the way down to her tailbone.

"It's getting dark," Lindsey said. "I need to turn on my headlights."

"Do it, but I'm watching your every move."

Lindsey felt the gun press against her temple again, and she had to squash a surge of anger. She hated feeling helpless, and she hated that this woman had them at her mercy. Never had she ever wanted to punch anyone in the face as much as she wanted to punch this woman now.

She switched on her headlights and put her hands back at ten and two.

"I don't understand," Beth said. "Why would he do this?"

"Because he was a failure," Astrid said. "A miserable, washed-up failure. He was like a high school football hero who doesn't get scouted for a college and spends the rest of his life as a townie, haunting the football field with a belly full of beer and bitterness."

Silence fell over the car, and Lindsey realized they were rapidly approaching the Briar Creek exit.

"So, because we figured out that you murdered Rick and Sydney, your plan is to kill us now?" she asked.

"It's nothing personal," Astrid said. "In fact, if

things were different, maybe we'd even be friends."

Lindsey did not have to meet Beth's gaze to know that she was thinking that was as likely as snowflakes in hell.

"What about Professor Cushion?" Beth asked. Then she cringed as if she'd given something away.

"Oh, please," Astrid said. "I wasn't stupid enough to let him see me. Given that he routinely gets naked in front of his students, it'll be easy to make a case that one of his students might have shot him for unrequited love, or maybe it was a jealous boyfriend. It can be spun in a million ways. By the time he's out of the hospital, there will be enough of a brouhaha going on that I sincerely doubt he'll remember talking to you two. And when you disappear, well, that'll be that."

Astrid looked so pleased with herself that Lindsey felt herself beginning to panic. How were they going to get away from her? The woman was a lunatic!

"It's going to be awfully hard to get rid of both of us without arousing suspicion," Beth said. "You know you don't have to do this. We'll promise to keep silent and never speak a word of this to anyone."

"Nice try," Astrid said. "But you're librarians, for Pete's sake. Freedom of information and all that. You probably consider it a moral imperative to turn me in. I can't have that."

Lindsey didn't bother to argue, because she knew all the way down in the marrow of her bones that she'd have to turn Astrid in, and she knew Beth well enough to know that even though she talked a good game, she felt the same way.

"All right, where to?" Lindsey asked.

They were now headed into town on Route 1. She wished she felt relieved to be coming home; instead, she felt as if the pendulum was swinging closer and closer to her neck.

"Let's go visit your library, shall we?" Astrid asked.

"It's closed," Beth said.

"Yeah, like you don't have a key."

Lindsey blew out a breath and drove them to the library. They parked in the back, and Astrid ordered them out of the car with their hands where she could see them.

She let Lindsey get the library keys out of her purse, and they made their way to the back door. Lindsey felt a flicker of hope sputter inside of her. The alarm. It would go off within fifteen seconds of their entry into the building and would bring the Briar Creek police screaming over to check it out. Shoot—she'd be so giddy to see Chief Daniels right now, she'd probably hug him.

She unlocked the back door and led the way in. The security lights were on, and they followed their glow into the main room.

"Now what tragedy can we have befall our two

290

spinsters?" Astrid asked. "Gas leak? No, too slow. I know. If I knock you out, and then light the building on fire, no one will expect you to be in here, since the library is closed. They'll put the fire out, but by the time they do, you'll be burnt to a crisp, a pile of ash that can only be identified by your teeth."

"You're crazy; you know that, right?" Beth asked.

"Keep your judgment to yourself please," Astrid said.

Lindsey looked at the clock on the wall. Minutes had passed since they'd entered the building, but the alarm hadn't gone off. Of all the days for someone to forget to set it, why did it have to be today, the one day they desperately needed it?

"Now where should I put you?" Astrid asked as she scoped out the library. She glanced at Lindsey. "You should probably be in your office." She turned and studied the library and then turned to Beth. "And you should definitely be in the children's area. It'll be so poetic, don't you think?"

"Forgive me, but I don't see it as poetic unless you're planning to let a boa constrictor eat me, as described in Shel Silverstein's poem," Beth said. "Death by a sociopath's immolation just doesn't have the same whimsical charm to it."

"Someone's getting cranky," Astrid said to Lindsey. "Let's get on with it, shall we?"

She took Beth's arm and shoved her none too gently in the direction of the sand-dune-shaped couch in the first-five-years area.

"I'm going," Beth snapped. "You don't have to get so pushy."

"Why don't you grab a few of your favorite books," Astrid suggested. "Then you won't have to die alone."

Lindsey felt her heart slam around her chest. This was really going to happen, and there was nothing she could do to stop it. This was completely unacceptable. She hadn't started her life all over in Briar Creek to have it abruptly cut short by a nutburger with a grudge.

She started scanning the room for a weapon. The computers were tied down by their cords; the furniture was heavy industrial-type stuff that took at least three people to move; the books in this section were narrow picture books that did not have the heft to do enough damage to be helpful. In the seconds she had taken to look around, Astrid had led Beth to the couch, and with one quick slam of the gun handle to her temple, Beth was out cold.

"No!" Lindsey yelled. She couldn't help it, and it echoed around the deserted library like the cry of a lonely seagull on the shore.

"Oh, really." Astrid looked at her as if she were disappointed. "You knew it was coming. Now, your office, please."

Lindsey led the way through the workroom toward her office. She started babbling, desperate to say the one thing that might change Astrid's mind.

"You can't do this," she said. "We have a sprinkler system. The building can't be burned down."

"I don't really need it to burn, do I?" Astrid asked. "I just need you and your nosy pal dead. I think there's enough paper in here to create a nice case of smoke inhalation to accomplish that. See? It's a no-brainer."

Lindsey didn't see any way out. If she didn't do as she was told, Astrid would shoot her like she did Tim. If she did do as she was told, she might be able to fake being knocked out and try to get Beth and herself out of here before Astrid torched the place. Neither option was terribly appealing, but she figured she had to go with the one that seemed to buy her more time.

She blew out a breath and stepped into her office. Astrid followed, and as Lindsey turned to face her, hoping she could dodge just enough to get hit but not knocked out, she heard a horrible *thwack,* and Astrid's eyes rolled back into her head and she slumped to the ground.

Lindsey felt her mouth slide open in surprise as she took in the sight of Ms. Cole clutching volume 9 of the *Oxford English Dictionary*, her weapon of choice.

"Nobody threatens my library," Ms. Cole said.

Lindsey nodded stupidly and bent down to retrieve the gun that Astrid had dropped. Then she reached for the phone on her desk and called 911. Ms. Cole remained stationed over Astrid, ready to swing again if the woman fluttered even an eyelash. She was awesome to behold, and Lindsey knew she had never been as glad to see anyone in her life as she was glad to see Ms. Cole at that very moment.

CHAPTER 27

Lindsey stayed by her side until Beth was loaded into the ambulance.

"I'm going to have my head examined, aren't I?" Beth asked with a small smile.

"Yep," Lindsey agreed.

"Probably overdue for it," Beth said.

"Don't worry. I'll explain everything to Detective Trimble, and I'll be in to see you as soon as I can."

"Excuse me, ma'am, but we have to go," the EMT said.

Lindsey squeezed Beth's hand and was about to move away when Beth pulled her back. "Hey, tell the lemon I said thanks."

"I will." Lindsey smiled. "I'm going to let her keep the *OED*, too."

"Good plan," Beth said. "Obviously it's a multi-purpose reference tool."

Lindsey stepped away and watched as Beth's stretcher was loaded into the ambulance. They drove away without lights or sirens but moving pretty quickly nonetheless.

Astrid Blunt had regained consciousness and was spitting and hissing like a cornered alley cat. Detective Trimble had let the EMTs check her, but there was no sign of a concussion so she'd been handcuffed and put in the back of the squad car.

Ms. Cole had been interviewed by both Detective Trimble and Chief Daniels. Luckily, she'd been in the library long enough to overhear most of Astrid's comments and was able to corroborate Beth and Lindsey's information. Detective Trimble had called the hospital where Tim Cushion was and planned to match the bullet they had pulled from his shoulder to the gun Lindsey had taken from Astrid.

Lindsey had given Detective Trimble and Chief Daniels the short version of the day's events, but she knew they wanted to question her further. So, she sat on a bench at the edge of the park and waited.

A thick, navy-blue fleece was tossed over her shoulders, and she glanced back to see Sully standing there. It was his fleece. She knew because it smelled like sun and salt, uniquely him.

Mary came running up beside him with a to-go bowl of chowder, a plastic spoon and a package of oyster crackers.

"You look like you're about to fall over," she said. "Now eat."

Lindsey did not have to be told twice. She couldn't remember how long it had been since she'd had any food. She must have been running on adrenaline for hours, which would explain why the hot soup sliding down her throat infused her entire body with a leaden lethargy that demanded nothing more than her fluffy comforter and pillows.

"I'm going to ask Detective Trimble if you can go home," Sully said. "I don't see why they need to question you anymore tonight."

"Do that," Mary said. "And don't ask them; tell them."

Sully gave her an exasperated look, shook his head and headed over to the cluster of officers.

"And don't you even think about going in to see Beth tonight," Mary said to Lindsey. She really was in full-on bossy mode. "I've got some chowder that Ian and I are going to smuggle to her as soon as she gets to her room. That hospital food can kill a body, you know."

Violet and Nancy were next to arrive. They bookended Lindsey, each sitting on one side of her. They didn't ask any questions—just gave her their warmth and support. As exhaustion crept over her, Lindsey couldn't have been more grateful that she had landed in this decidedly quirky but incredibly kind community.

Sully strode back over. Lindsey glanced into her bowl to find it was empty. He reached down, took her empty container and handed it back to Mary. Then he helped her to her feet and tucked her under his arm. She didn't dwell on how right it felt or how grateful she was to have him running interference. For once she just went with it.

"Come on," he said. "I'll take you home." And she let him.

The crafternoon club resumed meeting the next week. They had all finished reading Lynn Sheene's *The Last Time I Saw Paris*, and the knitting needles were flying as they dissected its literary merits. Lindsey had their copies stacked on the table, and she had bookmarked the reading guide in the back of the book to promote their discussion.

"I liked that the heroine knew how to take care of herself," Beth said. "Born into the life of a dirt farmer, Claire still found a way out."

"Yes, she reinvented herself," Violet agreed. "But she risked her life in doing it with phony papers and then spying on the Germans in occupied Paris. I couldn't stop reading I was so stressed."

"Sometimes you have to risk your life if what you're doing is right," Beth said.

She and Lindsey exchanged a look of understanding. They had spent a lot of time since Astrid's attempt to kill them, talking about how deluded she had been. How could she really believe no one would make the connection between her and Rick? How could she think that he and Sydney had deserved to die? Because no matter what he had done, Rick had not deserved such a horrible end.

Of course, the real corker had been that even after Astrid had tried to kill them and Ms. Cole had given witness to her plan, Chief Daniels had still been reluctant to let go of Beth as his primary suspect until Detective Trimble had blasted him in front of half of the town.

Lindsey took a moment to study her friend, who had fully recovered from being conked on the head and was now working on a baby afghan in peach for her sister-in-law's upcoming baby shower.

Beth looked to be over the worst of the past two weeks' upheaval. She seemed more rested, and her natural exuberance was coming back. She was even planning her first story time in days, which was going to be a teddy bear picnic.

"Well, I like that Sheene doesn't spare the grim realities of living in an occupied city during a war: the constant fear, the hunger, the persecution of the Jews and of all the French citizens, for that matter," Charlene said.

"And yet she is able to find beauty in her flowers and in the gardens," Nancy said. "As Claire's mentor, Madame Palain, teaches her in the book: 'Elegance is in the details.' "

"But best of all, she is even able to find love," Violet added with a satisfied sigh.

Charlene was knitting a scarf and hat set, red with white snowflakes, for her youngest daughter. Lindsey glanced down at the hat she'd been working on for her father for what seemed like an eternity.

She lowered it into her lap and said, "Did you know that Sheene was inspired to write this novel because of a French art deco brooch that she discovered?"

They all turned to look at her.

"Oh, no—here she goes again," Mary said. She shook her head and tsk-tsked at Lindsey. "She's annoyed with her knitting, and she's putting her scholarly voice on again."

"I am not," Lindsey protested.

"Yeah, you are," Nancy said. "Your voice goes up when you get all miffy with your project. Give it here. I'll take a look at it."

Lindsey handed it over, awaiting the peals of laughter that would no doubt accompany her first efforts with knitting needles. There were none. As Nancy turned it this way and that, the group studied the heather-blue rolled hat and then they all looked at her.

"What?" Lindsey asked.

"It came out really well," Nancy said. Her blue eyes shone. "Your dad is going to love it."

"You mean it's finished?" Lindsey asked.

"Well, you have to tie off the last row, but yes, you're done," Violet said. "You did good."

She reached over and patted Lindsey's knee.

"Good job," Mary said.

"It's perfect," Charlene added.

"You should be proud of yourself," Beth said. "It looks great."

Lindsey sat back and marveled that she had managed to wrestle that pretty blue ball of yarn into a hat. She put it on her hand and turned it this way and that. She could just see it on her dad's bald head, and she smiled.

Why this felt like the equivalent of climbing Mount Everest without a Sherpa, she didn't know, but she couldn't have wiped the grin off of her face if she tried. Such a little thing, and yet it brought her such a huge sense of herself and her possibilities.

She wished life could have been this simple for Ernie.

She'd thought a lot about Sydney Carlisle, Ernie Shadegg and Astrid Blunt over the past few weeks.

It turned out that Sydney had not known that Ernie had stolen Astrid's work and that she had believed that Astrid was a crazed stalker, not too far off the mark there, and had encouraged him to acquire the name Rick Eckman and sever all ties with his past so that Astrid couldn't find him.

And Rick, well, he'd been so desperate to prove his worth artistically that he'd betrayed the people who had cared about him the most, both Astrid and Beth. The lack of personal effects at his cabin turned out to be because he had already begun to ship his things out of the cottage. He had been planning to move away before the book came out, so his breakup with Beth at the Blue Anchor on that stormy night had really been quite convenient for him.

And then there was Astrid, who now a guest in the county jail and likely to acquire permanent residency in the state penitentiary. Her life decisions had particularly bothered Lindsey. Perhaps it was because Lindsey knew what the sharp blade of betrayal felt like when it was jammed right between the ribs, but still she couldn't imagine allowing herself to become so consumed with her bitterness that she would be driven to commit two, and almost four, acts of murder.

She glanced around the room at these women who had become her friends over the past few months. She valued them and the time they spent together. In the end, when she thought of Rick and Astrid, it was with pity. Life was full of so many precious gifts, and they had missed the greatest one of all: friendship.

She shook off her sad musings and glanced back down at her hat. She really was so pleased with it, but then a thought struck her and she frowned.

"Um, can someone show me how to tie it off?" she asked. "Or I'll be forced to go into a very long-winded monologue on how novels help us to understand historical events and put them in an appropriate contemporary construct."

All five of her crafternoon buddies roared forward in a mad scramble to help her with her rolled hat, and Lindsey grinned. She glanced around the room and down the hall to the main part of the building, where she could see the patrons come and go, and she noticed that at the moment, everything felt right in her world. As much as her life had changed over the past six months, she knew there was no other place she'd rather be.

THE BRIAR CREEK LIBRARY GUIDE TO CRAFTERNOONS

What is a crafternoon? Well, in Briar Creek, it is a meeting between close friends where they share a craft, a good book and some yummy food. Here are some ideas for having your own crafternoon.

Start with a good story. Lindsey recommends *The Last Time I Saw Paris* by Lynn Sheene, which comes with a handy discussion guide in the back of the book. The reading guide is also enclosed here to give you a sense of the novel.

Share a craft, such as knitting, where participants can work on their own projects at their own pace. See the next page for the pattern Lindsey used to make the rolled hat for her father.

Enjoy some delicious food. Nothing brings people together like good food. Recipes for Mary's clam chowder and Sully's hot chocolate follow the knitting pattern.

Lastly, the most important part of crafternoons is to relax and have fun with people you enjoy!

LINDSEY'S KNITTING PATTERN FOR A ROLLED HAT

One skein Loop-d-Loop River (90 percent
cotton, 10 percent cashmere), 103 yards
One size 10.5 US circular needle and one set
10.5 US double-pointed needles (or a second
10.5 circular needle) for working the top of
the hat
Scissors and yarn needle
Gauge
14 stitches and 20 rows per 4 inches in
stockinette stitch in the round. Take time to
check gauge.

Pattern size is for an average adult.

Cast on 76 stitches. Join in round, being careful
not to twist.
Work in stockinette stitch for 9 inches.
Next round, *knit 2, knit 2 together. Repeat
from * around.
Work in stockinette stitch for 1 round. Change
to double-pointed needles or work in second

to double-pointed needles or work in second circular when needed. Divide the stitches evenly among the needles.

Next round, *knit 1, knit 2 together. Repeat from * around.

Work stockinette stitch for 1 round.

Next round, *knit 2 together. Repeat from * around.

Work in stockinette stitch for 1 round.

*Knit 2 together. Repeat from *, ending knit 1.

Cut yarn, leaving a long tail. Thread tail onto the yarn needle, slip stitches onto needle and pull yarn tight, closing the top of the hat. Weave in ends.

RECIPES

SULLY'S HOT CHOCOLATE

¾ cup bittersweet chocolate chips
2 tablespoons sugar
1 tablespoon unsweetened cocoa powder
1 pinch salt
3 ½ cups milk
¾ teaspoon vanilla extract
½ cup half-and-half
¼ teaspoon fresh ground nutmeg
2 cinnamon sticks, broken into two pieces

Bring all ingredients (except cinnamon sticks) to a simmer in a medium saucepan, whisking often. Remove from heat, add cinnamon sticks, cover and let sit for five minutes. Remove cinnamon sticks, bring to a simmer again, whisking often. Pour into mugs and serve hot.

MARY'S CLAM CHOWDER

New England clam chowder is very particular; for example, don't even try to put a tomato in it or any self-respecting Yankee will not eat it. Also, those thick chowders that they serve in restaurants come from using too much flour. The real deal uses cream, which is much lighter and enhances the flavor of the clams instead of hiding it.

2 pounds chopped clams with liquid (quahogs, cherrystones or littleneck clams)
1 pound russet potatoes, peeled and cut into ½ inch cubes
2 cups onions, chopped
3 slices of bacon, diced
3 cups clam liquid, either broth from cooked clams or bottled clam juice, plus water to total 3 cups
1 cup milk
1 cup half-and-half or heavy cream
Kosher or sea salt and pepper to taste

Heat a heavy pot over medium heat and add bacon. Cook, stirring until lightly browned. Add onion and cook, stirring until soft and translucent. Add 3 cups reserved clam liquid or bottled clam juice and water, and increase heat to high. Add chopped potatoes and cook until potatoes are just soft—about 10 minutes.

Add milk and half-and-half or cream and chopped clams, lower heat and simmer until clams are cooked (4–8 minutes, depending upon the size of the chopped clams). Add salt and pepper to taste.

YIELDS 4 LARGE SERVINGS.

Center Point Publishing
600 Brooks Road ● PO Box 1
Thorndike ME 04986-0001 USA

(207) 568-3717

US & Canada:
1 800 929-9108
www.centerpointlargeprint.com